PLaYING BOTTICeLLI

Liza NELSON

PLaYING BOTTICeLLI

G.P. PUTNAM'S SONS *New York*

G. P. Putnam's Sons
Publishers since 1838
a member of
Penguin Putnam Inc.
375 Hudson Street
New York, NY 10014

Library of Congress Cataloging-in-Publication Data

Nelson, Liza.
Playing Botticelli / Liza Nelson.
p.   cm.
ISBN 0-399-14601-6
I. Title

PS3564.E4676 P57   2000   99-047292 CIP
813'.54—dc21

Printed in the United States of America
1   3   5   7   9   10   8   6   4   2

This book is printed on acid-free paper. ∞

Book design by Judith Stagnitto Abbate/Abbate Design

For Jacob and Rosie

ACKNOWLEDGMENTS

Sara Nelson, without whose encouragement, support and occasional needling I doubt I would have finished this book;

Pam Durban, teacher and friend;

Trish Hall, Pamela Harrison, Hilary Rosenfeld, Virginia Parker, Amelia Cook, Anne Lawson-Beerman, Nena Halford and Vinnie Rosenzwieg, each of whom succored my writing in her own way, whether through correspondence, conversation or chocolate;

Alice Martell, my agent, for her enthusiastic faith even when mine was wavering;

Laura Mathews, the editor every novelist dreams about;

and Rick Brown for sharing it all.

OnE

ONE

Well, this summer is over. Kaput. Finis. Down the tubes. Extinct. All gone. The end.

As far as I'm concerned, anyway.

It shut like a book this afternoon. One minute I was full of August, easing my way down Highway 12, windows down, music blasting, the hot wind whipping in thick ribbons against my neck. The next minute I was chilled to the bone.

To the bone.

I'd been at work. The teachers come back for pre-planning in a week, and I want no hassles from middle-aged women having nervous breakdowns because their chalkboards are dusty or their windows won't open. Life is too short and art is too long. Being a janitor—excuse me, custodian—is not exactly my life's work. I am an artist first, but I have to earn a living. If I were by myself it would be one thing, but with a daughter to feed, clothe, educate and all the rest, I've had to make my compromises, though fewer than most people, I'm glad to say. Bourgeois excuse, someone would have accused me in '68, back when the revolution was at hand. I'm kidding, sort of. Besides, I take pride in being a woman with Mechanical Skills, as Gulfside Elementary's esteemed principal Granger Morris would say.

It must have been around three o'clock when I finished painting the cafeteria ceiling an incredible azure blue, and I'd added the Pleiades and a few other constellations as my signature. There are ways to do a job, and then as Daddy used to say, there are ways to Do a job. Old Grange could always ask me to repaint it, but he never would. Certain teachers might complain among themselves, but not to me directly. A good janitor has clout, especially in a school with as few resources as Gulfside.

I gave the floor a good once-over with the mop, packed up and started home to Point Paradise. I was singing along with the oldies station out of Tallahassee, *"Don't you want somebody to love? Don't you need somebody to love?"* People have told me I look a little like a redheaded Grace Slick, or they used to when I lived where people had actually heard of her.

Then the news came on. Out in California, land of the seasonless season where all our dreams and nightmares bloom, a DC-9 and somebody's private jet had tried to thread the eye of the same needle.

"Eighty-one dead," according to the disembodied radio voice.

Just the idea. One minute you're looking out one of those little curved windows feeling godlike, casting your shadow across the earth; twenty seconds later you're bone chip and seared skin pierced with metal. Unless you're on the ground looking up, thinking what a pretty pattern those two planes make flying so close overhead, until the sky bursts wide open to surround and lift you up toward the deafening wreckage. Toward heaven, if only it existed.

Of course, people have been blowing up all summer, the innocent with the guilty. Not just in planes. In buses, in restaurants, in department stores. Wherever a bomb can be stowed. Frankly, I can handle the concept of terrorism. At least someone means death to happen. If I'm going to be blown away, I'd rather spend my last millisecond thinking I'm dying for a cause, even some idiot's insane idea of a cause that I find morally repugnant, than cursing the underpaid, undertrained air traffic controller, and probably a scab strike breaker at that, who has botched the job.

I'm willing to argue the point. I'm always willing to argue. As I've told Dylan over and over ever since she was a little girl, it's bad politics to accept the authority of an idea until you've examined both sides. Don't get me wrong. I'm not saying terrorists aren't scary people doing evil things. But let's face it, terrorists usually exist in the first place because some government screwed up, maybe months ago, maybe generations, maybe centuries ago. Maybe it was on purpose or maybe it was just a misjudgment on the part of an individual in some government department who set in motion the series of reactions, first to last, that led to the creation of people so angry and hopeless they'd commit desperate mayhem.

Not that I want to get into heavy political second-guessing. When I settled here, I pretty much left politics behind. That was the point of moving us to the edge of nowhere in the first place.

I'm out of the loop as they say a lot these days in Washington. Me and Vice President Bush. I mean who in their right mind wants to be in the loop? We thought Vietnam and Tricky Dick were bad, but the sixties were nothing. Let's face it, we're stuck in the middle of a decade that is spiritually pure shit, and Ronnie Reagan, with all his crummy little wars that keep breaking out on our collective chin, is leading the way.

Shit. Shat. Shitty. Wash my mouth out with soap. Nice girls and ladies do not talk that way around here, not that anyone would include me on her list of Esmeralda's nice ladies exactly, and not that I care. In any case, I do love the word. "Shit" has to be the quintessential female expletive. "Fuck" and "damn" are basically masculine, don't you think? Hard and sharp. "Shit" has the same number of letters but it's slower to say, softer across the tongue. A nice, nasty contradiction. Plus there's the mud pie in your eye against all those nice-nellyisms, like "ca-ca" and "poo-poo," our mothers taught us to use to keep us proper.

I mean really, in my deepest heart of hearts, I'm still twelve years old, the vinegar sting of my mother's slap hot on my cheek, pickle juice pooling at my bare feet that are pink from the blood trickling down my ankle where a glass sliver has lodged.

"Oh shit," was all I said when the jar hit the linoleum.

"Judy, please!" There was a splatter of small dark stains down the front of my mother's cashmere sweater. "I can't stand it when well-brought-up girls say that word."

The s-word. I was barefoot for God's sake and there was glass everywhere and that was all she could think about. Of course, now that I'm a mother I'll give her the benefit of a doubt. She could have been overwrought about something unconnected to me: the bad perm she got at the beauty parlor; trouble she was having getting the household checkbook to balance; Daddy coming home late from his insurance office yet again without calling. No matter. The devil had me by then. I laughed in her face and said it twice more, louder. That's when she slapped me, hard. Another in a series of intimate moments between Mom and me.

Don't get me wrong. I do not hate my mother. We talk almost every month. When she closed up the house in Connecticut seven years ago, I flew up to help her pack. The last time I was on a plane by the way. Since then, once or twice a year I drive Dylan—although she's getting old enough to send alone—to Hilton Head, where Mother has a condo with Jack, whom she refers to discreetly as her special gentleman friend. A perfectly nice man, Jack.

No one would ever have dared to describe Daddy as a nice man. That's what I loved about him, even during those two and a half years we didn't speak because he had decided I could not be his daughter Judy Blitch if I was also an unwed mother living in a commune "with a bunch of long-haired, commie bastards" and calling myself Godiva Blue. "Jesus Christ, you sound like you've turned Negro. If you've got to change your name, why not call yourself Virgin so we could all laugh at the joke?" Daddy never did mince his words.

Mom minces, dices and arranges on a platter with parsley and radish hearts every time she opens her mouth. As I said, I do not hate her or resent her or even dislike her any more. As I said, we talk on the phone with a certain regularity. But let's face it, all the phone calls in the world will not change the fact that we simply do not connect. She hasn't the slightest inkling what I'm about, never has.

She loves Dylan of course. Not that she wanted me to give birth to her—as if I had an alternative at the time—but once Dylan was born, Mom couldn't have given her up any more than I could, I'll hand her that. She has more or less adjusted to the terms of my motherhood. Her great joy is sending along articles she's clipped from earnest women's magazines about single mothers and how they cope. Coping is one of her big themes. She does not believe I am coping well. Of course, she believes coping is a good thing: make do, stiff upper lip, stoic forbearance, the Puritan spirit at work. What in her life, aside from Daddy dying over all those pain-filled months, has required coping I am not sure, but I don't bother to quibble because basically she's right. I do not cope.

I am against coping on principle and I tell her so. Coping is an acceptance of less than you want. I expect more and don't mind doing what it takes to get more. That's why I hammered and forged and sculpted until I built the life I wanted. And when I decided I needed to earn a living and find a job, I did not simply cope. I made the job fit me, not the other way around. Of course, that choice of jobs remains beyond my mother's comprehension. Needless to say, she never tells anyone in Hilton Head how I earn my living, and she can't understand why, if I'm going to call myself an artist, I choose to live in Esmeralda, where she's never been, instead of some overdeveloped artist-slash-tourist colony like the Vineyard or Greenwich Village.

"There are such limited opportunities."

"You mean to meet men." Men I can live without, as I have shown my entire adult life. Men are generally what I don't want to meet, and if Esmeralda has few to tempt me, the better off I am here. But I bite my tongue. My unwritten rule of etiquette states that if she's paying for the call, I try to avoid out-and-out confrontation. "Try" is the operative word.

"Not only men. Educated people." That cute little hurt in her voice could not be louder and clearer if she were standing next to me in the room shouting through a bullhorn. "And what about Di?" She loves calling Dylan "Di," as if she were named for Princess Diana, although, of course, Dylan was born long before the royal wedding. "What kind of education can she get there? Do they even have advanced-placement classes at the high school?"

"Dylan is happy."

"So you say."

I bite my tongue again. Dylan not happy? We have an almost perfect life. Not almost. Perfect. We play together, we create together. Dylan has never been merely my daughter, the way I was my mother's daughter, a responsibility to give birthday parties for and drive to dancing classes. Dylan is a mind in formation, a spirit I am helping to shape. She goes to the local, admittedly mediocre school, but I have been her primary teacher. I don't say it hasn't become a challenge lately, now that the demons of adolescence have begun to circle. She can be moody and a little prickly at times, but not like other girls with their parents. Our relationship is different. Being Dylan's mother is as intrinsic to my wholeness as a woman and an artist as being my daughter is intrinsic to her wholeness. Dylan, as much as myself, is the beneficiary of my quest for perfected vision.

That is what life is all about, isn't it? Seeing true and clear to the core, so that you know the essence of a thing despite the detritus. When we happened into Esmeralda ten years ago I was just beginning my search, trying to piece together the elements of a life that would allow me to slough off all that garbagey stuff that clings to most people, women especially. Most have no vision so they are trapped in what they call their lives—narrow alleyways cluttered with all the petty trivia of television, office politics, bill paying, dating. Those dancing classes and birthday parties that kept cornering my mother and me in my childhood. The prosaic routine of domestic dependency. I wanted more. I wanted to inhabit my space in the world as I pleased.

So after Daddy died, I turned the twenty thousand dollars he left me into traveler's checks, over my mother and her lawyer's strenuous objections. Then I loaded all our worldly possessions into the back of Miranda, my VW bus, and took off, clutching a map of America's back roads. Dylan was barely five, but she was a fine traveling companion for those three weeks, enthusiastic most of the time and surprisingly patient through the inevitable long stretches. I had not planned to stop in northwest Florida, but I fell in love with that barely visible line in the distance where sky and sea meet, how the roots of the scrub oaks dig in and take hold in the sandy soil. The spiky leaves of the palmettos. All that gnarled resilience. When I saw the FOR SALE sign at Point Paradise I knew we were home. It was destiny. Walking the marshy shore and looking out across the cove to flat open water and empty sky, watching Dylan's delight in the geckos and in the pelicans nesting on abandoned pilings, I knew this particular geography had been ripening for years while it waited for me.

Not that people hadn't stood there before, but no one who counted. Only a typical Florida land developer with King Midas dreams. Back in the fifties, he had cleared half the Point and built pastel bungalows to sell to rich retirees from Miami looking for a retreat from the sweltering heat of south Florida. Point Paradise was his name for the place and he gave each house its own title burnt into the lintel above the front door. Pelican's Landing, Hibiscus Haven. I've always liked him for those names.

Then Hurricane Margaret-Ann hit, the same week his ad campaign was scheduled to run, the same week his workmen were under rush orders to finish installing the pink and aqua kitchens; the same week it so happens that my grandparents took me to Madison Square Garden in New York City to see a rodeo with Roy Rogers and Dale Evans, my heroes I'm not ashamed to admit. Shaking hands with Roy and Dale counted as the peak experience of my six-year-old life. When we came outside afterward, the skies had darkened to an ashy charcoal gray the color of the sleeve of my grandfather's overcoat as he worked desperately to flag down a taxi cab. My first conscious sensory memory is the danger I could smell in the air, metallic and electric, smokey and moist.

My misguided get-rich-quick-now-bankrupt developer disappeared. I can see him, a small bald man who sweats through his linen suits, driving by his ruins one last time, his wife beside him, chipping off her nail polish and chewing her lip as they head north in a long-finned Cadillac whose back end sags under the weight of their hastily gathered possessions, the trunk's mouth roped down into a half open grin.

Eight of the ten cottages had been flattened by the storm and never touched since. I used most of what was left out of my traveler's checks—over half of my inheritance from Daddy—to pay cash for the twenty acres plus. God, it seems like so much land for so little money, but back then I was considered insanely fiscally brazen. Fiscally brazen, it sounds almost as bad as sexually promiscuous, which I was obviously considered by certain family members as well.

Rot and hibiscus overran the place. Even Paradise, the cottage most inland and least damaged, was falling in on itself by the time I moved into it with Dylan. I stripped the cottage down to its skeleton and rebuilt. The folks at Ace Hardware and Henry's Building Supplies were standoffish at first, as you can well imagine: Esmeralda, Florida, circa 1976: woman stranger who looks more than a little like a hippie coming around asking questions and buying supplies with traveler's checks written on a Hartford, Connecticut, bank while her little girl hangs on her leg and refuses to smile or take even one piece of Chicklets gum. The raised eyebrows I saw the first afternoon Dylan and I walked in stayed raised for months, but eventually the guys got used to me. And I even got used to them, overalls, chewing tobacco, ma'ams and all.

I did my own plumbing and pretty much all my own electrical. It was a learning experience, that's for sure. There is not one inch of surface, not a beam, not a nail hole, that I have not touched. Four rooms and a bath, that's all we needed—plus my studio in the old toolshed—filled with serenity and order amid the chaotic beauty of the land. Point Paradise. The embodiment of my, Dylan's and my, essential spirit.

And believe me, rebuilding Paradise was a spiritual act. I've been a studio potter, a weaver, a painter, even a glassblower. God, I had loved working the glory hole, but once I had Dylan I gave up my plans to go back. It was not a place to have a toddler crawling around. And I can't say I ever had what I could call a sense of purpose until I worked on my house. Fishing wires through the walls, framing doors, smoothing Sheetrock plaster, I discovered the energy of space and time within the set boundaries of a ten-by-twelve-foot room. The quality of space. How life can expand within an imposed, purely spatial structure. It all goes back to vision.

That's how I discovered my art. My boxes of wood—or clay or papier-mâché or whatever materials feel right—that I fill with my own constructions. My medium has become life enclosures. Not shrines. Not reliquaries. Though I like the spiritual nature of reliquaries, they're still about what is past and dead. My boxes are worlds unto themselves, filled with the shapes and colors and textures of my visions. Vision. Your vision forms your life. The seeing beyond takes you into the within and vice versa. As in waking dreams. As in visionary. My college roommate and ultimate mentor, Evangeline Pinkston, talked a lot about making her own inspiration, but Evie was a genius, a real genius. All I have is a strongly developed attentive unconscious. And thank the gods I have that.

I have always possessed the gift. My ability to lose myself, will myself lost within a given environment, has grown over the last ten years, but it has always been there inside, waiting for my recognition. I can do it anywhere, but out there on the Point is the best, at the tip of the peninsula, past the crumbling remains of the other bungalows. It takes some scrambling to get out there past the marsh, through the beach nettles, but once I make it to the thumbnail of limestone that sits like a turtle's back in the shallows, I'm home free. None of the noise of civilization to interfere with my inward hearing. Only the shushing of the tide, the shriek of the gulls, my own ragged breath. I become nebulae, like meditation without the mantra.

Even in this heat. Maybe the heat helps. Last Thursday was one of the hottest, muggiest days I can remember around here, and that's saying a lot. My toes squished deliciously deep into the wet muck of sand and dirt on what's left of the old road. The sand would have burned my soles but for the mud. My jeans and T-shirt stuck to my skin, so once I reached the Point I stripped them off, lay back, and opened my pores to melt into the natural sauna of salt spray, gray rock, and sky. I was transformed into leaf, cloud, foam, air. Bodiless, coming and going with the tides. My mother used to accuse me of daydreaming, but she had no idea.

So there I was peering into my own unconscious. A contradiction in terms, you might argue, but that is what happens. Like adjusting to the dark. Suddenly you see where everything fits despite, or even enhanced by, the blackness. Thursday, lying in that cocoon of heat, I traveled into a black room, windowless, doorless. I did not feel trapped. I felt the expansiveness of empty space. After a while, scissors cut slits in the walls and the walls curled like paper. Through the slits I saw blue sky filled with bleeding moons. Black to blue to red. Slices to circles to sharp moon points, silverfish bodies slithering, lines of unborn dead. And, strange or morbid as it may sound, a sense of profound peace.

I stayed there, inside wherever I was, for maybe an hour, maybe ten minutes, maybe only a few seconds. No matter. And then gradually it all faded back into the shimmer of sea and sky, the physical world I inhabit with everyone else. I could feel the physical reality of my body and the rock and the heat. I slipped off the turtle's back exhilarated by awareness that being alive was, is, the thing. Gray-green slime came off all over my arms and legs. Wet leaves and sand clung to my shoulder. Strings of seaweed wrapped around my ankle. They were life, life, life.

It is true that I am an unusually enthusiastic person.

I don't remember how I got back to the studio or sitting down to work. I was in a creative euphoria. But I do remember velvety browns and slippery blues and singing reds, a spiny silver. And the light. God, the light. Thick with heat. Tingly, stretching through the open double doors and along the walls, carrying me forward like a wave of energy as I sketched and cut and pieced.

Then the briefest shadow. I looked up. Dylan stood at the doorway beside a taller, dark-haired girl. Louise Culpepper's daughter, Cassie. For a fraction of a second, I thought they were another vision before I delineated the particulars of their presence. Identical black T-shirts and thigh-hugging skirts. Only, despite the multiple earrings and the painted eyebrows, Dylan, my Dylan, still chubby with baby fat, had not quite pulled off the look. She paled beside the other girl's theatrical, almost haggard disdain. Dylan's mouth and eyes formed small o's, the geometry of her horror quite wonderful from an artist's view.

But artist and mother are separate sensibilities sharing side-by-side space inside my brain. The mother side saw only disaster.

Maternal awareness moved in slow motion from Dylan's eyes to my knees, still covered with slime. Then I heard an intake of breath, hers and mine in discordant harmony.

"Shit."

I was stark naked. I grabbed an old shirt off the stool and buttoned it around me, not knowing whether to giggle or to sob. Even now the memory makes me smile and blush together. The absurdity. Those two painstakingly punked-out kids shocked by my less-than-youthful, far less-than-perfect body.

Needless to say, the mood was broken. I could not find my way back to any inner wisdom that day.

+   +   +

DR*i*VING along Highway 12 this afternoon, though, watching the clouds stretch over the Gulf as the radio cut from the news to a commercial for strawberry wine coolers, I decided my dream vision out on the Point had been some kind of real premonition: a sealed black room, a sky the color of the cafeteria ceiling, which is pretty spooky itself when you think about it, blood and death. My God, what had I seen coming? Someone who believes as strongly as I do in trusting my unconscious should have paid closer attention. *Let no sign slip away, remain on constant guard,* I began berating myself.

Then I saw the bicycle. Just barely noticed it, the way you half see a thing on the side of the road as you drive by. If I had not lifted my foot halfway off the gas and shifted my glance as I leaned across the seat for my cigarettes, the bike probably would not have registered at all, but in my state of heightened attentiveness it did register. As all wrong.

There were two bikes actually. One lay on its side. The other stood upended, halfway through a decrepit guard rail, the pedals revolving furiously in the breeze. I forced myself to get out of Miranda and walked toward the blue two-wheeler, an old-fashioned boy's Schwinn. Not Dylan's, was my first thought, as if Dylan has been near her bike in a year. Then I heard the cries and began to run.

A young boy, no more than seven or eight, lay several feet down the embankment. The bushy overgrowth had cut his fall, possibly saved him. *Let him be breathing*, I begged the powers that be, before I saw his face. He was awfully still, but his eyes stared up full of terrified life.

"There's blood. There's blood. Is he going to die? Is he going to die?" A second boy, the one whose screams I'd heard from the road, rushed at me as soon as I scrambled down to them. Tears were streaking sandy stains down his cheeks. He grabbed my arm and wouldn't let go.

He started sobbing, "We snuck off. I knew we shouldn't. I knew we shouldn't. Oh, is he going to die?"

"No, of course not." I needed to calm him down but had no idea how. "What's your name?"

"Philip."

"And his?"

"David."

"Well, Philip, let me take a look at David."

I let Philip keep hold of my shirtsleeve while I bent over the injured child. There was blood, red and oozy, a cut above his forehead, but it did not look terribly deep.

"Do you hurt real bad anywhere, David?" Dumb question but at least I kept my voice calm and used his name. I'd read somewhere that in a medical emergency you should use the victim's name whenever possible. The boy barely moved his lips. "I hurt okay." Whatever way I wanted to interpret that one, pain or terror.

"You're going to be fine. We're going to take good care of you." The gears had kicked in I guess, emergency automatic. By some act of fortune I had thrown a bathing suit and towel in the back-seat this morning. I stanched the cut with the suit, and used the towel as a blanket. Whether he had broken bones or internal injuries I could not tell, but I was not about to move him. I flagged down a car of teenagers and sent them off to phone 911.

Inside the cramped ambulance when it finally came, reality shifted somehow. David grew smaller strapped down on the stretcher, already attached to an IV-drip. Not small like a baby. More than anything else, he resembled at that moment a little old man, fear and pain stripping all the childhood out of his face. When the driver asked Philip if he wanted to sit up front, Philip shook his head and reached for my free hand. David already had my other. In a matter of an hour we had developed the visceral, physical intimacy of family.

Almost. As involved in the boys as I was, I also found myself thanking God, even if I didn't believe in him, that Dylan was safe. When she'd told me she was invited to dinner with the Reverend and Mrs. Brasleton after choir practice, I was not thrilled. This phase Dylan was going through, this flirtation with the Baptists, was annoying. But at least at this moment I knew where she was.

"What about my bike?"

I turned to Philip, but it was David speaking, worried even now about his bike.

"It's safe. I put the lock on," Philip answered before I could. Kids can be so amazing.

"David, you hang in there." I gave both boys' hands a quick squeeze. "You're being very brave, the two of you. Aren't they?" I turned to the medic sitting on the other side of David, a young guy with acne who had tried to describe the equipment to Philip earlier although the boy was too frightened to pay attention.

"Oh, yes, ma'am." He rubbed his palms along his knees as if to follow a musical beat the rest of us couldn't hear. "You have a very brave little boy here."

Gradually, David's grip lightened, exhaustion or painkiller. Philip stared straight ahead, holding on tight as ever.

What if I had not happened by? How long would the boys have waited before someone else stopped, and who, what kind of person? How would life be different, for them or that other passerby, now reaching another destination untouched? And what if I had not glanced over when I did, had kept driving, what other road would my thoughts be traveling now? Those planes colliding, finding these boys. What is life but the friction of one coincidence against another?

Thousands of miles away, victims and survivors were going through their private, enormous anguish. I tried to see them, but my imagination closed down. All I knew were these children's hands in mine, small and dry, dirt etched deep in the lines of the knuckles. I knew David, his dilated eyes, the matted damp hair above the bandages on his forehead, the blood drying to a muddy rust at the edges. And I knew Philip, his almond eyes the color of tree bark, the two pinpricks of nervous energy high on his otherwise drained cheeks, his narrow lips set in stubborn stoicism. For now at least, the ambulance had become the donut of my life. These boys had me completely claimed.

Other people's children. I almost wish those little boys had never entered my life. Or at least that I didn't have such a way with them, as everyone tells me I do. Saving people, being involved with them at all, creates burdens. Since finding those children, my life seems to be complicating in ways I do not want. I swear I don't.

The hospital waiting room when we finally got there was a dreadful place, too brightly lit and disinfected. A Muzak version of "You've Got a Friend" was playing along with a muted television talk show on a mounted TV in the center of the wall. Someone had decided primary colors would be cheerful for the furniture. David Franklin's mother somehow managed to arrive before the ambulance and was waiting for us, frantically pacing in front of a row of hideous green and purple chairs.

God, I hope I never have occasion to feel the way she looked, every muscle, every nerve ending taut with dread, fear and hope as she got her first glimpse of David. The rest of the world had stopped existing for her. Her eyes, her mind, her entire body could focus on nothing but her child. I introduced myself but doubt she heard me before the doctors whisked her down a hall beside David's gurney.

I was left with Philip still holding my hand. A doctor gave him a quick once-over. Not a scratch on him. Then we sat together waiting another ten minutes before his mother stepped off the elevator and rushed over to us.

Mrs. Rainey turned out to be one of those small-boned, pinched-cheeked women who never quite let loose. She was all porcelain delicacy in her aqua and beige suit with its little butterfly pin on the lapel, her smooth black hair pulled tight into a French knot. Obviously shaken, she hugged Philip stiffly against her chest. I felt for her, mother to mother, I truly did. But in the perfunctory glances of Thank-you and You're welcome that passed between us, I recognized her critical sizing up. Mine, too, if I'm honest. Each of us was everything the other was not. Instant antipathy. I began wondering how to make my graceful exit.

I was still wondering a few minutes later, when a thin weathered guy in work boots and a stained cowboy shirt walked up and Mari Rainey introduced her husband, Joe. What an unlikely couple. He was not unattractive exactly, but his rough-and-ready, slightly sweaty masculine edge did not mesh with her pastel precision. How these two ever found each other I couldn't imagine and didn't want to; their marriage was none of my business. Joe Rainey mumbled hello, his attention really on Philip, who was leaning against his mother and studying the linoleum.

We sat together, side by side by side, wanting to be anywhere else but riveted to the uncomfortable purple chairs. Philip sat on his mother's lap for a few minutes, then his dad's. I headed to the water cooler to give them some space and privacy, as if there is such a thing as privacy in a hospital waiting room. Finally a nurse came out to say that since the doctors would be running tests for some time, Mrs. Franklin suggested we go on home.

By now I was itching to get out of there, but I wasn't sure how. I decided to call good old Cleo. She'd love it that I was stooping to asking for a ride in that damn pink Lincoln Continental of hers she knows I hate to death. Cleo, unlike her car, I am crazy about. She is such a hoot. The citizenry of Esmeralda call her the Pink Duchess—God knows what they call me. She dresses only in pink, drives the pink Lincoln, two tones of pink, thank you, and lives pretty much in a bubble of pinkness, from the pink-frosted tip of her pageboy to the pink-painted nail of her big toe. She paints watercolors that have a pink quality all their own, and she is owner and operator of The Pink Heron, Esmeralda's one gallery and frame shop. She is also my patroness. Every artist deserves a Cleo Gallagher in her life, even if she does drive me nuts. She believes in me completely, and what is more, she sells my work as fast as I bring it in.

Not to the locals. Cleo has a whole different set of clients. She started out selling mainly to her various friends from resorts along the Florida coasts, but over the years, she's developed a reputation. If you're browsing for art or antiques along the Gulf, from Tampa to Destin, somebody along the way is bound to suggest The Pink Heron for one-of-a-kinds. Or maybe people come to see the Pink Duchess herself. Who cares as long as they buy, and they do buy. Along with the typical seascape crap you find everywhere in Florida, Cleo has her specialties. Local primitives, handcrafted furniture, her own watercolors, which do have a charm of their own, and my boxes for the more avant-garde fringe. Those boxes are turning into Dylan's college fund.

Basically, Cleo has been as close to a guardian angel as I'm likely to get. So I knew she'd be over in a flash if I asked her. I began rummaging in my purse for change for the pay phone.

"Why, Mrs. Blue, you need a ride back to your automobile, don't you?" Mari Rainey called across the room. "Joe, we have both our cars here. Why don't you give her a lift? It's the least we can do."

He looked as surprised as I was, but under the circumstances he could not exactly contradict her offer. I didn't care. I just knew I was ready to go.

"Hope you don't mind the truck," he said as I climbed in. "I'm a little like a turtle; I carry my office and factory on my back everywhere I go, work or home, or hospital." I had no idea what he was talking about, as I guess he noticed, but I was mildly charmed by his choice of words, thinking of my turtle-back rocks out on the Point. "I'm a farrier," he went on. "I shoe horses. You can't guess how many horses there are between here and Gainesville."

"No, I probably can't." I asked him would he mind if I smoked.

"Hell, no," he said, smiling for the first time, and I couldn't help noticing that he had one of those toothy, crooked smiles that can be lethal under certain conditions.

I rolled down my window, he slid in a Hank Williams tape, and I don't think either of us said another word until we reached Highway 12. I've never been much for country music, but it was oddly comforting listening to the sweet crooning while surrounded by the smell of leather and horse shit and fired iron. Leaning back against the torn seat cover beside Philip's father, whose arm stretched out behind me, not touching of course but giving off a welcome human warmth, I realized how badly I needed comforting. I could not stop thinking about David, about a nervousness I'd picked up in the nurse's voice. Was she holding information back?

Like how seriously he was hurt? I had told the child he would be fine and I had believed it, believed I had saved him. But what did I know?

It took one side of the tape and two cigarettes to get to the accident site, just enough time for me to regain my equilibrium. Joe Rainey made sure my car would start, as if Miranda has ever failed me. I helped him load the bicycles onto the truck.

"Thank you," he said, or I did, or we both did. He smiled again, and off he went.

In the morning, I rang up the hospital to find out David's condition. He was listed as stable. A few hours later, Mrs. Franklin phoned out here to say she was sorry she hadn't properly thanked me at the hospital. I could hear her exhaustion.

"You didn't need to call."

"Oh, but I did," she protested, maintaining her Southern good manners no matter what. Then she took a deep breath and told me about the spinal damage; how serious was not yet clear. I asked if I could visit in a few days. I felt a tremendous need to see David for myself.

"Of course, he may not even remember me."

"Oh no, he asked about the lady with red hair. I am assuming that's you."

"Yes, that's me." I laughed, overcome by a rush of protectiveness not only toward David but toward his mother, too.

I heard nothing from Philip's parents and did not expect to. Then two nights ago one of those coincidences happened, the kind that makes me wonder who's stirring the pot up there in the heavens. I was at The Pink Heron, dropping off some new pieces to Cleo, enjoying one of her little tirades.

"Oh my dear, the air in Esmeralda is getting worse and worse." I was barely inside the door when she started in. "Don't pretend you haven't noticed. If a breeze comes up from the south as it did today, carrying along those absolutely poisonous fumes from the mill, all clarity is lost. I cannot breathe. I cannot taste. I certainly cannot paint."

"You could move."

We have this conversation, or its variations, at least once a month. Bad air has developed into one of Cleo's favorite topics since she decided that Esmeralda could become the next Key West. She has been talking to moneyed friends about building a new marina, renovating the warehouses along Dock Street, even opening a bed-and-breakfast in the Guilfree house across the street from the gallery. Can you imagine a bed-and-breakfast in Esmeralda? The fact is that half the population here works at B&W Mill. Cleo's own adored husband ran the place until he keeled over with that stroke. He's the reason she ended up here and will probably never leave. The mill is the bane of her existence, and mine, too, half the time, but thank the gods for it. The mill keeps this town honest, the mill and the lack of a good beach like the ones you find once you get west of Port St. Joe. Imagine Esmeralda poked through with café awnings and T-shirt shops. Now *they* would keep me from breathing.

"I'm surprised George didn't take care of the odor problems for you when he was in charge," I teased, kicking off my shoes and dropping into one of the painted twig chairs Cleo gets from a man in his late eighties up near Weewahitchee.

"He had his engineers working on it when he had his stroke. But this new man"—who arrived right after George's death seven years ago, although to Cleo he will always be the new man—"he will never lift a finger."

"Oh well, there's always air-conditioning."

"Never. I love my fans and so do you."

"Yes, damn it, I do," I admitted. Air-conditioning is a sin of modern life, and I make that assertion as a licensed HVAC technician. "Why choose to live in a warm climate and then be chilly all the time?"

I studied the antique mahogany and wicker blades revolving slowly overhead pulling up the smoke from my cigarette in a dancing curve until some small creaking or shuffle pulled my attention toward the door.

Joe Rainey stood on the porch, framed by the pink molding around Cleo's window display. Of all the people I would not have expected to see. He was studying the grouping of my newest pieces we'd arranged out there the week before with my Egg of Life as the centerpiece.

"Come in, Joe, come in, come in," Cleo said with sudden gaiety.

"You know him?" I was about to ask, but Cleo was already flittering toward the front door, all aglow, the way she gets around certain favorite customers, although Joe Rainey seemed an unlikely candidate for Cleo's attentions. The man shoes horses, for God's sake. How much money, or interest, could he have to invest in art?

"Do you remember my painting *Florida Siesta*, Godiva?" I did actually, a small, rather exquisite re-creation of the midday view from Cleo's bedroom window. "Joe bought it, when was that, three years ago? I have not been able to convince him to buy anything since, but I keep trying." Cleo giggled, part aging coquette, part saleswoman. "At least he does drop by occasionally."

Not when I've been around. At least not until now. It was a little bizarre to cross paths again so soon. Definitely bizarre. He held out his hand. As I shook it, I noticed bits of blue paint around my cuticles and wished I'd cleaned up before coming over.

"I opened The Pink Heron eight months after George died, you know," Cleo said, picking up our previous conversation as if she'd never stopped, thrilled to have her audience enlarged. She patted Joe's arm apologetically. "I suppose I've told you this story before."

"I think you may have mentioned it." He smiled and took Cleo's long, bony, pink-nailed hand in his, ever gallant I must say. "But not the details."

"My Fairfield County friends were pressuring me to sell the house and move to Sarasota or Palm Springs. Starting the gallery was my excuse to stay. You know, I'd run one years before, but of course, my friends said the idea of an art gallery in Esmeralda was preposterous."

"They were right," I said on cue. I've heard this story a million times.

"Of course they were right. Opening the gallery was a preposterous idea. But George had left me plenty of money. And, of course, we'd been so happy here for those fifteen years."

"You're such a romantic, Cleo, under all the pink icing."

"Under all this pink icing, as you call it, I'm tough as life requires. Believe you me. I did steal the man away from his first wife, after all."

"Cleo!" I laughed, abashed that she had edited her familiar script to include that little bombshell. And in front of Joe Rainey, who was basically a stranger, not that he showed the slightest embarrassment. What a laconic Jimmy Stewart cowboy he was, leaning back in his dusty boots and smiling Cleo's story along.

"Just because I'm old, doesn't mean I haven't lived. We met at one of those awful bridge parties they were always having in New Canaan. The two of us had been assigned to different tables. Well, you know they like to put five at each table so someone's always rotated out. We ended up on the out rotation at the same time. There was a glorious deck overlooking the pool. We started talking, some mundane topic, olive varieties I believe. We'd both been to the south of France and agreed that American olives would never taste adequate again. And so it began.

"We weren't youngsters, but it was a grand passion I can tell you." Cleo turned to Joe. "That's what this one needs over in that dank little shack of hers."

"That is not what I need, and Paradise is no shack."

I could have wrung her elegant old neck or strangled her with her pink pearl choker. She was behaving like some bizarre, perverse version of my mother, talking about me in the third person. Besides, my antennae were definitely receiving signals, and I goddamn hated what they were telling me. Or not so much telling me as vibrating through me.

Coincidence can be a dangerously powerful aphrodisiac. Out of the void, this man Joe Rainey and I had been thrown together twice in a week. We had nothing in common to have so much in common. These newfound meaningful connecting points of his child and my patroness. Then, to top things off, coming out of the gallery, we discovered we were parked in the same direction and had to walk together another three blocks.

It was that creamy hour between late afternoon and early evening when the air softens and you want to move slower, to hold off the night. As we were passing by, the yellow light inside the Chit Chat looked so inviting, I don't remember which of us voiced the suggestion, but there was no way not to stop in for a slice of jam pie. We sat there in a corner booth talking for maybe half an hour, the only customers so near closing time.

At first we talked about David Franklin. Joe Rainey told me that the insurance companies and the lawyers were having a field day. "I know this is not a noble thought, not one that should be spoken out loud," he said and I felt temptingly at risk, "but I have to admit that I am relieved it was David's baby-sitter who was negligent. I could not have afforded a lawsuit."

"Wow, I've never considered issues of legal liability about anything," I blurted out.

Moral liability was another matter. In a few days David was being transferred to the hospital in Perry almost an hour away. They were still hoping he might walk eventually. I had visited him several times already and knew I'd be visiting him regularly from now until whenever. It might not be rational but I felt responsible.

"Something like this happens and everyone feels guilty, I guess. Last night was the first Philip has slept through without nightmares. Since the accident Mari is uncomfortable with baby-sitters at other people's houses, and frankly so am I. Baby-sitters period. I don't want him out of our sight. She gets off early when she can, but a lot of days she can't get home before six. So I pick him up after school and bring him along on shoeing jobs. Damn, if I don't find myself looking forward to those afternoons, having him by me handing me tools, picking up the old shoes, feeding the hoof scraps to the farm dogs."

"Philip is a good boy."

"He is, isn't he?" Joe smiled that crooked insidious smile, and I caught our reflection in the mirror above the jukebox, our two heads bent together over our mugs of tea and coffee. A cliché classic if ever there was one.

When he called last night, I was too surprised to hang up right away.

"Philip rode my horse today," he said with fatherly pride. "For the first time. Did real well, too."

"I'll bet he did." I smiled, picturing the two of them. Joe's attachment to Philip was pretty endearing.

"You should come out here and ride sometime. With a name like Godiva. Wasn't she a rider?"

"Well, yes."

"And your daughter, too. Young girls love horses. It would give Philip a kick." This line of talk seemed innocent enough. But still.

"I don't think so."

"Why not?"

"Actually, horses are one of the few things in the world that I am afraid of." It was true, I am; but when he laughed, I knew I should not have told him. The laughter was too comfortable. I remembered how I'd felt sitting in his truck, in the café. How at ease we were alone together with quiet between us.

Two nights later, he called again.

"It's me," he said and this time I was not surprised.

"Hello, me." I put down the book I'd been reading, stubbed out my cigarette and sighed. Some bridge had been crossed. The conversation took on its own rhythm, drifted to whatever came to mind. What we said was not the point. Charged with the velvety intimacy of the telephone late at night, we gradually reached that point, nothing left to be said, only the desire not to disconnect. It was lovely.

Not that it will go any further. He is a married man. I have never been a homewrecker and do not intend to become one now. My God, he is also Philip's father. I care about Philip. I owe Philip. Philip trusts me. So I'm staying clear, even if the marriage is breaking down. And I've been hit on by married men in this town enough to know better than to trust what a man says about his marriage. Not that Joe has said anything in so many words.

Anyhow, he's too short and he's stoop-shouldered, bending over all those horses' feet I suppose. I don't even know if he's intelligent. God, as if that's ever mattered before, as if I need to defend his mental pedigree just because he seems able to set off a few bells where I wish he couldn't.

What attracts a woman to a particular man, anyway? I swear, I have not the slightest clue why Joe Rainey might grab my heart. Of all the men I could possibly lose my head over, what makes him so special? Is it purely physical, some chemical reaction that came over me in the Chit Chat? He's too stoop-shouldered. I already used that one, didn't I? Well then, squinty-eyed. And there's that scar on his cheek. His ears point at the top. I have my mantra of his deficiencies, but it has proven as useless as bug repellent in the marshes around here. For every deficiency, I remember, what? His childlike nervousness, tearing up shreds of napkin as we talked. His hands, big, reliable worker hands. His brownness, the very male brownness of a man who works outdoors.

Listen to me. No, don't.

"Watch yourself. Men get in the way if you don't keep vigilance," clear-eyed, pure Evie Pinkston told me long ago in Ann Arbor, as I was walking out the kitchen door of our apartment on my way to meet some guy from my psychology class for pizza and, probably, sex. "Stay away from any man you might lose sleep over," she warned.

I have lost enough sleep in my time, and for what? I do not intend to lose any more. This Joe Rainey thing, I'm only playing with myself a little. I am going to put him out of my mind. I have no room in my life for any man. Nada. No room at the inn. No vacancy. Men need not apply.

THREE

I've never been all that enthusiastic about women cluttering up my life, either, come to think of it. I don't trust them, at least not the ones my age. They're too ready to bitch and moan over all their lost potential. "You lost it, you find it," I want to tell them, only they probably didn't lose it; they probably frittered it away. That's why I like Cleo. She may whine about the weather or the air but never about her own life. She's all, shut up and get it done. Like me. Okay, I'm not exactly tight-lipped, but I do not whine.

And now there's Louise Culpepper. My new pal. She doesn't strike me as a whiner, either. Although we've been acquainted one way or another for a while, it wasn't until school started back in September that we began what you'd call a friendship, which, I guess, I would call it. That morning, maybe the second week of school, I was on my way across the playground, grappling with a large rectangular carton full of lightbulbs, when I ran across Louise sitting on the cement steps, watching over her class's recess. She was catching a bit of breeze, an unconscious smile playing on her lips.

The thing I've noticed about teaching small children, and working around kids so much I've noticed a lot, is that a teacher can't turn her back for a second, *not one second,* or something disastrous, a fight, or an injury or tears of one sort or another, is bound to happen. She better be there on top of them all the time. So she—and let's face it, when I'm talking teacher, I'm talking she—better like children. Not all teachers do. Some teachers, I'd say a lot of Gulfside teachers, would admit without a tincture of shame that they hate the kids. Not to me they wouldn't, of course, but I hear them in their lounge while they catch a smoke. Complaining, complaining, complaining. I feel sorry for those poor kids they're supposed to be teaching. I feel sorry for the teachers, too. How do they face each day?

Now Louise Culpepper is not like that. Maybe because she didn't start back into teaching until her youngest began school himself, Louise has stayed enthusiastic. I can tell just looking at how much color she uses to decorate her room. Not to mention that she was the only teacher who actually came up to me after she saw my cafeteria constellations to say she was going to add them to her lesson plans. I was genuinely flattered.

Anyway, I followed Louise's smile from the steps to a gaggle of little girls trying cartwheels. What is it about little girls and cartwheels, some rite of passage we must all go through? As I was passing by, one of the girls, Carolyne Fenster I think is her name, put her right hand down flat and pointed her little rear end up to the sky, then crumpled when her left hand couldn't carry her weight.

"I love it!" I could not help calling over to her, she was trying so hard. I carefully put my carton aside and squatted down in the dusty dirt. These girls were a hell of a lot more interesting than my lightbulbs. "Okey dokey, who can do one more for me?"

I was wearing my standard work uniform: a bright purple T-shirt and overall shorts. I pulled off my baseball cap and pointed my own rear skyward. God, it had been a long time since I'd done a cartwheel, probably ten years, back when Dylan was learning. But over I went. When I came right side up, my face was burning with all the blood that had rushed up there, and my cheeks were probably the color of my hair—damn redhead's complexion does not give me a break—but I'd done one heck of a cartwheel.

I flashed Louise the victory sign. Now if she'd been Esther Parks, the other second-grade teacher, I'd probably have been in big trouble. Esther Parks can be funny about what she deems proper conduct. When Dylan was in her class, Dylan's reading improved dramatically, I admit it; but Esther was unwilling to give the least little bit of slack for Dylan's creative tendencies, the very tendencies I was trying so hard to nurture. Esther likes to run what she calls a tight ship, and that does not include her students fraternizing with the school's "lady custodian," as she has always referred to me. Fortunately, Esther was over near the jungle gym, too busy scolding some boys with sticks in their hands to notice me or anyone else.

I began actively coaching the girls. Brushing the gravel off her knees and grimacing, Carolyne Fenster tried again, without much more success than on her first try, but I got her friends clapping to encourage her. Not being a teacher, I can do things like have fun with the kids. If I were a man, I suppose there would be concern that I harbored dirty motives, but as a woman I'm deemed harmless.

"Beautiful! That was one incredible cartwheel, wasn't it?" I turned toward the steps to include Louise in our little charmed circle.

She nodded and smiled. Each of the girls did a cartwheel, more or less. I picked up my carton and walked over to Louise on the step. She was clearly surprised but not standoffish; more what I'd call shy, almost flustered.

"I've been meaning to talk to you," I said, setting the carton down again.

"Yes, well, me too." I could see a bead of pulse in her forehead between her brows. "According to the book of astronomy I took out of the library, you were very exact in your representation of the Florida night sky," she said.

"Well, I did try. Why do a thing halfway?" I sat on the step below her and waited for her to take her next conversational turn. Instead, we sat in a widening pool of silence.

I recognized that Louise was in a funny position. She would not want to be seen as presuming. Every teacher at Gulfside realizes, if she wants her classroom to run smoothly, she is pretty much dependent on yours truly. Mr. Jenks is supposed to handle major repairs, but Gulfside shares him with the middle school. So I am the crew of one who makes sure the lights are burning, the floors are mopped and no one has an air unit on the fritz; I am the one who can find extra shelves for a supply closet, and sometimes extra supplies as well.

"I guess we have some kids in common these days," I offered. "Dylan and Cass have struck up quite the friendship."

"Yes, it does seem to be lasting. So few of Cass's do."

"Oh?" That was interesting. Surprising as well. And a little worrisome. Dylan told me that Cass was popular, but she never mentioned fickle. If Cass dropped her, Dylan would be heartbroken. I pulled a pack of gum out of my breast pocket.

"When I can't smoke, I've gotta chew." I held out a stick of Wrigley's Spearmint which Louise declined. Gum chewing is not allowed at Gulfside.

"Dylan seems like such a nice girl. You must be proud of her," Louise said. She paused, then added, "I'm not just being polite. She really does seem a quiet, sensible, well-brought-up girl."

The irony was unavoidable. I knew, and Louise had to know, too, that anyone you asked in Esmeralda would assume it should be the other way around. Louise's daughter should be the one people describe as well brought-up, not mine. But Cass is evidently something of a tough nut. Not that I've ever said more than two words to the girl, but the way she dresses and makes herself up like Miss Punk Rock of 1986 has to drive a conventional woman like Louise crazy.

"Cassie is going through such a stage. I hope she is not a bad influence."

"I'm not worried. Dylan's not that easily influenced. Besides a girl like Cass, I like her spirit. Dylan is crazy about her." And if she hurts Dylan's feelings I'll kill her.

"Darryl complains about the hair, the makeup, the jewelry. He says she is not wearing those crosses of hers out of religious conviction. Of course she isn't, but it can be hard to know anymore when to keep the parental reins tight and when to let go."

"Tell me about it," I agreed, not that I really had that problem with Dylan. I've raised her in Esmeralda knowing she'd have to learn early how to stand on her own because there was no way she and I would just blend in, and she has learned. I like her black T-shirts better than Peter Pan collars or polyester stretch pants, that's for sure. Dylan might be a little self-conscious, what teenager isn't? But she is a great kid, the kid every mother wants. She's her own person, but she knows how to get along with all kinds of people. I must say I've done a good job of child-rearing. Her classmates' parents have to give me that, whatever else they think of me. God knows what they do think, and only God cares. Of course, at the moment, I'm a hero because of the bicycle accident, but I imagine Esmeralda's usual thinking about Ms. Godiva Blue lies more along the lines of crackpot eccentric Yankee, also mannish and possibly atheist or Jew. Some of which may or may not be true; I'm certainly not telling.

It doesn't help that I'm better educated than most of the teachers whose rooms I clean. I can see their little brains calculating, wondering why, if I'm so smart, do I keep this shitty job? Their attitude is a lot like my mother's, come to think of it. Why are people so uptight, so ready to judge and ready to blame? Of course, my artistic nature sets them off, too. My boxes on display at The Pink Heron, some of them are worth hundreds of dollars, but people around here don't know what to make of them. Esmeraldans think art means landscapes and the occasional still life, if they think about art at all.

"I find those boxes of yours fascinating," Louise Culpepper said out of nowhere. Was she reading my mind or what?

"Yeah, be honest now."

"I do, even if they are a tad unsettling."

"A tad?" We both laughed.

"Well, you're a tad unsettling in general."

"I probably am." We laughed again. Let's face it, a six-foot-tall redhead is going to stand out wherever she goes—I'm used to it—and in Esmeralda, where women my age still wear flower-print dresses and go to the beauty parlor, I am a regular freak. Me and the Pink Duchess.

"Dylan and Cass, they're a hoot, aren't they?" I thought shifting the subject back to our daughters might be wise.

Louise nodded. "I hope, I truly do, that Dylan is the friend Cass has been looking for. She needs a close girlfriend like Dylan.

I don't have a clue what goes on in my daughter's brain. I truly think I could live with everything if I didn't feel so in the dark about Cass all the time." Her hint of desperation felt foreign and a little pathetic. After all, I know Dylan as well as I know myself.

As I struggled to strike the right note of proper empathetic commiseration, I noticed Philip Rainey moping along the edge of the field as if he'd lost something in the weeds. I'd seen and talked to him at school half a dozen times since the accident, but I don't think I'd realized before how small Philip was, dark and small with chicken-skinny arms and legs. I looked for but could not see the father in the son. It occurred to me then that, as special as Philip seemed to me, in his schoolyard life he was the kind of almost invisible little boy usually passed over by teachers as well as classmates.

"Hey, Philip, aren't you going to come by and say hi?"

"He's in my room," Louise said as Philip slowly walked over.

"No kidding. Another child we have in common." I jumped up from the step and bounded down to meet Philip halfway across the field. I swooped him into a hug, trying not to remember my conversation with his father the night before, a conversation I'd already decided was best forgotten. Out of the blue, Joe had begun a story.

"A year ago we went to Tallahassee to have a family photograph made for Christmas, the cards they make you up," he told me. "Only something went wrong at Sears, the man in charge of developing negatives went berserk, destroyed a whole day's worth of families. Not just ours. By the time the money came back with the form apology it was too late to make another appointment. For months I wondered if I should drive back down there. Raise hell. I never did. The beginning of the end."

"Why are you telling me this?" I'd asked, but Joe didn't answer. Now here was his son swinging on my arms.

"So why did the lobster blush?" I asked Philip.

He shook his head, his eyes on the sandy plot of grass in front of us.

I leaned down and whispered, "Because the sea weed."

He looked up straight at me then, shocked that I'd tell what I guess is a dirty joke to a seven-year-old. Which was the point, because despite himself his cheeks puffed and all his missing teeth showed as he broke into giggles. Little-boy giggles are hard to beat. All of a sudden he was laughing like crazy, and I had two more jokes up my sleeve. When I gave him a push toward a group playing Star Wars near the teeter-totters, he actually let himself be pulled into the play.

"You're great with kids," Louise said when I came back to the step.

"Well, Philip and I have a kind of pact." I looked at my watch and sat back down. No one was actually waiting on the lightbulbs. "That was one scary afternoon. Whew, when I saw the bicycle wheel spinning in the wind. You're a mother, you know what I'm talking about."

"I do. I know exactly. Whenever I looked at Philip in the last two weeks, I could not help thinking of David Franklin in a hospital bed in Perry and then of my own kids, knock on wood, safe and sound. I know how selfish that sounds."

"It sounds honest to me. I felt the same way." But we both knew that most of Louise's neighbors would consider such a remark, hinting at the comfort taken from another's grief, unseemly. Louise's openness was refreshing.

"So how is he doing, do you know?" she asked.

"He's hanging in there. I saw him yesterday, as a matter of fact. I visit as often as I can. I have to. David's recovery is in my hands. Not literally, I realize, but there's this basic primitive reaction when you're involved in saving a person's life. Nothing altruistic about it, either, believe me. Some kind of instinctual higher primate drive."

I told her about stopping the car, how part of my mind had seen something was wrong before I looked back and saw the bikes in reality.

"God, it was awful, full-of-awe awful. I mean, somewhere out there David's parents were going about their day's business without a clue, their thoughts wrapped around the number forty-five or the peppermint flavor of their chewing gum or whatever adult epiphany they might be wafting through."

Louise looked across the playground, considering. "We couldn't survive if we didn't block out bad possibilities," she said.

"That's the goddamn truth. Imagination is glorious. I'm an artist. How could I create without it? But imagination can be paralyzing. Especially if we're talking mother and child. Believe me, try riding in an ambulance with someone else's kid hooked up to monitors measuring God-knows-what, knowing that at any moment, as soon as the driver radios the hospital and some social worker at the hospital dials her number, the karma of that kid's mother's moment will shatter into a thousand pieces, every one sharp enough to cut glass. Meanwhile, I was the one rocketing down the highway, holding her kid's hand."

I looked at Louise and shut my mouth, considering whether she wanted to hear all this. Aside from the fact that she happened to be Philip's teacher, I had no reason to drop these ruminations on her head. What I was saying was extremely personal, after all. Of course, it was also rather interesting, if I say so myself. And the way Louise was sitting, her pale skin slightly flushed, her hands clenched in her lap with the effort of following what I was saying, she was obviously fascinated.

I explained about my daydream foretelling the accident. Louise did not even flinch. Instead, she leaned forward and spoke intently.

"You know I have read in a book how someone was 'transported.' The author said it was as if a door were opening up and she could see a whole new world on the other side, brighter colored, more boldly outlined."

"Yes," I said, impressed. "That's it exactly."

"You know," she went on in that innocent north Florida twang, "all my relatives and the girlfriends I grew up with here, I love them dearly, but I know them all so well, know exactly what to expect." Louise shifted on the step, crossed and recrossed her legs. "Well, it's just that my friends and I, we can practically finish each other's sentences, but we would never talk like this."

Whatever chemical or spiritual mingling must occur for a friendship to ignite between two women began occurring right about then. The same slight tingle of recognition I'd felt along my spine so many years ago back in West Hartford, when I knew, without knowing their names or anything else about them, which two or three among the group of twenty almost indistinguishable little girls in Mrs. Crispin's first-grade class would become my friends. The same knowing I'd had in high school, in college, in any crowd of women, but different from the sexual ignition light that clicks on around certain men. I can't put my finger on the particular frisson of impending friendship, but when I've felt it I've known, and I felt it then sitting on the step with Louise, the children cartwheeling and chasing each other around us.

As I began to describe another dream, Louise stole a glance toward Esther Parks still sitting on the bench by the jungle gym, grading worksheets, her skirt scrunched around her thighs so it wouldn't blow up unexpectedly.

"Such a tight ass," I said, and Louise tried to swallow the giggle that slipped up her throat.

"Anyway, I am driving with Dylan, not in Miranda, in some kind of red convertible. Me in a red convertible, can you picture it?" She shook her head, grinning. "Anyway, we have to cross a body of water. Now usually, in my dreams, I am a man. It makes sense I guess. But last night I was me. Very female. More female than ever in real life."

"You don't think you're feminine?" Louise asked.

"Feminine enough. So anyway, there is a bridge and we start across and the bridge gets lower and lower, closer and closer to the water. Soon the waves are lapping at the tires, and I am still driving, wondering whether I have enough speed to skim across the surface and save our lives, Dylan's and mine. I can see the shore the whole time."

"Can you just see it!" I slammed my hand against the carton so hard that the glass bulbs rattled like crazy. We both looked and held our breaths as if we could repair any broken bulbs that way.

"What's one broken lightbulb more or less?" I shrugged.

"Is this how you come up with your boxes?" Louise asked.

"Sometimes."

"I love how you fill them. I go out of my way to check out new boxes in Mrs. Gallagher's display window whenever I go downtown. They remind me of when I was a little girl and used to collect shells, ribbons, hair barrettes, whatever I happened to pick up. My momma used to look at all the bits of this and that gathered in my room and call it turkey stuffing, as in 'Clear all that turkey stuffing off your bed, young lady.' That's how I think of your boxes. In a good way, I mean. I don't pretend most of the combinations make logical sense to me, but they are so pretty, and a few seem almost funny although don't ask me to say why. They all have your stamp. All those tiny sculptures and miniature paintings of yours, the pieces of machinery, the beads and weavings. They're like your dreams."

"Well, thanks," I said. "Really. Thank you, Louise. I can call you Louise, can't I?" Teachers can be touchy about how they're addressed, as I have learned thanks to Esther Parks among others.

"Louise is fine." Her cheeks reddened. "Of course."

"Well, Louise, would you like to have a cup of coffee or something after school this afternoon?"

Louise was clearly flummoxed. I might as well have been a boy asking her to the high school prom.

"I don't think I can," she started to say, then stopped herself. "Well, come to think of it, my boys have Scouts until five." She smiled. "Sure, why not."

I looked across the playground. The sun had turned a corner in the sky and now light was outlining the kids, turning them into cutouts against the landscape. God, it was beautiful, the sheen that slips over everything down here at odd hours of the day sometimes.

I stood up and stretched my arms toward the flat pancake of sun overhead. Pulled forward by its force, I began to dance toward the teeter-totters. The kids gathered in a ragged circle around me and began to follow. Philip, awkward and hesitant at first, was there with the others stepping and swaying, lifting their arms, singing a nonsense song we made up as we went.

All those bare legs and arms going going going. Like notes on a flute. I mean for that moment I could not imagine myself anywhere else in this world.

"Will you look at that?" I called over my shoulder to Louise.

But the period bell was ringing and Louise didn't hear me or look upward to see the migrating birds flying high above in a thin black blade that left only the barest shadow in their wake.

FOUR

"*You* one selfish bitch of a white girl."

Evie Pinkston tongue-lashing me. July 15, 1970, shortly after three in the afternoon. Was it a condemnation, a warning or a statement of fact? Whichever, it has been blowing in across the Gulf at me these last weeks, distracting me in the studio, sometimes even rousing me from my bed. I can't seem to shut Evie out like I could sixteen and a half years ago. But back then who was listening? Anyway, it was too hot to listen in that airless University Avenue apartment, heavy with heat and the odor of last night's burnt rice.

I had just confided—proclaimed might be the better word—that I was pregnant.

"Preggers, with child, in the family way, pick your euphemism." I'd laughed, probably half-hysterical, though I would never have admitted it. Hell, I don't like admitting it now.

"No," Evie said, slowly putting down her pencil and placing the sheet music she was transcribing back into its folder.

"Yes, and I'm keeping my baby. No one"—meaning my parents—"is going to change my mind."

"What about the father?"

"Believe me, a baby and parenthood is not part of his life plan. Let's just say he's out of the picture."

That was when she called me a selfish bitch of a white girl, obviously thinking worse. What did I expect her to say? I should have known, must have known how she'd react. We'd been sharing the apartment for six months by then, a lifetime in those days, ever since my original roommate dropped out of school to join an ashram in Nevada. Evie's music scholarship didn't cover board, she told me when she answered my ad, so she was always looking for a cheap deal on rent. Once she moved in, we spent the typical roommate hours together. Meals, an occasional movie, weekend afternoons at the laundromat. Having my first black roommate, God knows I was eager for the friendship. What lefty, hippie college girl with lofty ideas of universal love wouldn't have been? But were we really friends? No, not really.

Our lives ran on separate paths. Race was only one difference. And race aside, Evie was not an easy person to know. The truth? The truth is that I never was confident I knew her. She unsettled me; not many people can claim that ability. I've always been pretty damn comfortable with who I am, but around Evie's deep amber elegance, her exquisite self-control, I felt unkempt, illogical, shallow. Like a selfish white girl. Which, in fact, I was. So, why out of all my women friends—and believe me that was a season when sisterhood was powerful and plentiful—did I go to Evie Pinkston about my pregnancy? Shit, it's obvious, isn't it?

"Only us black girls do that 'cause we got no choice." Ms. Evangeline Pinkston of Little Rock, who normally spoke with clipped precision, slipping on dialect like a favorite old sweater conveniently rediscovered at the back of her closet. A joke that was no joke. Infuriating.

"I've got news for you," I threw at her, full of myself and my righteous womanhood. "Every white girl I know, if her period's late or she forgot to go by the infirmary before class for her morning-after pill, starts fantasizing, 'What if I am?' "

"That's why I stay away from men," Evie shot back, and I shut up because she had me. She was not about to let anyone or anything sidetrack her ambition. Not Evie.

"So you're going to have this baby, and then what?" She shook her head, more to herself than to me. "O Lord, have mercy."

Her fierceness shamed me. Fierceness might seem a strange way to describe Evie. Not a hundred pounds with her coat on, that husky whisper of a voice, and the permanent expression of calm about her light brown eyes. But those eyes streaked with yellow sparks whenever she played her violin. I loved to sketch while she practiced, although I'd lose my focus, drifting upon the billows of music, gossamer as the orange blossom fragrance she wore—who else but Evie would wear cologne in 1970? Who else but a black girl who dressed only in pastels and pearls, who claimed she didn't know Huey Newton from Fig Newtons. Delicate as that music was, even my untrained ear heard the muscle rippling and flexing underneath. People talk about my intensity; God knows I cut quite the figure around here. Well, compared to Evangeline Pinkston, I've been a lightweight my whole life. A featherweight. Weightless. I mean, she was a genius.

And a truth-teller. "Your instrument won't let you lie if you're a genuine musician which I certifiably am," she'd explain with that little smile.

Who else could I possibly have gone to?

Of course, there was no way of knowing that six months later I'd be the only white person at Evie's funeral; not one member of the music department showed up. Which is a whole other story, except that after all her lectures about not letting anyone get in the way of her music, she had let that very thing happen, and in the worst way.

Not on purpose, of course. Evie was not expecting anything like death. Home in Little Rock for Thanksgiving break, she'd walked to the corner store to buy her mother some chicken parts. There was a robbery.

"Always a lot of them the month before Christmas," Evie's brother explained, carrying me into town from the airport in the beat-up taxi cab he drove for a living. In the trunk were three not-very-full boxes of Evie's clothes and books from the apartment, and her violin in its small black casket.

I should have learned my lesson then. Once the gun went off, there was no retracing of steps. Evie, so sure yet so lost.

"That's why I stay away from men," she'd said, secure in her self-protection. "They are a threat to my artistic selfhood."

Threat comes when you least expect, doesn't it?

+   +   +

LiKE last Wednesday afternoon. A normal autumn day at Gulfside, no hint of incoming fire, not a cloud in the sky, not a dream to disturb my sleep the night before, not even a call from Joe Rainey to upset my psycho-sexual balance—he does keep calling, and I do keep wondering if friendship with a man is possible. Louise Culpepper and I went out again after work. Wednesdays were becoming our day to play. This time I'd suggested The Oyster Shack, a sawdust-on-the-floor, whiskey-at-the-bar joint down by the marina with the best oysters you have ever tasted. I couldn't believe Louise had lived in Esmeralda her entire life without once stepping foot inside The Oyster Shack, although I guess it's not a restaurant where you'd go with the family after church for Sunday dinner, which is the main meal most Esmeraldans eat out.

"Darryl won't touch an oyster," Louise explained. "He says he choked on one once as a child and never got over it."

"Really?" I leaned forward across the varnished wood table scratched with penknife initials and littered with torn cellophane and squeezed-out lemon rinds. The smoke from my Pall Mall wavered up in a thin line above the platter of empty oyster shells the waitress was clearing away. "But you eat them?"

"Oh my, yes." She nodded gaily. "The sweetest in the world can be found right around here; everyone knows Gulf oysters are the best. I used to gather buckets full with my aunt Sally up near Apalachicola. We would not even bother to rinse the shells, just clean off the barnacles, then roast the oysters over a wood fire as soon as we got back to Sally's house, but only for a minute or so to make it easier to pry them open. Then we'd sit on Sally's screened porch and eat dozens at a time, stirring them around in a special horseradish catsup Sally mixed. I swear we got drunk on those oysters, laughing away as we scooped them up on our little forked plastic spoons. We'd swallow them down so fast they hardly tasted more than salt and bitter and sweet."

"You know oysters are aphrodisiacs?"

"Well, no. Are they truly?" She sounded interested but not shocked. Even as a small child I think Louise knew—and this is what I do appreciate about her, that she knew and was happy in her knowledge—that what she was doing was extravagant, decadent, sensuous. All those heavens people give negative words to once they're too old to accept them pure and unadulterated.

We ordered our oysters and looked around. Every table was filled. In the middle of the afternoon. Burly men in business suits, shrimpers in ball caps, even a few yachtsmen from one of the boats that occasionally put in at the marina which the town had recently voted to spend a ton of money fixing up in order to attract more tourists. Probably thanks to Cleo's lobbying.

"You know I do not recognize a single soul," Louise said with amazement.

"No kidding." I had to smile. It was obviously a revelation to her.

"I cannot think of a time," she went on, "at the grocery store or Shoney's or the public library, when I haven't had to nod hello or small talk my way past acquaintances."

"You know your layer, but even in a place as small as Esmeralda, there have to be other layers above and below yours that never intersect." Not a great metaphor but she knew what I meant. "Coming in here, you've jumped layers. You're not used to being anonymous."

As if I were. I'm used to the stares and whispers, not necessarily flattering either, I get everywhere in Esmeralda, especially in a male domain like The Oyster Shack. I'd felt the eyes at my back earlier as we followed the hostess across the room.

"Enjoy it while you can," I said and laughed, lifting off my hat to unfasten the barrette that held my ponytail in place. "Someone's bound to show up you do know, even in here."

As I shook my hair free, I caught a young shrimper at the next table staring. He was all wiry muscle in his Dolphins T-shirt and tanned a golden caramel that stopped just short of his sleeves and collar to show narrow bands of vulnerable, white skin.

"Do you come here much?" Louise asked me. If she noticed the shrimper she gave no clue, and I wasn't about to let him know I had. There was a time when I would have, but no more.

"Every so often. It's a nice change of scene." I turned my attention to the platter the waitress set before us. I speared an oyster onto a saltine, dabbed the oyster in horseradish, squirted it with lemon and threw my head back to swallow it. Then I drank down the juice left in the half shell. Louise took an oyster on her fork and did the same. The oysters were small but very fresh, as salty-sweet as the best. I turned the platter clockwise so we each had a new oyster in front of us. We forked and dabbed and swallowed. I turned it again and we repeated the routine, six times until the platter was empty.

"I could easily eat another dozen oysters, but what an extravagance that would be on my salary," I said and took out a Pall Mall. Louise began fiddling with my plastic lighter trying to balance it on its edge.

"I stopped smoking three years ago," she said.

"I suppose I should. God knows, it's out of keeping with most of what I believe about how we should live our lives, but hey, as an artist it's my right don't you think. A little inconsistency is energizing." A thought of Joe Rainey flashed across my inner eye.

I let Louise keep playing with my lighter and instead struck a match from the pack that said THE OYSTER SHACK over a picture of a shrimp and an oyster jitterbugging. The waitress was clearing away the shrimper's empty plates. She held out the coffeepot, but he shook his head so she took his cup, too. He stood up, dug into his pocket for tip change, slapped on his cap and grabbed his check. As he headed to the cashier, I took a drag off my cigarette and studied his walk. Not bad.

When I turned back I realized Louise was blushing a bright crimson. She had noticed him after all, and noticed me noticing him, too. We looked at each other and cracked up.

We were still feeling slightly naughty a few minutes later as we drove away from The Oyster Shack in Miranda. Rolling down my window, I signaled a left turn with my arm because Miranda does not have blinkers.

"What would your friends think if they saw you putter past in my beat-up Volkswagen van, complete with yellow daisies painted on each door?" I asked.

Louise threw up her hands with a carefree toss of her head.

"Well, they probably won't." I wasn't sure if Dylan was pleased or not that I was becoming friends with Cass's mother. When I'd suggested that the four of us might want to get together for a mothers-and-daughters dinner one night, Dylan had shrugged, noncommittal.

"Oh," I remembered out loud. "I have to stop at the Quick Mart. More apples for Dylan. All she'll eat these days are apples and vanilla yogurt. Here we are in Florida and she won't touch an orange. Says the acid is bad for her skin."

"Her skin is lovely."

"Yes, but you know kids. I have to keep reminding myself this is just a phase Dylan's going through. Like her new interest in Baptists—no hard feelings, Lou."

"No hard feelings." Louise grinned. "I admit I was a little surprised to see her at morning worship last Sunday."

"Right up there beside Elvira Brasleton I bet."

For all I knew Louise considered Elvira Brasleton her best friend, but I doubted it. Elvira was too nice to be trusted, even for a preacher's wife.

"Actually, Elvira did mention to me, probably because she knows Dylan and Cass are friendly, what a fine girl Dylan is. She told me she and Reverend Brasleton hope Dylan joins the youth choir as a soprano to take Mitzi Grabler's place now that she's off to college in Tallahassee."

"She was trying to feel me out through you, huh?" I could just hear that wheedling voice of hers. "Worried that I would raise some opposition." As if I would stop Dylan from anything she really wanted to do, even joining the Baptist choir.

I was driving a block from Quick Mart, past the post office when Louise sheepishly mentioned that Darryl had asked her to get him stamped envelopes three days ago. "I hate to ask you," she said.

"No problemo. We both have our errands to run for the ones we love." Without missing a beat, I whisked Miranda into an empty parking space in front of the post office and came along with Louise into the building.

It was empty as usual. Mr. Peden, who's run the post office ever since he lost his eye in World War II, started talking to Louise about Disney World. Mr. Peden is a bachelor. The rumor is that his girl dumped him while he was overseas, but that is always the rumor, isn't it? As long as I've lived here, Mr. Peden has directed all his unused affection toward Disney World. Every weekend he takes one group of kids or another with him to Orlando. Dylan knows my opinion of Disney World and has never asked to go, thank the gods. The smell of desperation is too strong on that man to make me comfortable, although the kids always seem to come back in one piece and happier for their vacation. I suppose he is doing a good service, especially when he takes children who could never afford to go otherwise.

Evidently, he was just back from Epcot and eager to describe the space exhibit to Louise.

"Despite my being a good Christian and all, I have to say I can't help holding out hope there is reincarnation in heaven." He leaned over the counter and almost winked in Louise's face as he went on. "You won't tell the Pastor, but I like to think I'd be an astronaut. I truly do."

As he talked to Louise I wandered over to the stamp machine and began studying the commemorative choices up on the wall by the photographs of missing children. My glance drifted to the wanted posters, drifted away, then snapped back, hooked like a fishing line on the big catch. There was Hank.

My Hank. In the first flush of recognition I did not consider, did not even completely remember Dylan's connection to him. I saw his face and thought, "My God, Hank, what are you doing here?" When I looked back and forth fast enough, I could swear that what Hank was doing was staring intently at Mr. Peden's freckled bald head while Mr. Peden laboriously counted out change for Louise.

It was too bizarrely comic. I stood in the middle of that ugly brown room laughing to myself, dying to get out of there, but warmed with a certain tenderness, too. Hank, that's whom the young shrimper had reminded me of, like a physical, in-the-flesh premonition. But of what? Of seeing Hank's picture on a wall? How many years, yet that face was as familiar as the palm of my hand. I could still feel the hollow under his cheekbone in that dank church basement where we had talked and talked as I have never talked to another human being in my life. Talked and touched as if they were the same thing. I knew those eyes, that chin, those lips. I slipped the poster from the ring-bind holder.

"We've got to get out of here," I half-whispered as Louise walked up to me stuffing a dollar bill in her purse.

"Have you taken sick?" She looked at me with friendly concern and already the fact of Hank's face folded in my shoulder bag began to change shape like molten glass on the blower's pipe.

"Only in the head." I grabbed Louise's arm and pulled her through the door so hard she almost dropped the envelopes for Darryl.

"This is really strange. I mean, I don't know whether to laugh or to cry." I was walking to the car fast, dragging her along.

"I need to take a long ride to nowhere."

Louise did not speak. I did not expect her to. "Can you come along? I think I need the company."

"Darryl is with the boys at Scouts until at least seven." That's all she said, but it was all I needed.

We stopped at the Quick Mart as planned, but instead of apples and yogurt, I loaded the cart with a twelve-pack of Miller Lite, a carton of Pall Malls and two family-size bags of barbeque-flavor chips. Louise followed me up and down the aisles. God knows what she was thinking. God knows what I was thinking.

"Hell, Louise, we are friends, aren't we?" I asked as we headed up Gulf Road.

Louise nodded. "Sure."

"Then why don't you ever ask me the juicy questions I'd ask if I were you?"

"Like what?" Out the open window, the breeze had picked up among the scrub pines. Dust and sand and the rotten-egg odor of the paper-mill stacks blew through the car, across my cheeks and down under my collar.

"Like where is Dylan's father?"

"Well, I guess I figured he was someone you'd rather not talk about."

"The truth. Come on, out with it, girl."

"The truth? I assumed we needed to be better friends before I brought up painful subjects like divorce."

"Good point, well taken." I snorted and hit the accelerator. Louise gripped the edge of her seat. We were going close to sixty-five miles an hour, and Gulf Road was narrow and curvy. Finally I slowed down some, took a deep breath and reached for a fresh pack of Pall Malls.

"I'm sorry if I'm acting a little strange." I took another deep breath and pulled the car over to the side of the road. I see now that I should not have been so quick to share my own little truth, but I was bursting, wild with the strangeness, a little out of my head. And I had already decided I wanted to trust Louise. I realized that, in many ways, she was your conventional Southern woman, the kind of woman who pressed her husband's jeans. Still, I sensed a yearning to break out of her rut if someone would only show her how. Someone like me. But even in my crazed state, I saw the risk I was taking, guessing what a friendship can weather, especially a baby friendship like ours.

"I just saw Dylan's father for the first time in almost seventeen years," I blurted out. "At the post office."

Louise stared at me. No one had been in there besides the two of us and Mr. Peden. I knew she was racking her brain, wondering if I'd had one of my visions, wondering probably if I was psycho.

"What do you mean?" she said finally.

"On a wanted poster." The words rattled out like nails.

"Good Lord, what did he do?"

"I haven't had time to find out yet." It was true. I had been so absorbed in his face, I'd not bothered to read the words under it. I reached into the recesses of my bag lying on the seat between us and pulled out the wadded page of printed paper.

I'm not sure why I handed it to Louise, but I did. She smoothed out the page on her lap. I wanted to study her reaction to what she was looking at: two not very clear photographs of a man in his early twenties, good-looking in a scruffy, rough way. Hard-eyed, with a birthmark between his long thin nose and his rather full lips. No mustache or beard, but coarse dark hair that hung down almost to his shoulders. Not someone Louise would ever have brought home or introduced to her folks as her fiancé. The name printed under the pictures was Henry Howard Fierstein. The paper shook gently between Louise's fingers. Three or four aliases were listed as well.

"Well, what's the bad news?" As if I weren't reading along with her.

"A bombing." Louise could barely get the word out. "Conspiracy to bomb, it says."

"Does it say what he bombed?"

"No, not that I can tell."

"Does it say when?"

"Nineteen seventy-one."

"Well, back then it didn't necessarily mean all it does now." I reached an arm over the seat and pulled out two cans of beer from the Quick Mart bag. "In the sixties we all did things that seem dangerous now."

"Dangerous? That's not exactly the word I would have used."

"No, I guess not."

Louise fell silent. At The Oyster Shack she'd mentioned that she did not like beer's thick, sour taste, but now she took one long swallow after another.

"I cannot imagine holding a wanted poster of Darryl," she sighed.

"Try," I said.

She shook her head and looked out the window. I assumed she was angry at the question.

"Well, he was in the service before we got together," she said eventually.

"Vietnam?"

"No, Germany. He was lucky. Someone had to be posted to Europe I guess. Anyway it is not impossible that he could have done something, a prankish theft or even a little experimentation with drugs, but nothing like this. Darryl is my husband, the father of my children, my life." She looked at me apologetically. "An ex-husband is different. Less devastating I suppose. But my heavens, a terrorist?"

I drove on to the old municipal park. No one went there anymore, especially not during the week, so we had it entirely to ourselves. We opened two more cans, then lugged what was left of the twelve-pack to the old splintered picnic table.

Near the picnic table was an old swing set with two swings left from the original five, the kind that when you let go, bits of rust and cold metal smell stick to your hands. I sat in one, looping my arm around the chain so I wouldn't have to put down my beer. Louise sat on the splintery bench. She was ashen-faced, and I couldn't blame her. Two beers in less than half an hour, yet here she was, hanging in there for me. I could have hugged her.

"There's going to be rain by evening," Louise said licking a finger and holding it up to test the air. As soon as she spoke, I knew she was right. The sky was clouding up, while the wind had died down to the spooky soft calm that so often anticipates a storm along the coast.

It kept running through my brain like a bad song, Hank was a wanted criminal. I began to swing. Why not? The skirt I'd changed into on a whim after school dragged along the ground when the swing went up, then billowed behind when I came back down.

The skirt was one of these gauzy peasant deals, printed with multicolored flowers, and I felt as if petals were falling in my wake. A lovely sensation. I thought of the shrimper back at the restaurant. He was more or less the same age as Hank when those pictures were taken, except the pictures were fifteen years old. Men change a lot in fifteen years.

I stopped swinging. "What's the worst secret you've ever had?" I asked Louise.

"Me?" Louise yelped. Then she looked down and we both realized she was still clutching the wanted poster. She folded it neatly by quarters into a small square and handed it back to me. "This is."

"No, I mean before now. Of your own."

She concentrated earnestly. "Well, once in a while I have these fears. I'll get home after being out somewhere by myself and stand on the grass by the carport, and Darryl's old broken motorcycle will be lying on its side, or there will be a soccer ball with all the air kicked out of it in the azaleas, or the screen on the porch by the kitchen will be torn again. And I'll have this overwhelming knowledge that everyone inside is dead. Part of me is gripped in horror, but—and this is what is hard to admit—part of me is relieved. I have to force myself to walk up to the door, to turn my key in the latch. Sometimes I'll actually turn back to the car before I can force myself forward."

"Wow!" I must have shifted my weight because the swing tipped back suddenly, so far that the ends of my hair grazed the ground. "That was beautiful, really." I resettled myself on the seat. "But is there anything more concrete?"

A thin red line creased Louise's forehead between her eyes. She had just poured her heart out, against all better judgment, and here I was telling her it wasn't enough.

"I can't imagine any secret deeper or darker."

"Oh, Lou." I hurried reassurance like the condescending ass I admit I can be. "Don't think I don't appreciate your candor, but I wasn't thinking of anything quite that profound. I was hoping for something that might bring you down in the dirt with me. Just a run-of-the-mill dirty little secret was all I meant."

Louise swigged her beer, and I swigged mine.

"I do pick my nose. In the car driving and under the covers at night, ever since I was a little girl."

"I love it." I pushed the swing away from the ground on the balls of my feet. "Now we're even."

"Well, nose-picking doesn't compare to this," Louise said, giggling despite herself. She was definitely getting a little tipsy, maybe more than a little. So was I. Everything was coming to me as if I were coated in Jell-O armor.

"I've always been perfectly straight with Dylan about her father."

Taking another swig from her can, Louise's eyes widened with curiosity, and her lips twitched with unease.

"I mean, she knows I was not married."

"Goodness."

"Is that better or worse than a bomber-terrorist's ex-wife?"

She began to giggle again, but I was serious.

"I've told Dylan the basic story of her father and me. Our time together, what little there was, was as genuine and romantic in its way as most stories parents tell their children about how they came to be born." I doubted Esmeraldans ever told children anything about their births. "Also, I thought she deserved the truth."

"Which was?" The question evidently jumped out of her mouth before Louise could stop it.

"Kent State. Student demonstrators against the war in Vietnam were shot by the National Guard." I squinted at Louise. "I don't know if you remember."

"Yes, of course I do. It was the spring of 1970. I was one year out of college and teaching kindergarten. Also in the middle of getting engaged to Darryl. Most evenings, before we left my parents' house for wherever we were going, Darryl made a point of sitting with Daddy in the living room for half an hour to catch Walter Cronkite. I remember how impatient I'd get, wanting to be alone with Darryl."

I thought of asking whether they were sleeping together already, but I didn't dare. Her secrets were hers to tell me herself, and that wasn't one she'd offered.

"The picture of that young girl looking up from her dead friend on the cover of all those magazines gave me goose bumps all over," Louise said.

"It was May," I said, remembering the slightly humid scent of freshly mowed grass on the quad. The semester had finished, but I was hanging around for an extra spring semester to make up some of the credits I'd lost while blowing glass in Seattle the previous fall.

"A demonstration was called in D.C. I'm not sure why I decided to go. Probably because I was bored; my roommate had gone home to Little Rock for the week before classes started again. Or maybe because I'd already missed one big march that November. Anyway, it was organized the same as they all were. A score of rented buses left from the Union at seven in the evening to get there by the morning. Seats were assigned first come, first serve. Once the buses were filled, they rented cars. A former communist owned the local budget rental agency and didn't mind being taken advantage of.

"We thought of him as so old," I sighed, "and he was probably younger than I am now.

"I was smack in the middle of a big project that spring, a giant mural I was creating with kids from the Ann Arbor Free School. I couldn't decide if I should leave it, and by the time I decided for sure, I was too late for the bus. I ended up in a gray Chevrolet. Remember 'See the USA in a Chevrolet'? Somehow, I don't think they meant six strangers heading to D.C. with no plans to tour the White House. Twelve hours it took us, maybe thirteen. We sang. We ate candy bars. We played Botticelli."

"The painter?"

"The game. It's a variation on Twenty Questions, more intricate and insinuating. The person who's 'it' comes up with a name but tells only the initials. Then, to get him to answer a question you have to stump him by offering a clue and initials to a name of your own—you know, I can't remember if the initials have to be the same for both names or not; I haven't played for so long. It can take hours, believe me, circling in, slowly, on the identity. God, it was fun that night."

"You played word games?"

I nodded, hoping I was giving her the right mental picture. The intimacy, the intensity of the six of us singing at the top of our lungs in a car with the windows rolled up.

"You probably never thought the kind of people I'm talking about allowed themselves to have fun. They never looked as if they were having fun in those news reports, did they?"

"No, Godiva honey, they really did not."

"Well, we were upset. And we did everything in extremes in those days, didn't we?" As if Louise had been there, too. "Rage against injustice one moment, sing the rock-and-roll pleasure of being shit-kicking alive the next. God, it was intense being young, wasn't it?"

I unfolded the square of paper with extreme care and ran one blunt fingertip along the creases.

"Hank was assigned to my car. He didn't play the Botticelli game, but he could sing, a voice like choppy water, and he knew all the lyrics. Blues, folk, you name it. His eyes, you can't tell from this crappy snapshot, but they were amazing. Light, light blue, like a dream of blueness."

"Like Dylan's?" Louise asked.

I pushed the swing back and forth a few times, jerky but not hard enough to lift my feet off the ground. Without knowing it, she'd hit a nerve.

"You're absolutely right. Like Dylan's." A connection I'd never consciously made before by myself. Incredible.

Louise smiled. We were obviously on some kind of new wavelength. She came over and sat in the swing next to mine.

"Anyway, we didn't pull out of the Union parking lot until almost midnight so a lot of the driving was at night. Every so often we'd stop at a Howard Johnson's—ah, the innocent days of black raspberry ice cream and saltwater taffy—but no more than we had to. We drove and we drove and we drove."

I was swinging more regularly now. I let my voice follow the rhythm of the chains scraping back and forth, the story building and ebbing as the memories surfaced. God, how long ago it had been.

"When we finally made it to Washington, the actual demonstration was a downer. There hadn't been enough time to organize properly. People gathered as usual at the Justice Department to get tear-gassed, but no one was much in the mood for marches or chants. By late afternoon there was nothing to do.

"Somehow Hank and I got separated from the rest of our traveling cadre." Boy, that was a word I hadn't used in years. "We had agreed that, whatever happened, we would meet at the car at eight that night to find the church where we'd been assigned to sleep.

"Away from the others, Hank was much more boyish and playful. I think he decided to take a vacation from his politics for a little while. He took out his harmonica and serenaded me as we walked. He bought us hot roasted peanuts and soft ice cream from the truck vendors that catered to D.C. tourists. We began to pretend we were tourists. We window-shopped in some ritzy neighborhood full of what you'd call yuppies now, then strolled into a fairly grand hotel where we had drinks and cocktail sandwiches in the lobby."

"They let you in?"

"You mean despite our wild radical good looks?"

"Well, yes."

"We didn't look that outrageous. Remember, most young people in 1970 were a little scruffy around the edges. I'll bet even you had a pair of patched jeans and a peasant blouse or two. Besides, Hank told one of the managers we were trying to decide where to hold our wedding."

"And they believed him?"

"He was pretty charming. They gave us the food. Anyway, we didn't stay very long. We ended up on the mall. The cherry blossoms were out. Folks had taken off their shoes and were wading into the reflecting pools. But we all knew we were spending this lovely day together in the name of those dead students. It was definitely surreal. Like a scene right out of a Fellini movie, if you've ever seen one."

"All of them. *Satyricon* Fellini or *La Dolce Vita* Fellini?" Louise nodded to her beer. "That's what brought Darryl and me together—movies. We both loved them. All kinds. Ones I imagine you would never expect."

"You guys as movie buffs. You're right, I'd never expect."

"Well, Darryl had seen a lot of foreign films in Germany, and the one summer I worked in Orlando, all I had to do was go to movies. The first one we saw together was *Easy Rider*. I hated it. Darryl loved it." Louise laughed. "We argued all the way home and I was sure that he would not be asking me out again. But he called the next week for a double bill over in Gainesville. *The Seven Samurai* and *The Magnificent Seven*—Darryl said that if I didn't like watching *Easy Rider,* I'd *really* hate them."

Louise smiled dreamily and pushed her swing in a kind of stationary circle. I didn't have the heart to interrupt while she was taking a turn with her past.

"For months I lived for going to the movies with him. Driving back to Esmeralda late at night, knowing I had to be at work at 8:30 the next morning, I felt nothing existed but Darryl and me in his Rambler. There were few lights along the road, not even stars most of the time. The radio would be on low, and that late at night there would be few commercials. Song after song, we'd pass a single cigarette back and forth, or a bottle of cheap wine Darryl picked up somewhere. Finally, when the soft unbroken dark around and between us became too much, Darryl would pull off the road. There was always that heartbeat as he turned off the ignition, the complete silence before he touched me."

"Fellini, cars late at night, we have more in common than I thought. Did you go to Bergman films, too?" I tried to picture Darryl Culpepper reading the subtitles.

"Yes, as a matter of fact, we did."

"I have to admit I am impressed."

"Thank you." Louise grinned as I started to swing again.

"It's funny that I never painted it, though, the soft, tissuey cherry blossoms filling the background, the water spraying in pearly arcs over and onto hundreds of half naked bodies, the strong, beautiful bodies of youth. All of us middle-class kids splashing and laughing knew that four of our own had been killed on that campus in Ohio. Some protective bubble had been invaded. Responsibility for one's beliefs was finally being demanded. It was almost a relief.

"Hank was wearing a baseball cap with VENCEREMOS stitched across the bill. I remember I knocked it off his head, and he retaliated by pushing me into the reflecting pool." I stopped swinging. "Does all this sound too bizarre to you? God, it was long ago."

"Don't stop now." Louise hiccupped, and reached for the bag of chips on the ground beside her. "You're just getting to the good part," she said and ripped open the bag with her teeth.

I shook my head, and Louise flushed at her own indelicacy.

"You had to be there, I guess, in that renta-Chevy and at the fountain," I said carefully. Those few days probably could not be described in words after all. They existed only within the emotions and experience of the people there. I nibbled a chip.

"I don't know," Louise said, almost pouting. "You've been doing a pretty good job of bringing the experience to life."

"There isn't much more to tell. We met the others as planned, spent the night at a local church where there was some kind of organizational meeting, and drove back to Michigan. He wasn't a student. He lived in Toledo or Detroit, I didn't find out exactly where, working for the movement."

"Did he come back for you?"

"For me? No way." I left the swings with a push and a short leap. "I never saw him again." A bank of clouds was moving in fast. "It could never have worked." We had reached the end of what I was willing to share even now. There are feelings better left unstated, even to oneself. "He was too political for me. I stayed at the edge of things political because they distracted. He, on the other hand, was clearly at the center of the struggle."

"What struggle was that?" Louise hiccupped again despite her best efforts.

I reached over and grabbed a handful of chips.

"I don't remember."

Then I began to laugh. So did Louise. We dropped into the weedy dirt. I think we were flat on our backs by then, holding our sides, spitting the word "struggle" back and forth along with bits of potato chip and saliva.

"Let's face it, marriage is not my style," I said. "But I have always loved children."

"No kidding," Louise sputtered, preening her new wittiness. "Kidding—get it?—*kid*-ding."

"I get it, I get it. I mean there I am in the post office, minding my own business, and there is Hank Firestone on the wall staring down at me."

"Fireman." Louise corrected me through a spasm of giggles.

"Whatever."

Our last hoots of laughter subsided, floating away on woozy, newly discovered affection.

"Wait until I show Dylan."

"Show her what?" Louise asked and something hard, a pebble or a stick end, pressed into the small of my back, forcing me to sit up.

The wanted poster, crumpled and smudged, lay in the dirt by my straw hat and lighter, inches from Louise. I saw her fist clench and had a sudden horrible vision, no, not a vision but a déjà vu in reverse of what I might be about to see, the lighter flicking open into flame, Hank's face burning away. Quickly, with strained casualness, I picked up the sheet of paper and dusted it off.

"I've always been straight with my daughter."

"I guess I'd handle things a little differently," Louise said, sitting up and brushing the dirt off her stockings. There was no mistaking the splintery edge in her voice.

"Would you really?" The beer had left an ugly taste in my mouth. I stood up. "Look how dark the sky has turned," I said, pointing. "And so quickly."

Louise did look. What she saw brought her to her feet. She tossed the empty cans into a trash bin and ran with what was left to Miranda, squeezing inside just as the sky opened up. I waited, just a few seconds, to let the rain come.

By the time I climbed in on the driver's side and rolled up my window, my seat was already wet but it didn't matter since I was soaking. My arms glistened as I reached for the key. But I managed to keep Hank's picture dry.

"Have you ever thrown the *I Ching?*" Sealed in the steamy hot car, I had to shout to be heard over the rain pounding from all sides.

Louise shook her head.

"I only use it for major questions myself. Do you have any major questions?"

"Yes. Of course. Everyone has questions."

"Well, I'm game if you are."

Throwing the *I Ching* may have been my biggest mistake, because here I sit banished from the garden of ignorant certainty. For the first time in my life, I'm not sure what to say to my own daughter. But that afternoon, how could I resist?

Sitting cross-legged on my living room rug, Louise looked entranced when I got out my book, lit the candles and removed the pennies one by one from my satin box. She giggled before she wrote her question out. I took the slip of paper without reading it. I didn't need to. The frizzle of her nervous hilarity electrified my hands as the pennies rolled on the stitched satin square.

They came up *k'un* under *ch'ien*—stagnation. Shit, she looked so vulnerable, smoothing her wrinkled shirtwaist over her radishy knees. How could I tell her? The next page happened to be Community, a much more optimistic sign for new endeavors.

Yep, I compromised the *I Ching*. Not a red letter day in my life, was it? Maybe that's why the pennies fell out no better for me. Fire above excess: Contradiction. No answer at all. Either the *I*

Ching had no opinion or there is no right answer. Either I tell Dylan or I don't. Damn Louise. Those filings of doubt she left behind cling like magnets however much I try to dust them away.

Meanwhile, across from me Dylan is eating her carton of yogurt. Her pudgy hand wraps around the spoon like a much smaller child's, hardly bigger than David's or Philip's clutching mine in the ambulance. She is sitting farther away from me at this moment than they were that day. Yellow yogurt dribbles down the side of her chin. If I try to dab it, she'll jerk away; I certainly would have at her age if my mother tried. Not that I am to Dylan what my mother was to me: the bane of my existence.

We often eat in companionable silence this way. I assume she's thinking about what girls her age always think about. School, boys, the magic art of popularity. But I want to know *how* she thinks. She doesn't think in straight lines anymore. Girls don't after puberty. I've tried to myself, but it goes against the sex. So I have to wonder, if I showed her Hank's picture, how would Dylan react? A year ago I know she'd have been tickled. Now, though, I'm not sure: Would she care or would she be embarrassed at being connected to such a man? Inevitable adolescent embarrassment. "You mean, people could have walked into the post office and seen him!" I can just hear her.

When she was little, Dylan loved me to tell her stories about herself as a baby. All kids do, don't they? The day came, as I knew all along it would, when she started asking about a daddy. That spring we were living in Magic House, a commune of artists and artisans near New Hope, Pennsylvania. She was no more than three years old, maybe four, and the only child. One of the potters was particularly nice to her. Dylan asked me if he could be her father and I had to explain that no, Jake was only a friend. Friendship was all I wanted from him. Don't get me wrong. I was no righteous celibate, but Jake the potter made me nervous. His dark Jesus eyes never seemed to blink, and he'd begun demanding the illusion of permanence; that's all it is between a man and a woman—smoke and mirrors. I was not interested. One thing about Hank, he never pretended to offer more than the moment at hand. Not casual, not grab-someone-to-fuck, but life in the concentrated present, so intense the air was heavier around him. No yesterday, no tomorrow.

Of course, parenthood, that's the long haul. A whole truckload of yesterdays and tomorrows, a fleet of trucks. No illusion there. The bottomless glass is always full. Love as infinity. The deepest subject if women were the composers, painters, poets.

When Dylan came back from playing in Jake's studio one morning—God, was it over eleven years ago?—she asked me about fathers. I was tempted to make up something respectable to carry her into the middle-class acceptance I had already rejected for myself. It would have been easy enough. Instead, I pulled out the old scrapbook I'd been carting around since high school. My own childhood was on the pages already. I told Dylan we were going to bring the scrapbook up to date and then keep it current. She didn't completely understand but she was thrilled. Children are always thrilled by the smell of truth.

So, for a couple of weeks we collected newspaper clippings, ticket stubs from concerts, photographs, doodles I'd sketched while bored in lectures or meetings or sit-ins. There was Dylan's infant foot print, her first paintings, the frayed book of nursery rhymes. Then I tried to sketch Hank from memory, but it came out all wrong. I'm an artist, I can draw for godsake, but Hank's face kept eluding me. I could see him in my head, could describe him, but I couldn't capture him on paper. He's on paper now, isn't he, though not captured. Dylan loved the sketch, of course. She colored a big messy heart frame and taped it on its own page.

Those were the days of my mother's weekly, we'll-keep-this-a-secret-from-Daddy calls, before he was diagnosed. Daddy refused to speak to me, and she always swore he was out of the house, as if I could not hear his voice bellowing a running commentary in the background.

"How could you be so irresponsible?" she wailed as soon as I took the receiver from Dylan. For weeks, months, she called and asked the same question.

"What would you prefer I tell her?" I teased with my new possibility-of-the-week, each more elaborate and less likely to satisfy Mom than the one before: "Your father died." "We got divorced and he disappeared." "He moved to Canada before you were born to avoid the draft and became an Eskimo." "He is a prisoner of war in Hanoi." "He has joined a religious cult and moved to India." "He's a bomber for the Weather Underground." (Oops on that one as it turns out.) "He's an international spy, code name Zebra." That some of these suggestions were actual possibilities I neglected to mention or really did not know.

"Why don't I tell her she's the result of a virgin birth and be done with it?" I suggested finally.

"Really, Judith, you are a trial." She slammed down her receiver but quit badgering.

Soon after, Jake the potter moved to Oregon, and Daddy's cancer was diagnosed. I moved us back to Connecticut, and Dylan's interest shifted from her parentage to printing her name in snaky, unsteady lines. I never really had to confront the issue again. Dylan and I have lived exactly the way I always envisioned we would. Plenty of time and space. The Blues against the world if it ever came to that. Not that it ever has.

After Daddy died and we moved down here, I worried at first how the good people of Esmeralda would take to an unwed mother working in their schools. I filled out the application honestly enough, leaving certain spaces blank. No one noticed. At least, no one chose to ask. The Esmeralda Board of Education had a job to fill and no other applicants. Otherwise, they'd never have taken a woman in the first place.

Dylan has lined up her apple cores in a row on her plate. The peelings are in a neat pile. She is ready to leave the table. But we have not shared our nightly "cuppa." That's when to talk things over with her. I set the kettle on the stove.

"So, anything new at school?" Does every mother begin every conversation the same way?

Dylan shakes her head. That feigned boredom I know so damn well. She's not about to admit she's been spending more time with the holy rollers in their choir, but I know she has. What attracts Dylan, that's what I cannot figure. How could she be infatuated with a plastic purse of a woman like Elvira Brasleton?

It will pass. I know my Dylan. Despite the Elvira Brasletons of the world, Dylan is my constant, part of myself, as permanent as my hand. As permanent as Hank was not. The man who happened to be her father is merely a face on a poster, a scrap to cut out and paste into a collage of the past. A story I might tell on myself to explain how then became now.

A story I might tell. Louise was warning me, wasn't she, not to live by a rule no one could follow to the letter anyway. That's the kicker. Honesty only goes so far.

The tea kettle begins to whistle. The little cap over the spout shoots off like a bullet, hits the wall inches from my head.

"Watch out," Dylan shouts, startled.

"Too late," I laugh. We're both laughing. I reach over and tousle her hair. "You are growing so fast."

"Oh, Mother," Dylan says.

I pour the boiling water into a ceramic pot I threw for her years ago to resemble a sleeping cat because she was too allergic for a live cat and too old by then for stuffed ones. The tea steeps in the cat's belly, the scent of orange peel rising in the steam.

Dylan has taken down two mugs from the open shelf. She fills our cups and stands beside me in the mauve shadow of dusk. What a joy it is to have a daughter in my life, what a comfort. Lightly, lightly, I rest my arm across her shoulder. She does not pull away. She sips her tea. She may actually be smiling. To hold such a moment, even briefly, should be enough, to have such a moment at all.

SIX

What is happening to my universe? What door did I leave unlocked to let the gremlins in? They're running all over, poking around where they're not wanted, mucking up my clean ordered life. Okay, maybe there are no gremlins, but something is wrong, off, out of whack. Up until now, my life has always run in declarative sentences. Sure there have been plenty of adjectives and adverbs along the way and maybe the punctuation was by exclamation mark. But basically the sentences were straightforward subject-verb-predicate. Now I'm all questions. What to tell about what? Who to talk to? What to feel? I don't like it one bit.

Not one bit. Evangeline Pinkston was so damn right about men. Why have I ever bothered with them? Shit, another question. Well, here's another: Why have I ever let them bother me? I must be crazy. Once a man slips into your brain, the circuits twist and the cells atrophy.

Damn Hank's picture. As if I needed that reminder, that unnecessary intrusion. Well, I'm not going to let him muck things up.

At least I can fold Hank away until I've decided what to do, and I will decide soon. I will. But Joe Rainey is another matter. I can't fold him up and I don't seem able to make him go away, either. He's like a crab that won't let go. The more I resist, the more he hangs on, gripping with those pincers tighter and tighter. If I could cut off his claw, maybe then I could flush him out of my life. He made me so mad this afternoon I swear I almost did cut him, or would have given half a chance.

It was my weekly visit to David at the hospital. (Damn all the men but bless the little boys.) I try dropping by other days when I can, but Fridays always. I need to see David at least once a week to reassure myself. David's such a stoic, his pain is hard to gauge except by the degree his freckles pale or brighten. So I need to touch him, hear his voice, make sure he is not hurting unduly.

Not more than five minutes after I sat down by David's bed, in sauntered Joe Rainey with this shit-eating grin on his face and a gigantic, I mean gigantic, stuffed gorilla under his arm.

"What a coincidence," I said and stuck out my tongue. Fortunately, no one but Joe saw or heard me. His smile just widened and got more crooked than ever.

"I had to be down this way for work," he told Myra Franklin, who stood up and started straightening the room as soon as she saw him. "Thought I'd stop by and see how the boy is doing."

"Now wasn't that the most thoughtful thing. And Mari over with Philip only two days ago."

"Well, yes." He nodded. She'd thrown him a curve, but he recovered quickly enough. "As a matter of fact Philip picked this fellow out." He held up the gorilla to David. "If you poke him in the stomach like this, he lifts his arms and sticks a banana in his ear. If you poke him here, he sticks it in his eye. What do you think?"

"Cool."

Cool all right. Chilling would be more like it. A regular ice cube dropping into my glass of life. Who was he trying to impress exactly? It was exactly the kind of oddball, crazy, useless toy I'd love, as he damn well had to know. David, too old for regular stuffed animals, couldn't put it down. Even Myra laughed, Myra Franklin who wears flowered blouses with lace around the collar and tortoiseshell hairbands. She seemed to think it the most natural thing in the world that Philip's father would visit her boy.

"How nice of you." She twisted the rings on her fingers the way she does whenever she's trying to find something to say, which with me is most of the time. "Have you met Godiva Blue, the woman who found the boys that day?"

"Yes, we met in the emergency waiting room."

"Of course you did." She blinked and twisted some more.

"But it's nice to see you again," he went on, nodding in my general direction.

"Uh-huh," I said, avoiding his eye, aware of the color rising in my cheeks. What did he think he was doing there? What was he trying to prove? I was not going to be invaded upon. I quickly turned to David and pulled out *Treasure Island*.

"David's not much for books," Myra Franklin had said with a sigh the first time I suggested reading aloud. It took all of ten minutes to capture him completely. Myra, too, for that matter. I have a hunch my *Treasure Island* visits are the only time that the TV looming over David's bed is ever turned off.

I am a damn good reader aloud. I even mesmerize myself, and you should see the two of them, mother and son, David lying still under his covers, watching me while Myra holds his hand, her eyes glued to the intravenous tubes running silently from his arm to the machine. The three of us enter a state of grace, into that circle of light I've entered before only with Dylan.

I was not going to let Joe Rainey pierce that magic circle. When he pulled up a straight chair and sat down just behind me, I opened the book where I'd left off last time and began as if he were not there.

I had reached the moment when Jim is fighting for his life.

"The hammer fell, but there followed neither flash nor sound; the priming was useless with sea water. I cursed myself for my neglect. Why had not I, long before, reprimed and reloaded my only weapons? Then I should not have been as now, a mere fleeing sheep before this butcher."

With Joe Rainey's eyes boring into my back, the inevitable was closing in.

"Wounded as he was, it was wonderful how fast he could move, his grizzled hair tumbling over his face, and his face itself as red as a red ensign with his haste and fury. I had no time to try my other pistol, nor, indeed, much inclination, for I was sure it would be useless. One thing I saw plainly: I must not simply retreat before him."

On and on I read, dread and anticipation knotting at the base of my spine. I knew when I stopped I would once again find myself walking with Joe Rainey out of a building into the electricity of twilight. I had not seen him since the night at Cleo's but there had been the phone calls. They were disconcerting but at least I could hang up. Lately, worse offense, he was sliding into my unarmed dreams. Another kind of premonition. Shit, what a disaster.

I have told myself repeatedly, for weeks, that I do not want Joe Rainey in my life. God knows the question of what to do about Hank's picture has been bad enough. I do not need the complication of another man, especially one who comes with moral complications. So I have told myself, but who am I kidding? His phone calls have hooked me. I sit with the phone on my lap, watching the moon through the kitchen window, wondering where he is, trying not to imagine. As the righteous Nancy Reagans of the world have been warning, it is only a matter of time until I move up to the hard stuff. I mean Joe showing up in that hospital room was no coincidence. I probably mentioned David and my visits in one of our half-awake, half-dreaming conversations. But I fervently wished that he had not brought that gorilla.

The nurse came in with David's supper tray.

"Aren't you ahead of schedule?"

"No, right on time."

I glanced at my watch. So much later than I thought, almost five. My God, I'd promised Dylan to be home early.

"Oh shit."

Myra's head jerked up.

"I'm sorry. Have to vamoose." I stood up and pushed out my chair, too hard evidently. It fell into David's bedside table. Over went a vase of half-dead daisies, the TV remote control, a pitcher of water, a pile of comic books and my open purse. Dimes and quarters rolled under the radiator and halfway across the room. The remote control cracked into pieces and began to squawk. First it was me down on hands and knees, then me and Joe.

Shoulder-to-shoulder under the bed, among wet dust balls, sogging up the few dollar bills that had wafted there, we stared at each other, my heart galloping like a herd of butterflies. Myra passed down a towel; David began giggling in short hiccupy gulps. Puddles of water spread everywhere I put my hand, stagnant, stinking of dead flowers. Wet scraps of paper and petal stuck to every available surface. We're talking gigantic fucking mess.

Somehow I got myself out of there, but talk about frazzled. I kissed Myra goodbye, which I never do. I almost forgot to kiss David. And I shook Joe's hand. Shook his hand, for God's sake.

Then who should be in the elevator when I stepped in but Louise Culpepper.

"My heavens," she said, evidently as surprised as I was.

"Small world." I tried to smile. "Sometimes there's nothing like a good cliché, is there?"

"What are you doing here, Godiva honey?"

"David Franklin."

"Oh, yes."

"And you?"

"My neighbor, Dorothy Bander, has cancer."

"Oh, is she here for chemotherapy?"

"She's been through the chemo and the radiation. She's finished with treatment now." Louise seemed oddly distracted, lost in her own thoughts. "I have known Dorothy Bander all my life." Louise opened her purse and started rummaging, then glanced at me almost as an afterthought. "You want to get a cup of coffee?"

"I'd love to but I have to get Dylan over to First Baptist."

"Oh yes, the lock-in," she repeated absentmindedly. "Is Dylan going? That's nice."

"Despite my better judgment, but I'm sure she'll have a ball even if it is all a crock. Dylan's simply experimenting. The attraction of the group norm. Shit, the vibes over there must be thick as the incense, if Baptists even use incense. What do they do, anyhow, all those adolescent hormones locked in the church basement all night?"

"Beats me." Louise's smile was halfhearted at best. "But I'm sure they're well supervised."

"I'm sure they are, Louise. I didn't mean to offend you."

"No matter," Louise said vaguely. I realized her attention was elsewhere.

The elevator lurched, stopped, then started again. I looked at the wet spots on my sleeve and pictured Joe up in David's room. How much longer would he stay?

"She has two little boys, four and nine," Louise said as the elevator reached the main floor.

"Oh?" I said, trying to remember at what level of the garage I'd parked Miranda.

"Our parents sat in the same row at First Baptist. I dated her brother's best friend for a couple of months my senior year in high school. Then living in each other's yards so to speak for the last ten years—her house is the brick with the carport you see out my kitchen window. There's not a fence, not so much a line of rocks to mark where her yard ends and mine begins. We probably talked every day about something or other yet just now up in her room was probably the first time either of us ever spoke from the heart about something that truly mattered. And it had to be about dying, her dying.

"She told me she is perfectly willing to die. She's cheerful, almost lighthearted. She's not merely resigned to it. It's more than that. She's almost eager. She says that she's accepted God's will. Can you imagine?"

I couldn't. I didn't want to. Then I looked at Louise, really looked at her, concentrated on that homely, open face. She was upset to a degree I had not bothered to notice.

"What troubles me most is how she is completely wrapped up in the lives of people on TV, you know, soap operas. I think she finds them more real now than her own friends and family that love her."

The woman lying up on the fourth floor watching soap operas was not real to me the way she was to Louise, but death was real enough. I hadn't watched Daddy die without learning that much.

"Louise, I am sorry. I wish I had more time."

"I know you do, Godiva honey," she said, but the sorrow and puzzlement on Louise's face as I reached out to hug her pulled me up short. She wouldn't say so, but I had failed her as a friend. And what about Dylan waiting at home for me? She would be worried sick by now. I was never late like this. I was never so oblivious.

I could blame Joe Rainey all I wanted, but I was angriest with myself, my foolish ridiculous self. Somewhere I'd lost control. "Get a lid on it, kid," I told myself as I swung up to the house and honked for Dylan.

TWo

Dylan Blue lies crosswise on her bed, ankles dangling over one side, arms and head over the other, a habit she knows Godiva hates. "Damn, if you don't look like a carcass," she'd say, standing in the doorway uninvited, the smoke from her Pall Mall spiraling up. "Like those sad-eyed deer your grandfather used to tie on his hood to show off to the neighborhood every time he went on one of his annual damn hunting forays." Godiva is more or less a vegetarian of course, refusing all red meat; Dylan is not, not anymore, not for weeks. Besides she likes lying with her head weighted down and the blood pooling somewhere behind her eyes, the rest of her body floating above the bedspread momentarily lighter. Heavy. Light. Heavy. It relaxes her.

"Lock-in." When she closes her eyes the words swirl around in red blackness. She says it out loud and it sounds ominous, as if secrets are to be unveiled only to those willing to undergo dark rites of religious passage. What they would do exactly she has not quite figured out. Sing hymns and read scripture? Listen to Amy Grant tapes? Talk about God's role in their lives?

"You guys aren't going to T-group with Jesus all night?" Godiva laughed through her smoke rings when Dylan first asked her to sign the permission slip.

"What's a T-group?"

"Another lost phrase, Honeybunch. Another slice of my past disintegrating into dust. Sometimes I envision the sixties as a strange clay statue we all slapped together in a crazy artistic ecstasy. You know I'm all for artistic ecstasy, but no one had the fol-low-through to get the damn thing fired, and now it's crumbling away bit by bit. It's already lost its original shape, and eventually it will just be a pile of sweepings." As Dylan knows, her mother tends to get carried away. Then she'll remember and come back down to earth.

"A T-group is when you sit in a circle and share your fears, desires and deep psychological problems. I don't remember what the letter 'T' stands for, therapy or togetherness or tell-all."

"I don't think that's what we're doing," Dylan answered quickly, unnerved at such a possibility, however remote.

When she opens her eyes, she is slightly dizzy. She tries to focus on the knob of her bottom dresser drawer. It is chipped on one side. Of course. Everything in the house is beat up and sec-ondhand, what Godiva calls collectibles but most people consider junk. Mrs. Brasleton has all new furniture from Sears in her house, with matching chairs and a dining room set sort of like Gram's at Hilton Head. Dylan has been invited to dinner at the Brasletons' twice: chicken spaghetti the first time, pork chops the second. As the pastor's wife, Mrs. Brasleton will be chaperoning tonight. She has bent the rules so Dylan can attend as if she were already an official member of the congregation.

Reverend and Mrs. Brasleton do not have children of their own even though they're old, even older than Godiva. Dylan has been wondering lately what it would be like to have a mother like Mrs. Brasleton, who wore perfume and watched television and believed in God. Someone normal who would raise her to be normal without even trying. Normal people take being normal for granted, Dylan has noticed.

She likes Reverend Brasleton, too, although there is something disconcerting about the bullet-headed erectness he never loosens, not even after supper when he's supposed to be relaxing over *Wheel of Fortune* in his recliner. But maybe all men are like that. Dylan has been around so few. She does like his way of dressing, the way she can see the sleeves of his undershirt through his white dress shirt. Dylan is seriously considering being baptized.

Godiva will go ballistic. Godiva has no interest in doing what normal people do. There is no way Dylan could hope to turn out like everybody else, the way Godiva has been raising her. It isn't the single-mother routine; lots of kids Dylan knows have divorced parents. But no one else has a mother like Godiva Blue. For starters, the way she looks. Six feet tall, orangy hair flying in all directions except when she wears it in a long braid that reaches her waist. She buys her clothes from thrift stores. And she is almost forty years old. A forty-year-old woman in braids and high-tops. But the way she acts is worse. Those "outbursts of public conscience," as Godiva likes to call them. Why must her letters to the editor of the *Esmeralda Weekly Gazette* always take the opposite view of everyone else about everything, from garbage pickup to President Reagan's policy on Nicaragua?

Then there is her art. Not that kids from the high school would ever be caught dead inside The Pink Heron, but Miss Cleo always sticks Godiva's most outrageous pieces in the window for anyone walking by to see and comment about. Even Godiva's job is weird. She couldn't be a nurse or a secretary or a teacher like Cass's mother. No, she has to be a janitor, "down and dirty where I like to be," even though, as Gram tries to explain to Godiva all the time, it is a pure waste of brain and talent.

Dylan puts her hands flat on the floor. The wooden planks are splintery and hard against her palms as she pushes herself up. The clock radio says 4:45. Godiva promised to be home by 4:30. Dylan wanders into the front room to look out the window. Nothing. She tells herself not to worry. Godiva should be home any minute. There is still plenty of time to get to the church. But she cannot relax. She keeps thinking how everyone is going to be there, even Cass, who always scoffs. Of course, Cass can afford to scoff. Everyone knows Cass Culpepper is the coolest girl at Esmeralda High.

Hair dyed black and cut at a jagged angle everyone is copying, pole thin in acid-washed jeans, Cass Culpepper is totally punk. And she knows just how far to go with it. All the girls want to be like her, though none of them has the guts to cop the whole attitude. And practically every guy in the school has a crush on her. Dylan couldn't believe her luck this summer at camp when she and Cass were assigned together to the five- and six-year-olds. Who would ever have predicted that they would actually become friends? But they did. Amazing as it seems, Cass seems genuinely to like Dylan, to seek her out, even since the most embarrassing, mortifying moment in Dylan's life.

Cass got her license in August and began driving Dylan home from camp. Cass kept saying she'd always wanted to see what a real artist's studio looked like, but Dylan avoided going into the studio—it was hard to describe, but she respected that it was Godiva's private place—but then one afternoon when she and

Cass drove up, the doors were open wide, inviting them in it seemed, and Cass was practically begging. So in they walked.

Cass saw, all right. Godiva stark naked practically, humming away, up to her elbows in clay. Cass was chill, pretending not to be shocked. For days afterward, Dylan kept waiting for Cass to make her the butt of some sarcastic joke. Instead, Cass became friendlier than ever. The only difference was that she began asking questions about Godiva a lot, about what it was like living with an artist.

"Your mother is an iconoclast, that's really cool," she told Dylan one day after school started. It was an amazing word for her to use. Dylan had to look up the meaning in the dictionary that night even though she's always had straight As in English. "Iconoclast" turned out to mean exactly what Dylan doesn't want to be, what she lives in fear that people might think Godiva is. Now she has begun to recognize, with some bemusement, that having an eccentric for a mother, an "iconoclast," somehow makes her more interesting to Cass. Which realization does not stop Dylan from jumping at the chance to tag along whenever Cass invites her, especially when Cass is heading to the Dairy Queen.

If you are a girl between fifteen and twenty, there is nothing better to do of an evening in Esmeralda than to find yourself leaning on someone's silver Camaro in the Dairy Queen parking lot, chewing the straw of a milkshake and giggling at some boy's dumb jokes. Jimmy Cryder smiled at Dylan this morning when she walked past his locker after History. Cass, who always mysteriously knows these things, has been dropping clues all week that he is interested. And Jimmy will be at the lock-in tonight.

Dylan grabs a cassette, the first her fingers touch, and shoves it in the tape deck. Randy Travis is singing "Too Gone Too Long."

Godiva has discovered country music lately. The refrain hammers in. Dylan hates it. She switches the music off. She tries not to look at her watch. Godiva promised 4:30.

"No sweat," she said yesterday, standing barefoot at her work-table, shaking silver paint from a thin brush in spatters across a square of stretched silk. Dylan hates a lot of Godiva's stuff, but sometimes one is pretty wonderful.

"I won't even come in to embarrass you." Godiva went on sprinkling silver raindrops. Although Dylan has been living in a state of perpetual secret embarrassment for the last two years, she was surprised Godiva had noticed.

"But are you sure, absolutely certain, you want to spend all night in a church?"

"Fellowship Hall."

"Whatever."

Surrounded by the kiln, the loom, the remnants of unfinished projects, Godiva could still cast quite a spell. Dylan watched her mother's arm swing the brush, watched her shoulders hunch and stretch. For as long as she can remember, there has been Godiva's back at work while she talked. In those moments when all that matters is to be loved, to be someone's child, Dylan closes her eyes and sees its broad reassurance, smells the slightly acrid mix of sweat and paint and clay and cigarette, finds herself filled with longing for that simpler time when Godiva's love was an impene-trable wall surrounding them from the rest of the world.

"You know I don't trust religion." Godiva picked up a tray hold-ing small pieces of wood and metal.

"That's because you don't believe in God."

"Oh, Honeybunch, God is beside the point. Besides I don't know if I believe in God any more or less than you do. Hell, I'm a regular browser in the supermarket of the spirit. You know me. I'll try anything."

Dylan could not help smiling back. One thing about Godiva, she can poke fun at herself.

"It's the idea of you being sucked up inside a group mentality that scares the shit out of me. Like what happened to Coyote Sikes."

"Your roommate who ran off to the desert with a snake-swallowing guru and never came back, right?" Dylan has always thought Coyote Sikes was a dumb name to change to, even dumber than Godiva Blue. What kind of people changed their names all the time?

"Other kids did that kind of thing, too, freaked out." Godiva put down her brush. "But Coyote—Ellen—seemed so unlikely. So normal. I always admired her good sense as well as her intelligence. The same as I admire yours as a matter of fact, Honeybunch. So don't you dare Coyote out on me."

Dylan cannot imagine turning out like Coyote Sikes for reasons Godiva would never understand. Being sucked into a group is what Godiva worries about. How to suck up to the group is exactly what Dylan still wants to figure out. Coyote Sikes really believed her guru's line or else she fell in love with him, a matter of the heart. Coyote was vulnerable because she was secure in the first place. Not Dylan. Coyote could do something everyone thought was crazy because she'd taken everyone's approval for granted for so long. She was probably a cheerleader in high school and a Girl Scout before that. Dylan remembers second grade, the little girls wearing their Brownie uniforms to school every Tuesday. Godiva would not have stopped Dylan from joining, but Dylan knew she couldn't be a Brownie. Being a Brownie was the antithesis of all

Godiva stood for. How could Godiva Blue's daughter want to participate in such a regimented organization? As if being a daughter should have to stand for anything. It is not that she loves Godiva less now, but that she recognizes Godiva is, as Mrs. Brasleton would say, a heavy cross to bear.

Dylan sits by the front window and stares at her hands. 5:37 by her watch. The clock in the kitchen says 5:40. If Dylan is going to the lock-in at all, she has to be there by 6:30. Everybody will be there by 6:30. Most of the girls are getting there by six. It is a long twenty-minute drive from the Point to First Baptist. If Godiva is not home in another fifteen minutes, Dylan might as well forget the lock-in.

She strains to hear a car as it rounds the last bend in the shore road, but there is no car. There is nothing at all. The air is dangerously still. Even the gulls have stopped their usual afternoon swooping to disappear into the gray horizon. Dylan thinks she will suffocate in the thick stillness. She walks slowly, counting the steps, back into her room. Her clock radio says 5:43. She knows for a certainty then that Godiva is not coming, knows but does not, cannot believe.

In the bathroom she stares at herself in the mirror over the sink. She can call Gulfside, but why would Godiva be working this late? A new pimple has erupted on her chin since she checked the mirror half an hour ago. She worries it with her pinky, then pinches to squeeze the pus to the surface. The school secretary would be long gone by now anyway. Her chin is turning blotchy red under her prodding. Could Godiva have gone to visit that stupid Franklin kid all the way over in Perry? If so, and if she is still there, the situation is hopeless. Dylan might as well forget the lock-in. But it isn't possible Godiva would do this to her.

At the front door, listening to the emptiness, Dylan aches to get to the lock-in. She pictures Jimmy scanning the room for her before some other girl snatches away his interest. She pictures Mrs. Brasleton at choral practice next Monday nodding understandingly when Dylan makes excuses for Godiva. She is so tired of feeling she has to explain Godiva. But this is different. Usually Godiva is all-too present, unavoidable in her diligence. She has never before failed to be where she said she'd be. But Mrs. Brasleton won't know this; she'll assume Godiva is irresponsible on top of everything else.

Godiva's old sleeping bag lies bunched on its side where she left it by the door this morning. A faint odor of mildew and incense clings to the flannel underbelly as Dylan uncurls and re-rolls it. She sets the tight, neat cylinder next to her overnight case, the white Bible from Mrs. Brasleton poking out from an unzipped corner.

Dylan cannot sit still. She wanders over to what Godiva self-mockingly refers to as her sacred corner. For someone who does not trust organized religion, Godiva is a sucker for her I Ching and tarot cards. On the second row of shelves above Godiva's inlaid table sits the purple satin box where Godiva keeps her polished throwing pennies. Indian heads. Dylan wants them for herself suddenly. She doesn't know where the urge comes from, whether she is about to roll the pennies to read her fortune or about to toss them into the Gulf. She only knows she has to have them.

The shelf is higher than she expected. She has to stretch on tiptoe for the box. Even then she cannot quite grasp it. She is reaching beyond some awkwardly placed incense sticks when her wrist knocks a heavy book that falls forward off the shelf, bringing with it the penny box and a silk-covered notebook. An unmarked, unsealed envelope comes loose from inside the notebook flap as it drops.

The notebook is all blank pages. Dylan opens the envelope and removes two folded sheets. At the top of the first LOUISE CULPEPPER is printed in block letters, followed by rows of long and short vowel markings and what look like Chinese symbols. The combination has a rhythmic, even musical quality. Dylan is amazed. Mrs. Culpepper. Why would Godiva throw the *I Ching* about her? Dylan runs her finger across the writing. It is spooky, voodooish. Dylan wonders if Mrs. Culpepper knows Godiva has thrown in her name.

The other sheet, some kind of flyer, has been folded over and over, down to a small thick bundle. Impatient as she's been for the last hour, Dylan takes her time. Crease by crease, she unfolds the fragile paper speckled with water and grease stains. Not until she has smoothed the page against her thigh and shaken it gently does she let herself look at what she is holding.

Her father's face in the palm of her hand. Though she's never seen him before, she knows. He stares up at her, and she stares back. She reads a list of vital statistics: Middle name Howard. Height, 6'1". Weight, 180 pounds. Born 1945, Shaker Heights, Ohio. His face on a wanted poster torn at the top where it has been ripped from a ring binder. Her father wanted by the federal government. "Conspiracy to bomb." Where or how not mentioned. Or if he succeeded. Only his aliases. Henry Fireman, H. Firely, Frank Heeny, Firefly. And his face. Long black hair. Mole above lip. Expressionless eyes she is sure she has seen somewhere before.

It does not occur to her to keep the picture. Nothing occurs to her. She breathes through a cloud, her arms weighed down by the thin sheet of paper, overcome by the same combination of terror and relief she feels whenever she wakes from her recurring night-mare of being chased across a rope bridge by unseen assailants.

With excruciating care she folds the poster back the way she found it and places it in the envelope with Mrs. Culpepper's *I Ching*. The pennies have scattered across Godiva's handwoven rug. It takes a few minutes to find where several have rolled under a chair, but Dylan keeps count until she finds them all. She is putting the notebook back on the shelf when she hears Miranda sputter on the gravel where Godiva always swerves in to park. Godiva honks the horn and calls Dylan's name.

"I know, I know. I am so goddamn sorry," Godiva says as Dylan stuffs the sleeping bag into the backseat. "But I'll get you there yet."

The clock on the dash says 6:20. Godiva is flushed and more disheveled than usual. She inhales her cigarette and blows smoke out one corner of her mouth.

"I was visiting David at the hospital and got caught in traffic."

Lacing her fingers in her lap, Dylan does not open her mouth. She does not ask the questions she knows Godiva expects. Godiva answers anyway.

"He seems to be doing better. The physical therapy has started."

Dylan wills herself not to listen. The storm she sensed in the air earlier has spread into an approaching darkness over the water. Along the side of the coast road, the weeds and sea oats lean against the wind.

Just get me there in time, Dylan prays into her hands. Just get me there in time.

THReE

I am on my way. You know, don't you, that this is the happiest day of my life, so far. I keep pretending to read my magazine, but I can't keep from smiling at the two old ladies sitting across from me. You should see them. They have a big box of popcorn they must have bought at the station before they got on the bus, and they keep offering me some, like we're at the movies or something. Every time they look over and nod, I have to bite my tongue to keep from standing up in the aisle and declaring to everyone, "I'm on my way to my dad, and you can't stop me."

It was so easy to leave. Godiva did not suspect a thing. Usually, she is so nervous about cars—the only thing she's overprotective about—but she agreed just like that when I suggested that Cass and I drive to Gram's in Cass's new car. Probably she didn't want to offend Cass's mom, her new best friend. Anyway, who cares why she said okay. She did, and here I am. "Thank you, Jesus," as Mrs. Brasleton would say.

Traveling by bus is a snap. SEE AMERICA FIRST; that's what the coupon says. I have it tucked in the zippered pouch in my purse so I don't lose it. Twenty-eight days of unlimited travel for the price of one cashed-in savings bond from Gram. "Thank you, Gram" is more like it. According to the schedule the ticket agent in Atlanta gave me, I can be in Eden, Delaware, by late tomorrow if I push it. So there is a good chance I'll see you sooner than I even imagined.

Only I can't tell if this bus is on time or not because my watch stopped. When I got off at the Thomasville depot to buy some chips and an orange soda, Minnie Mouse pointed to 9:30, and when we turned off the exit for Atlanta, Minnie's thumb had only moved to 10:15 even though I knew we'd been on the road for hours. The second hand had stopped twitching forward altogether. Minnie had breathed her last, so I wrapped her in a Reese's Cup paper and buried her in a trash can in the Atlanta bus station.

It's not like I'm on a set schedule. If you're not at the farm outside Eden, there's bound to be somebody there who can tell me where you are. Because I am going to find you. I am not going back. I mean it. I am going to find you. I am.

The sun is tilting up left of the bus. Is that east or west, I never can remember. Without my watch or a coastline to define beginnings and endings, it's hard to keep track. I have no idea where I am or when I am. All I am sure is that I am heading north and it's one day since yesterday.

Godiva would explain that time doesn't follow clock minutes and hours anyway. She told me once that at important intersections in her life, time speeded up and slowed down at the same time. For instance, the six months she shared an apartment with that friend Evangeline she named me after—Evangeline Dylan Blue—who was killed, or the first three months after I was born, or whenever she was working full throttle on a new enclosure. I thought she was just spouting another of her crazy ideas, and you may remember she has plenty, but I have to admit I understand now what she meant. Since the lock-in, there have been more hours in the day, more minutes in every hour, especially more seconds in each minute, and yet everything has happened so fast. Not at Esmeralda speed, that's for sure. In Esmeralda the days just dragged out and I had to look for ways to fill them. If I were there now, I'd probably be asleep. I'd be asleep and Godiva would already have taken her dawn walk and gone out to the studio hours ago. That's where she is right now I would bet. You wouldn't believe how much energy she has; five hours of sleep is all she needs most nights. Now I'm doing the same thing. Wouldn't she be surprised.

I don't know what I expected exactly. I'm right out there on the edge it feels like. If Godiva lives this intensely all the time, no wonder she's so difficult to live with, not that she ever looks for an excuse. I mean, she manufactures her intensity on purpose; for me the intensity is situational. It has to do with being keyed up looking for you and at the same time penned up on the bus. But Godiva Blue, she's keyed up on ordinary life.

Godiva, Godiva, Godiva. Godiva Blue, does the name ring some bells? How about Judy Blitch? I'm not sure when her name changed. You have no idea what she's like now. She couldn't have been like that when you knew her, or you wouldn't have felt the way you must have. I don't know why I am wasting so much energy thinking about her myself except, maybe, that if all goes well (no, no matter what, even if I gave up searching for you tomorrow, which I won't) my life with her is never going back to the way it was. I do not fit inside any of her boxes anymore.

Godiva and her boxes. I broke one about three months ago B.D. Before Discovery. That's how I divide life now, before I discovered your picture and after. This is a secret I could share only with you. The details are probably not that interesting to anyone else. But to me, you can imagine.

Cass had dragged me to The Pink Heron. She has this sick fascination with Godiva. I told her I hated going in there because Cleo makes such a big deal. The Pink Duchess is a little weird. She wears pink muumuus all the time and uses some kind of pink rinse on her hair. Not punk pink, believe me. She likes me to call her Aunt, but don't worry, I don't.

Cass thinks she's a kick. And it's hard to say no to Cass, believe me. Or it was, when I was still an innocent and Cass was the Queen of Punk.

Anyway, Cleo fussed around us for a few minutes, then disappeared back to her office. I suspect she was finishing her afternoon round of sherry. She is a tippler according to Gram. Gram hates Cleo. Not that they've ever met. Gram hates the idea of Cleo.

Cass wandered around the gallery, almost shy for the first time since I've known her. I explained the stuff to her, like the papier-mâché tube hung like a telescope inside fake alligator jaws. It is one of Godiva's cooler pieces. The way Godiva set it up, you would think the telescope cuts right through the ceiling and roof toward a sky full of stars and purple clouds. Cass stopped in front of a miniature coffin in which Godiva had placed a necklace and matching earrings of glass beads and stone and wood. Cleo had suggested that jewelry sells, so Godiva was experimenting. "It's not art, but it would sure beat janitoring," she told me.

I swear it was like magic, the transformation in Cass when she put on the earrings and necklace. She became a sort of priestess. Looking at her sudden, unexpected glamour, how the necklace hugged the bones of her throat, I was a little stung. Jealous, I guess. I wondered what it would take to transform me. (Remember, this was B.D. Finding your picture did the trick, didn't it?)

"This is really boring," I said to Cass, but she didn't answer.

She was completely absorbed by her new image framed in the mirror, touching with one finger her lips, her cheek, the soft skin beneath each eye, lost in the wonder of who she might be.

For lack of anything else to do, I rummaged carelessly among the other boxes on the shelves and on the small table in the center of the room, where Cleo put work she was rotating to and from her window displays. I picked up pieces and put them down without really looking. I had seen them all before.

When I heard the sharp, metallic crack, I didn't move. I thought it was a gunshot, although I have never heard a gun fired in my life. Then Cass was standing in front of me, the glittery dangle of earrings swinging. I half-expected to see blood.

"Shit, shit, shit." She was whispering under her breath as my hands floated up in front of my chest, the palms up to prove their innocence.

"Shit, you've really broken it," Cass said loud and clear this time. I closed my eyes so I would not have to see. My cheeks burned, and I knew my face must be puffing up like a jellyfish's. But finally I had to look.

I had knocked one of the boxes onto the floor. The domed lid was shattered, or at least broken into many, many pieces. The oblong ceramic body of the box was cracked in half down the middle, like an egg. But instead of spilled yolk, small silver oblongs, half the length of matchsticks, lay scattered between the blood-red halves. They looked like small miniatures of the box itself, but I knew what they were. I'd seen Godiva spray paint them. Perfect silver babies, and I had just helped them hatch prematurely. I picked up one and handed it to Cass so I could register the shock on her face. Instead, she giggled.

"How cool. It's a plastic baby just like the ones Aunt Lureen stuck in the cupcakes at Marcie's baby shower."

There were dozens of them. The trick for Godiva had been to fit them inside one at a time through a small hole at the end. I'd sat watching her for two hours one Saturday morning, and even then she was not half finished. "Art is long," she liked to tell me.

"It was one of her favorites," I accused Cass as if she were the one who'd broken it. "She was asking over two hundred dollars."

By then Cleo was clicking across the room in her pink mules. Before I could say a thing, Cass turned and said, "It's all my fault. I'll pay for it."

I didn't contradict. But I begged Cleo not to tell Godiva.

Cleo's eyes scrunched up so that hundreds of papery wrinkles popped out at the corners.

"Don't you think she would rather be told," she said, her voice slathered in layers of pink gauze. Cass again offered to pay for it, and Cleo said they would work something out. I could tell Cleo liked the idea of not telling, of keeping someone's secret. I didn't listen to the details. Cass never suggested visiting The Pink Heron again, that's for sure.

Cleo never did tell Godiva. I'd know if she had. And I don't think she ever made Cass pay because Cass never asked me to pay her back. The whole incident evaporated into dreamlike memory. Meanwhile, I'd set those babies free.

+   +   +

aND now I am free. Godiva was always warning me about getting boxed in by other people's expectations, meaning mostly Reverend and Mrs. Brasleton's. Well, the joke's on Godiva because her boxes are the ones I won't fit inside anymore. That's the one thing I am sure of. Maybe the only thing. Last night I was so certain of everything, but now it's hard to think straight. The bus is so hot and stuffy it's making me sick. I have to keep pressing my face against the window to cool my cheeks, and so no one on the way to the toilet can see the tears slithering down my nose.

What if this whole plan was a terrible mistake. What if I never find you. No, I am going to find you. I am. But so much depends on I don't know what, like, what if Godiva had not been late the night of the lock-in?

Every ten minutes this old guy, at least fifty, goes past me on his way to the toilet. He's got a chin full of stubble, stringy hair weaseling out from under his ball cap, and definitely crazy eyes, the kind that swivel around to the sides. Every time he goes by he gives me this creepy smile and nods. I'd be scared if he weren't so pathetic.

I don't know what I expected exactly. That everything in the world would be a little shinier, touched by the magic wand of my quest. Well, it's not. All I've seen, I swear, since I crossed the Florida state line into Georgia, has been pure dreariness. The sky is gray brown, the fields are dead, the ponds scummy. There don't seem to be any towns, just exit ramps leading to gas stations, eight-dollar-a-night motels and fast-food neon signs. I swear, if I do end up back in Esmeralda, I don't care what Cass says, I'll never step foot in that Dairy Queen again. (Why did I even think about going back? I cannot believe I am homesick. I am not going back.) For sure, I'll never eat french fries again.

The worst are the houses. Either broken down shacks or else these surreal settlements plopped down on crisscrosses of blacktop that don't lead anywhere, definitely not to a town. Like they're imitations of houses, all so new, all basically identical, whether they're fake brick or fake wood. Treeless backyards smack against the highway. Plastic Big Wheel tricycles lying on their sides under spokes of flapping laundry. I'd worry about the kids getting run over except I can't believe anyone real lives there.

What if you live in a place like that? On purpose, incognito, invisible the way those houses must make a person? What if I find you in one of those houses, sitting in a vinyl easy chair, drinking beer and watching *I Love Lucy* reruns? Godiva used to joke that *I Love Lucy* was the beginning of the dissolution of Western civilization.

But what does she know anyway? I am not going to let myself start thinking this way. I can't. You would never let yourself go that far. You would never give up your soul.

It's just this bus that's depressing me. I mean it smells depressing, disinfectant and old people's sweat. Did you know that most people who ride buses are old? Except there's a baby toward the front who's been squawking on and off for, like, an hour. No watch anymore, remember, so maybe it only seems that long. Despite myself, I keep thinking of that long ride with Godiva from Connecticut to Esmeralda. The same landscape but completely different. North to south then, south to north now.

Washington was the only city we went through. We must have stopped to sleep but I don't remember. It seemed to me then as if we drove forever. When I was a little kid, time and space seemed bigger and wider than they do now. And thrilling, or Godiva's running commentary made it thrilling. The way the thick green trees of Connecticut suburbs gave way to the rolling pastures of Delaware and Virginia, the scrub pines of Georgia, the orange juice souvenir stands of north Florida.

Godiva had no idea herself where we were heading, at least not in specific geographic terms. It didn't matter to me one bit. Actually, what I remember most clearly is her pack of Pall Malls open on the seat between us, her eyes on the road ahead, as she passed the hours explaining what she planned to accomplish moving us to a place where no one knew her, where our lives, hers and mine, were a blank slate.

"Total integration, Noodle." She flicked ashes out the window and let the wind carry them off into the Virginia hills. "Total integration. All that passion I've pissed away on men and the bullshit talk they pass off as their idealism. All that passion is going into what's important. I'll think for myself from now on, I'll raise you, I'll perfect my art." She gave me one of her warm-the-earth smiles. "We are all each other has in the world, and I promise we'll be each other's best friend for the rest of our lives.

"We are on our way to Paradise," she sang. Too young to know better, I sang along with her.

But then everything about Esmeralda turned out wrong, a big fat disappointment as far as I was concerned, although I'd have died before admitting it at the time. The ocean was there all right, the town smack against the Gulf of Mexico, but the coast turned out to have a marsh and rock shoreline. The nearest beach was over an hour away. There were none of the orange trees Godiva promised either, only dusty palms. And no sun, just a flat, dirty blanket of cloud hanging over the car wherever we drove. Worst of all, the whole town smelled, and smelled bad.

"Don't worry, Noodle," Godiva kept saying that first week, every time we caught another whiff. "We'll find a place to live upwind of the mill, out of its range altogether."

Meanwhile we stayed in a boardinghouse on Magnolia run by a Mrs. Mims. "Call me Aunt Glad." She squinted at me with an angry smile. Short and red-faced, Mrs. Mims (I refused to call her anything else) made huge breakfasts of pancakes and biscuits and sausage and grits and became silently broody if her paying guests did not eat every bit. She also had a dog she doted on, a big black dog that used to snarl whenever he saw me. "Darling is not used to kiddies," Mrs. Mims would say every time.

Darling slept on the bathroom-floor rug. If I had to pee in the middle of the night, I lay in the bed next to Godiva with my legs pressed tight, holding off getting up as long as I could, wavering between the temptation to wake Godiva so she would walk me in there and my determination that I would manage myself. Finally, almost doubled over with pain and effort, I would make my way down the unlit hallway. I'd graze my fingertips along the cracked plaster on the wall until I came to the wooden door frame. The light switch was just inside. I could reach around and in. My breath plugged up in my throat as I prayed that Darling would assume from the light that I was not an intruder. Ever so slowly, I'd step around the door and over his mangy back into the room. I always wore leather shoes out of fear that naked feet would be too tantalizing so long after his supper.

And always, Darling would be awake, watching. As I sat on the toilet, unable to hold back another second, I'd stare into his yellowy eyes until, invariably, he'd lay his head on his paws with a bored yawn and fall asleep. I'd lower the lid without flushing and tiptoe back to our room, vowing never to admit I was the one if anyone complained the next morning.

It was the loneliest I have ever been in my life. Until now. No, I am not lonely. You are out there. In Eden or somewhere like it. I know you are. You have to be.

That night at the lock-in, all I could think about was your face purposely hidden from me. And for how long? What I felt about Godiva went way beyond anger. Dry ice, frozen fire. The evening passed in a blur. Basketball game, pizzas, treasure hunt, circle of prayer. I let Jimmy Cryder make out with me during the movie. I had never made out with anyone before. After we'd kissed awhile, he pulled out a little bottle of what looked like cold medicine.

"Brandy from my dad's office cabinet. He keeps it locked, but I know where he keeps the key." I pretended to take the swallow he offered. I hate the taste of liquor. "My dad says he sold your mom the house you live in. He says it's a pretty strange place. He thought your mom was crazy when she bought it."

Usually, hearing someone say something like that would trigger all kinds of defensive loyalty from me, but not that night, not anymore. I just let him keep kissing me to keep him quiet.

Near dawn I woke in a chilled daze. I tried to curl back into the flannel warmth of my sleeping bag, but sleep would not come. Leaning up on an elbow, I breathed in the closeness of too many people sharing air in a closed space. Stale and sour, yet faintly sweet, a flicker of déjà vu.

Somewhere nearby Jimmy was asleep, and Cass. No, Cass never showed up after all, but Suzanne and Mickey Searcy, and the Baxter boys were all there. For so long I had positively ached for their acceptance. I could name every occupant zippered into the sleeping bags scattered across the Fellowship Hall, the boys' side and the girls'. Someone sighed, someone else snored, several coughed. Turning slowly this way and that, like so many caterpillars weaving themselves into new beings for the day to come, they knew nothing of gray darkness that muffled shape and sound, nothing of chill or dull, achy tiredness shot through with wiry threads of anticipation.

I had been, what, four years old, the one time someone directly addressed me as "bastard." Not as a curse but as a simple descriptive fact. I was sitting in a sandbox three backyards down from Gram's with a child named Melissa Pafford. Her mother had gone to high school with Godiva and told me over milk and graham crackers that she'd always admired "your mommy's artistic ability."

Lissa, with her curly dark hair and green eyes, was bossy the way admired children are, and I admired her greatly. We were shaping wet sand into a castle when she announced in her scratchy voice, "Dylan, you're a bastard."

I put down my plastic spoon and watched Lissa pour a torrent of dry sand from one cup to another. Then Lissa stood up and brushed the sand off her knees, out of the folds in her pink skirt. The colors remain strangely vivid still, the yellow spoon, the pink skirt, the sky eggshell blue.

"I'm sick of this sandbox," Melissa Pafford said and stepped daintily out and onto the gravel path toward the sliding board.

I had never heard the word "bastard" before, had no exact idea of its meaning, but I knew, the way you always know an unwanted truth when you hear it. Melissa Pafford had described an actual state of being, had labeled the vague but undeniable difference already present between me and everyone else.

"All it means is that I never married the man who is your father," Godiva explained that night as she tucked me into the canopied bed she'd slept in when she was a child. "But I've already told you that, just not named it." Then she told the story once more, how the day I was born, all of Godiva's friends brought oranges and chocolate to the hospital and scattered gold sprinkles as a kind of baptism into the spirit of creative life.

Gold sprinkles.

When Godiva drove us through Washington, D.C., on our way to Florida, we sat across the street from a Catholic church to eat lunch, White Castle burgers for me, fruit and cheese for Godiva.

The front was massive, gray stone with deeply glowing stained-glass windows, ruby and emerald and gold. Nothing like First Baptist, that's for sure. Looking up at the stained-glass angels over the church's front door as she peeled her orange, Godiva described a night she had spent in there once long ago.

"Before I was born?"

"Yes, Noodle, before you were born. Everyone else slept in the sanctuary, in the pews themselves, but those glorious windows would have kept me awake, all that fire and ice within each pane had to glow even in the blackest night.

"So I went looking and I found a windowless cubicle. I woke up surrounded by a circle of nodding priests. It freaked me out. Then I blinked and saw they were only choir gowns draped over hangers. But for half a second, I thought maybe I'd become a saint or something."

At the time I was spellbound. It sounded like Godiva's personal ghost story, her version of Rip Van Winkle or the Headless Horseman. But remembering back as I lay wrapped in Godiva's sleeping bag on the floor of First Baptist, a possibility took shape that my heart and soul raced to embrace.

I could see you, can still see you, waking, rubbing your eyes, smoothing the black hair matted above your ear, stretching the stiffness from a night on the floor out of legs and shoulders, casting a glance at the redheaded young woman beside you, your mind crackling alert, your every nerve alive to the risks and potential everywhere around you. And I am there, too, unborn but there in your pores and your eyes and your brain, smelling your smell, hearing your pulse tap out *Do not forget me,* waiting for the chance, waiting to be given life. *My turn,* shouting through your lungs, through your heart, through your fingernails. *My turn.*

That's when this all started. I knew what I had to do. I had to find you. First, though, I had to figure out how to find you and without anyone, Godiva especially, getting suspicious. I didn't know where to begin, but considering how resourceful you've been all these years, I figured I must have some resourcefulness in my genes. I just had to call it up. If I was going to find you I had to do some research.

N I N E

GRASSLY MUNICIPAL LIBRARY WAS ERECTED IN 1837 AS A
FAMILY HOME BY THE GRASSLY FAMILY WHOSE LAST HEIR,
CLEVELAND AGENCY GRASSLY, DONATED HIS ELEGANT
BIRTHPLACE TO THE ESMERALDA FREE LIBRARY COMMIT-
TEE IN 1933, AN ACT OF GRAND GENEROSITY.

I read that plaque the first Monday after the lock-in. Afterward I was glad that Mr. Grassly forgot to leave any kind of endow-
ment for upkeep. As dark, dank and hard to get around in as it
must have been when Mr. Grassly removed his last elderly aunt to
the nursing home, his old house is everything a library should not
be. That's why I loved it. I loved the green odor of the books slowly
molding in disuse and the warrens of high-ceilinged rooms lined
and partitioned by unsteady shelves. I loved particularly the other
patrons, I guess you'd call them, though I preferred to think of
them as guests: a scattering of old men who nodded over their
copies of *Sports Illustrated* and *Life*. The two librarians, inter-

changeable in their identical beige skirts and cardigan sweaters, paid no attention to what went on beyond the Circulation Desk until 5:05 when they shooed the old men out. The cashiers at Winn-Dixie were more interested in the vegetables they rang up, especially if Godiva was buying one of her mangoes, than those librarians were in the books they stamped with the old blotter. I could read or check out whatever I wanted without a question asked.

On my first visit, that Monday after the lock-in, I wasn't quite sure how to begin. For half an hour I wandered around the American History section, trailing my eyes along the dusty spines, hoping some Geiger counter would go off when I saw what I needed. Then I riffled through yellowed index cards in the subject catalogue. No computers in this library, thank you, though there was an old but reliable copier I fed all my change to. Under "Crimes and Criminals" I discovered a book written in 1973 by an FBI informer, *A Life on the Run: Three Years with the Weather Underground.* You can imagine my excitement. My future clicked into place, not only how to proceed, but what exactly I was looking for. Even in Esmeralda, the library's *Readers' Guide to Periodical Literature* was a rich mine. I began to hang out at the library after school as many afternoons a week as I could.

I thought of little else but said nothing to anyone, and on the surface at least, nothing much changed. If anything, Godiva and I started getting along better. All the small irritations and embarrassments she had been causing me now seemed irrelevant, of juvenile concern. I wasn't going to let my anger at my mother, immeasurable as it was, get in the way of finding you.

One afternoon late in October, I was thumbing through one of the library's picture books on nature—I did that sometimes to relax from the intensity of the research—when I turned a page and there was a series of time-release photographs of a molting snake. I felt such a rush of recognition I couldn't believe it. That snake was me, the same and different, growing new insides under old skin. Me, and you, too. A symbol for us both. A bond.

Godiva never asked why I taped pictures of a snake on my bedroom mirror. She was probably too relieved that I'd lost interest in being born-again to notice anything else. After Mrs. Brasleton called to ask Godiva, politely, why I had stopped attending services and choir practice, Godiva was full of gloating indignation.

"She kept asking about a crisis in the home, as if I had locked you in a tower until you promised never to attend church again or something. A crisis in your home life, can you believe it?" Godiva could mimic Mrs. Brasleton perfectly, I'll give her that, the way she drops her voice and smiles at the edges when she has something unpleasant to say.

"I told her I was disappointed myself since, actually, I'd been looking forward to visiting the Church again to hear you sing." Godiva leaned over to brush my bangs out of my eyes. Why did she always do that? "Which is true, by the way."

Godiva had come to First Baptist exactly one time. She'd attempted, in her fashion, to blend in, but I heard the rustle as the worshipers' attention shifted to the back row. You should have seen her squeezing past the other ladies in her magenta-and-white checked dress with matching wide-brimmed hat, perfect church-going attire for 1955, white gloves and all. Vintage Godiva, courtesy of The Way We Were shop in Gainesville. Afterward she had marched up to Reverend Brasleton and shaken his hand heartily.

"What were you saying to him?" I asked on the way home.

"Only that the music was lovely and God was probably enjoying it immensely from Her place on high." Typical Godiva, so full of herself.

Once she thought I had returned to her way of seeing things, she became almost unbearable in her patronizing.

"I think Mrs. Brasleton believes I've beaten you into atheistic submission. I told her, and I mean this, Noodle, honestly, that I hope you did not make your about-face on my account. I want you to live by your own beliefs, whether I agree with them or not."

Then she began to grill me on the lock-in. Mrs. Brasleton's call gave her the opening she'd probably been looking for. Had there been an incident of some sort, she wanted to know, had I been made uncomfortable in some way, or disillusioned.

"Nothing bad happened." I did not lie. "I simply realized I was not meant to be a Baptist."

My answer more or less satisfied Godiva. She was glad to believe I was over my religious phase. Godiva is big into phases, whether of the moon or of people's lives. Besides, she was so busy herself all fall that she wasn't quite as obsessive as usual about every nook and cranny of my life. She was spending hours in her studio every night, all excited about a new creative breakthrough. Godiva has always had lots of creative breakthroughs. She was also visiting that little Franklin kid all the time. For some reason witnessing his accident really shook her up. She went to the hospital in Perry at least once a week, almost an hour each way. She was also over at the gallery more, plotting her new show with Cleo.

And then there was Godiva's friendship with Mrs. Culpepper. It was pretty weird that they would be friends. B.D. (Before Discovery, remember), I would have resented Godiva horning in, but now I was almost glad because, since Mrs. Culpepper was her friend, Godiva was less concerned if I went off alone with Cass. So Cass and I came up with covers for each other all the time, and she gave me rides home in the afternoons. Sometimes she even took me all the way into the university library. While I researched, she shopped or visited some guys she knew from Esmeralda who had rented a house off-campus. It was tricky, but there were books and magazines that dear old Grassly didn't have.

One Saturday night early in November, I was late getting back from a trek to Gainesville, so I was relieved not to see Miranda parked in front of the house yet. I was just taking off my jacket when the phone rang.

"I stopped by Cleo's and she wants to talk about the show setup," Godiva said. "Can you get your own dinner?"

"I'll manage."

"So what will you do tonight? No parties?" As if I went to parties. "If I'm later than ten, I'll call." Over the phone her voice sounded older, more sedate, almost motherly. "There's plenty of food in the fridge, yogurt and fruit if you're still dieting."

"Don't worry, I won't starve." I was not dieting anymore (I smuggled bags of M&M's into the Grassly all the time despite the handwritten sign barring food or drink from the building), but of course Godiva had no idea.

"So, you're all set, then." She sounded a million miles away. "I love you."

I went straight to the *I Ching* shelf and took down the envelope. It was still there as if completely forgotten, as if no one had ever discovered it. I had made my own copy on the Grassly's copier, just one. Any more would be tempting fate. I have it with me now, but somehow the original, wrinkled and dirt-smudged, brought me closer to you. Of course, now I am closer for real.

Anyway, I had developed a little ritual. First, close the doors, unsash the curtains, turn off all the lights but the glass lamp. Then line up the candles, two short pinkish ones and a tall amber one, and light them one at a time. Wait until the scents of cinnamon and rose overwhelm the room's usual salty musk before opening the envelope. Unfold carefully, kissing each corner before laying it flat under the lamp to study.

I always found something new. That evening it was how, instead of holding your head straight like most people would for a police photo, you pulled your chin in toward your neck. Pressing your jaw down pulled the corners of your mouth into a thin frown, as if you were humming a deep-throated scale to yourself when the photographer snapped. I like to think you are less stern, or less sad, in person. And if you are sad, I will make you less sad. Our reunion was obviously meant to be or I wouldn't have heard that newscast. I wonder, did you hear it, too? Over Thanksgiving? On Public Radio.

We'd spent Thanksgiving afternoon the same as we'd spent it every year since we got to Esmeralda—at Cleo's. We got there around noon. Cleo, in her pink muumuu, swept us in. Her friends Hudson Something and Matty and Gordon Somethingelse were already slugging down their pink mimosas. "Aunt" Matty hugged, the "uncles" patted and pinched, as if they had been waiting all year just to see their little non-niece again. Actually, they came for Thanksgiving at Cleo's because it was a good stopover on their way from wherever they came from in the Midwest to wherever they were heading in southern Florida for the winter. But everyone always pretended to be family at Cleo's Thanksgivings. I never minded because they always brought me inappropriate but outrageously expensive gifts that cracked me up. This year I got a Miss America Barbie doll from Mattie and a bottle of Chanel No. 5 from Hudson. I swear when he handed it over, his eyes glinted with a dirty-old-man leer but no one else noticed.

Soon more people arrived. Harry Somebody had worked with Cleo's husband at the mill. He brought his new wife. It was fairly obscene, that old guy holding hands with a girl who was maybe five years older than me. The Bosell sisters showed up again. They are so strange. They're Cleo's neighbors, and they never go anywhere without each other. Beatrice is taller and Grace is darker, but they are basically interchangeable, and they share a hissing lisp that I suppose they can't help but that gives me the creeps. Then Cleo led in a couple with a little boy. All three wore uncomfortable, slightly dazed smiles as if they weren't sure they were supposed to be there, or that they wanted to be. There were always a few stragglers like these at Cleo's. She made a point of inviting anyone she assumed would not have a grand enough Thanksgiving otherwise. When Godiva saw the couple, she gave Cleo a look but then galloped right over to the boy, who looked about eight, one of those skinny kids who always has snot dripping out their nose.

"Well, Philip Rainey, I didn't expect to see you today. And so spiffy in that bow tie." Godiva acted all thrilled that he was there. It turns out he was the other kid from the famous accident. Cleo obviously wanted the Raineys around so she could tell her friends from out of town all about Godiva's big moment of heroism. Good for sales and all that.

Mrs. Rainey looked pretty, dainty and elegant in her plain dark suit. I felt sorry for her. Mr. Rainey was ugly, with scarred, leathery skin. And the kid was a brat. When we went into Cleo's bedroom to watch TV, he kept switching channels. By the time I left him in there, he was using Cleo's eyeliner as a pencil to draw all over Cleo's pink bedspread.

Back in the living room, Cleo was describing her plans to bring tourists to Esmeralda. I don't know why they'd want to come; there's not even a movie theater, let alone a water park. But Cleo kept talking about copying Key West.

"I want to build on the mystique of being located in the middle of nowhere," she was explaining to Mrs. Rainey, who looked uncomfortable and out of place, as if all Cleo's pink were making her a little ill. "So how do you like my watercolor? Has it worn well?"

One of the Bosells stood trapped in a corner with Uncle Hudson. He was always trapping someone in a corner to talk gardens. Mr. Rainey was talking to the newlyweds. Godiva glided among them all, decked out in her off-the-shoulders pineapple blouse and multicolored skirt that whirled like a rainbow in a blender whenever she moved. All she was missing was a hat of bananas. She kept disappearing into the kitchen, her skirt twirling through the doorway behind her.

The turkey was served a little after one and then Cleo brought out the games, board games like Parcheesi and Chinese Checkers no one else plays anymore. We were home by five. Godiva immediately announced she was going to bake some bread. She always does this. We've been somewhere and she decides she has too much energy left over so she starts some giant project. Around Thanksgiving it's usually bread.

As she arranged her ingredients on the table and started mixing stuff, she sang at the top of her lungs, old Beatles and Joni Mitchell and Bob Dylan (my other namesake, I hate him!). Every so often she'd break into free-form dance steps that caused flour to rise from the open bag in dusty clouds.

I sat at the one uninvaded corner of the table, eating leftover yam and fruit casserole. To a stranger we'd have looked as cozy as a greeting card. That was the thing, for everything to seem just fine, as if the same old ground rules still applied. I forced myself to hang around because she expected me to.

"You used to love to help bake. Remember those little baking tins you had?"

"I guess."

"We had so much fun." When Godiva tossed her hair back, flour sprinkled down. "You'll come back to it. You're just at an age when making bread is a little too sensual to handle."

I cringed inwardly but said nothing. B.D. I might have exploded at such a ridiculous comment, but I was not going to waste energy on scenes with Godiva Blue anymore. Godiva shook more flour across her bread slab, a jagged piece of marble she'd found abandoned years ago and used only for her annual baking splurge at Thanksgiving. Watching Godiva punch and knead, it was hard not to be lulled by the familiarity of the warm room full of the sweet scent of yeast and cinnamon and chocolate—Godiva makes a killer chocolate bread.

"God, I do love Thanksgiving." Godiva set a blob of dough in the unlit oven to rise and took another blob out. "The idea of a holiday when all you do is stuff yourself and be thankful. Done right it transcends religion. After all, nothing says you can't pick which god, or gods, to thank."

The same old ranting, easily ignored. Bits of dough clung to her cheek; flour had tamed her hair to a dull mud color. Godiva is an extremely messy cook. She had on a stained green turtleneck that pulled unflatteringly at her breasts and showed her heaviness. This is mean, I guess, but I swear she resembled a turkey.

The phone rang. Godiva has always hated the phone but since September, the stupid accident and all, she was getting more calls. At first we both ignored the ringing the way we often did unless one of us was expecting a call (and since the lock-in I'd stopped expecting or wanting calls). Then suddenly Godiva leaped toward it. Her hands were covered with flour so she cradled the receiver between her jaw and shoulder as she worked over her dough. Whoever was on the other end caught her attention. I swear she flushed.

"No." Almost formal. "I'm baking bread with my daughter." She wiped her hands on her apron and started to pace as she talked.

I took another helping of casserole. Godiva's back rounded into the phone. She wandered into the other room, the long phone cord slinking after her. After a minute or two, she wandered back and reached for her lighter on the table.

"Yes." She held the flame at arm's length before she lit her cigarette. "I'm not sure." She casually glanced in my general direction. "I'm not sure. Maybe later."

As Godiva hung up, I had this fleeting hope even I recognized was crazy, that you were calling to say you wanted to meet with us and that Godiva was agreeing.

"I'm sorry, Noodle. It wasn't important." Godiva punched my arm lightly, then suddenly full of energy, tousled my hair the way she used to. I tried not to flinch before she gave it up.

"I'm crazy to hear more about the Iran-Contra thing," she said and switched on the radio. Godiva listens to National Public Radio every night for about half an hour, as close to mass media as she gets, although she let me have a black-and-white portable television in my room because, she said, she didn't want me to feel deprived and sneak to other people's houses for my favorite programs.

I was playing with my fork, mashing my yam into hills and valleys when I realized what I was hearing on the radio. Instead of Iran-Contra, a reporter was describing some drug bust in South Carolina.

"Lehman and Tremp have been identified as members of the A.R.M., the American Radical Movement, an offshoot of the Weather Underground movement of the late sixties and early seventies."

I could not quite believe my ears. Godiva was kneading dough, oblivious.

"Arrested Monday night as they were about to board a shrimp boat laden with one and a half tons of marijuana twenty miles north of Charleston, South Carolina, the suspects have been sought for years in connection with various terrorist activities including several bombings."

I did not dare stop chewing my mouthful of casserole, afraid Godiva would notice, but Godiva was staring out the window, her hands in the dough.

"This arrest, like the Brinks robbery several years ago, raises the question for many who came of age in the nineteen-sixties— what happened to the idealism of that era?" The woman reporter's confiding, slightly puzzled tone was gratingly similar to Godiva's at times. "Why did college radicalism turn ugly, first to violence, now criminality."

I did not want to hear any more. I was desperate to get out of the kitchen.

"Speaking with us now is Gerry Flint, a former Weather Underground member who has lived under a false name for the last eight years. You worked as a garage mechanic until you turned yourself in and received a full pardon last August, is that right, Mr. Flint?"

Gerry Flint had the high-pitched, rattling voice of a college professor. He explained how he'd married and fathered two children, how the family lived in a solidly working-class neighborhood in Toledo, Ohio, where they were completely accepted. Accepted as what? I wondered.

"And do you still participate in political activism?"

"I don't vote or anything." He either cleared his throat or chuckled. "I've signed a few petitions with my new name, abortion rights, environmental issues, that sort of thing, but I'm no activist. No anti-nuclear groups or stuff like that. I wouldn't be fool enough. Not that I really had done much of anything to make me worth seeking out in the first place. Nope, I've just been an average Joe. My one passion was, well still is, my son Hank's soccer team, which I coached until my legal situation came up. We're talking about my coaching again next spring in fact. The parents are standing behind me."

I could not breathe. Could not move. Had he really named his son Hank? I glanced at Godiva punching her dough. No reaction visible.

"Why did you turn yourself in?"

"Well, I knew my parents were getting older, and now that I'm a parent, I wanted to clear things up, wanted Hank and Eden to meet their grandmother and grandfather. My folks have been great by the way. Extremely understanding."

"Do you know the men who were arrested yesterday?"

"I'd heard their names round and about before Toledo when I was still on the move, but I never met them personally. Living underground is a funny existence."

If I'd only had a tape recorder I could play this for you sometime. But I remember every word.

"It can go either way. You can fit yourself right in, carve a safe place for yourself, or you can keep on the loose, move around, switch identities. If you go that way, you're less likely to get caught I suppose but you're also pretty much on your own. You might maintain some old contacts, keep in the political swim on the periphery. Well, not always on the periphery if you still want to blow things up, not that I ever did. But basically you're isolated. That way of living was too lonely for me. I'm a nest builder. I'm a people person."

"Is that what drew you into politics in the first place?"

"Sure. Good parties, good dope, if I can say that here, pretty girls."

"The dough is on its own for a while," Godiva said. I was listening so hard to the radio I almost didn't hear her, had to swim back to the present of being together with her in our kitchen. "I'm heading out to the studio."

She spoke nonchalantly, but I wasn't sure. I felt as if I were watching a silent film of Godiva walking across the kitchen in slow motion. At that moment I almost wished I could tell her, could let the words out into the space between us, say in a clear clipped tone, "I know." But there was no way. Meanwhile, being in the room with Godiva was unbearable. I thought I would scream.

The report had lasted no more than a minute or two, and Gerry Flint had said little that was exactly surprising. I already knew from my research most of the survival techniques of the hunted, how you get a phony ID, how you send messages to your families. However, he'd given me something far more important.

A paperweight Godiva made years ago sat in the middle of the table holding down some striped napkins. I picked it up. Although heavy in my palm, the glass ball filled with aqua and rose bubbles had an airiness, as if it were on the verge of floating away. For over a month, I had been searching old newspaper clippings and autobiographical books for some acknowledgment of your existence, and here it was. Gerry Flint knew you. His son's name could not be coincidence. I knew I could look up his name, the real one and the fake one, in the Toledo phone book at the Grassly library. I could find out where Flint had been and find you.

That's how I zeroed in on Eden. Flint wouldn't actually talk to me when I called his house pretending I was a reporter, but there were articles about him in the newspapers the next few days. One mentioned some time he'd spent on a collective farm in Delaware. Eden, like his daughter. A little paradise for people who needed to disappear. Gerry Flint had stayed there long enough to name his daughter after the place. He had named his son Hank. After you, it had to be. Gerry Flint must have known you. Where else could your paths have crossed but Eden. There is no other possible connection. I am sure I am on the right path.

At first, when Randall Spider Gervais sat down, pulled off his red snakeskin boots and said, "Don't worry, my feet don't smell," I pretended to be too busy reading a magazine to hear him, but, in fact, I sat up a little straighter. I guess I've already told you, but bus travelers are pretty creepy, like they've been old forever. The sitting dead. So it was not all that flattering that he'd picked me to sit next to. Besides, by yesterday afternoon all the window seats were taken. But still, a little thrill ran through me that he was a guy, and an older guy, at least nineteen, maybe even in his twenties.

As for me, I was just starting to feel a little better, or at least less totally depressed. At least I'd stopped crying. But I was ready to back out. I mean, not really. I knew I had to find you. But had the wrong person decided to sit next to me, some responsible grown-up who looked at me hard and asked questions in that concerned adult-stranger tone, I admit I might have given up and slunk back to Esmeralda, your picture to remain in my wallet forevermore untouched.

If Randall Spider Gervais was sent as a first test of my will, he is a whole different kind of test. In his silvery cowboy shirt and those red boots, he does not appear to have one extra inch of fat, or skin for that matter, anywhere on his body. His head balances above his shoulders on a popsicle stick neck. The skin is pulled tight across his face from ear to ear, so that his nose looks like a folded sheet of paper. He could be two-dimensional. A fish with an eye on either side but no front. Not that he is ugly. He is not ugly at all. Just different. Dramatic. Mesmerizing. No just-one-of-the-guys Jimmy Cryder, either, that's for sure. Boy, Jimmy Cryder was a whole other lifetime.

"Your feet stink," I told Randall Spider Gervais after a few minutes. Did they ever. The smell was sour and moldy. Randall Spider Gervais was wearing black socks out of some nylony material that emphasized his bony arches.

"Yeah, but those boots like to kill me, they're so tight." His Adam's apple bobbed with each syllable, but his skin was smooth in a tan, manly way. "Are you on your way to the D. of C., too?"

I nodded.

"Business or pleasure?"

"Excuse me?"

"Business or pleasure, ma'am?"

I just looked at him.

He wasn't kidding. I mean, he was talking to me the way Jimmy's dad might to a client in Esmeralda, but he was not a middle-aged real estate agent. Not by a long shot. I took the time to consider seriously what my correct answer should be.

You have to realize, he was the first person I'd seen anywhere near my age, not counting that crying baby, since Cass dropped me off, and then I was so nervous I barely said goodbye to her. I was trying to squeeze Godiva's knapsack into the overhead rack when I looked out the window and there was Reverend Brasleton locking his car door in the Waffle House lot across the street. Squinting right at the bus like he was trying to see inside. It was probably the sun he was squinting against actually. Besides, the bus windows were tinted so I'm pretty sure he couldn't see anything even if he tried.

Not that Reverend Brasleton was likely to talk to Godiva. Hardly. But if he'd seen me, I would have had to make conversation, explaining why I was in Perry taking the Atlanta bus or pretending I wasn't. I could easily have ended up missing the bus altogether. Luckily Cass was parking the car around the corner, but when she came back, even though he was inside by then, ordering his chili fries or pecan waffle, all I wanted was for her to leave fast.

I'm assuming everything's working out on her end. If they call Gram's, they'll assume we're out shopping or eating somewhere, as long as Cass remembered to call her mother last night so Mrs. Culpepper would let Godiva know we arrived safely. I wonder where exactly Cass went with her friend. A male friend, I'm sure, although she didn't say. She's so mysterious. That's why I trust her. She has her own secrets.

Meanwhile, I decided that the best approach with Randall Spider Gervais was to stay above it all.

"Personal business," I said, looking straight ahead.

"I'm on a mission for the United States government myself. Highly confidential." He spoke in a low drawl, not a whisper, but conspiratorial, as if he'd sized me up and I'd passed.

"Right, and I'm on my way to join a commune of bomb-throwing terrorists." You'd have been proud of me, the way I didn't miss a beat. There was no way he'd believe the truth put that way.

"A commune?"

I figured he didn't know what I meant and started explaining how I'd already lived on a commune once, even if I didn't exactly remember much about it, when I was really little, before we went to Gram's because Poppo was dying. Godiva has told me stories about Magic House, but it's hard to picture Godiva part of some group of friends, sharing everything, making group decisions. Now all she does is warn me against stuff like peer pressure. Isolation is her big thing these days. Only she'd call it independence.

Spider stopped me before I said much. Held his finger to my lips. Very gentle but spooky kind of.

"We might be adversaries someday," he said. Adversaries! Imagine Jimmy Cryder talking like that. When I started to giggle, he looked offended.

"You'll begin to understand soon enough."

It was very weird. I didn't believe for a second he was on a mission for anybody, but then again, who'd believe I was going to a commune of bomb throwers? I felt exposed, almost. Part of me was saying this guy is a nut case. But another part was curious. What made him say he was on a mission? Besides, he was taking me so seriously. A cute older guy taking me seriously. That was a first.

Evening was catching up with us. The countryside looked different, more exotic, the distant lights turning everything a kind of pewter. The world softened and I felt a reawakening of life's possibilities. Everything and anything was possible. Did you ever have a moment like that? Now that your life is constricted, with so many options closed because of your past (not that I'm critical of any choice you made; I'm sure there were reasons), do you ever look back and remember a time when anything could have happened next? That's how I felt last night.

Randall Spider Gervais started talking about his childhood, telling me how his mother was the belle of Meridian, before she married Spider's daddy and started traveling in a downward spiral that ended when his daddy disappeared with all their savings while she was giving birth to Spider.

"When she died, so many roses and lilies came from all over to the funeral home, my step-daddy had to rent a tent, a big striped tent like they use for weddings, to hold them all." Spider was seven years old at the time. "Next thing I knew, I was shipped off to military school, a junior junior cadet." He pressed my finger against what he said was a scar above his chest. I couldn't see it in the dark, but he said it was from his first fight defending his mother's name. "Since that day I have never been without a weapon at my disposal."

I let the idea of weapons settle in. His voice was so sweet, how dangerous could he be? I realized we were holding hands, had been for a while. I didn't mind. His life had been so tragic really, even if his stories didn't make sense.

Then he kissed me, and there in the dark bus, it felt wonderfully right, romantic as a movie. He was a man, not a boy, who trusted me as a woman. He needed me. The other passengers just faded away. Except for the driver, who didn't count because he couldn't look back, we were the only people awake on the bus, anyway. The forward rocking of the bus, the drone of the engine blocking out all sound except Spider's burred twang so close to my ear, made the outside world seem unreal. We were locked in our own little private night. Only the whisper of cold air escaping in along the rubberized window frame reminded me where I was.

I don't know if I slept at all. I remember a neon gas station sign somewhere, a gold shell lit up like a perfect jewel on black velvet.

Sometime after that, gray streaks began to stain the sky. When a few people lumbered past us on their way to the toilet, I wondered briefly, a passing thought I didn't try to hold, what it would be like with Spider once the sun came up. It was almost light enough to see his face clearly, but my eyes wouldn't open. Not that I fell asleep exactly, just my eyes. The rest of my body was aware of every lurch and turn and brake of the bus, every slowdown and speed-up. Here and there I'd let myself sink into a luxurious blank undertow, but then I'd feel the pressure of responding weight against my shoulder and float back into semiconscious awareness of Spider next to me, wide awake. He didn't seem to need sleep at all. By the time we got to the Shoney's we're at now, Spider had only to touch my arm and I was awake. Eyes-open awake and starving.

As soon as we got here, Spider took his zippered bag of quarters and went off to the pay phone. He should be back any minute. Meanwhile, I'm stuffing my face. This is my first real meal since Thursday night. I was too nervous Friday to eat anything before I left, and since then it's been chips and candy bars washed down with orange soda. But Spider ordered the breakfast buffet for two before he went off. I'm having bacon, scrambled eggs, a blueberry muffin, hash browns, pancakes. It's amazing how hungry sitting in a bus seat can make a person. If Godiva were here now, she'd be sipping tea and smoking, blowing smoke rings and tapping ashes into the little tin ashtray. That's what most people here are doing, drinking coffee, but I can see Godiva so clearly because even doing almost the same as everybody else she's always out of place. She'd dwarf them all.

Outside in the parking lot a man keeps wandering up to the door and then wandering back. It's really kind of sad. He's wearing three layers of sweaters and one of those hats with earflaps. His hair sticks out in knotted spikes and he's real dirty besides. A street person, I guess, but when he peeked in the last time, he had the clearest, bluest eyes.

What if I get to the farm and they don't know where you are? Hiding from the police and the FBI all these years could damage a person's spirit. I suppose street persons are able to get by without social-security numbers. If your spirit is broken, I'll rehabilitate you. I'll get a job and learn to cook. But what about your parents? Are they accepting, like Gerry Flint's? Do you send them postcards occasionally? We could go to their house in Michigan or wherever. They'd probably be overjoyed to get back their son; a granddaughter would be a bonus. Only we wouldn't go right away. I'd get you good and healthy first so you could cope. Not that you're going to need rehabilitating. You're going to be great.

It turns out the schedule was misleading. I can't make it to Eden before late tonight at the earliest. But I am going to get there and I will find you. I almost hope Spider doesn't come back, although I know he will because his briefcase is here next to me. I could look inside if I wanted. It is tempting, but no, I do not think I will peek. One glance at me and Spider could tell. Even though we hardly know each other, he seems to see into my heart somehow. It's kind of cool.

Don't worry, he won't get in the way of my finding you. He is a little bit of a distraction, but in a good way because he makes the traveling less lonely. Even if only half of what he says is true, his life has certainly not been dull. He's a renegade, same as me. He told me this whole philosophy he has about living by the inner light, what he calls self-actualizing. Not like Godiva at all even if it sounds that way. Well, maybe a little like her.

I do wonder how it's going—if Godiva is suspicious by now. I'm worried about Cass when she gets back. She thinks Godiva is so interesting. She could mess me up although I've warned her that Godiva is tricky, that she sucks people right in if they're not careful. She'll talk to Cass as an equal, ask her questions that hit little pings of truth Cass won't be able to imagine Godiva has recognized. Cass will be flattered, but I think she'll hold out. She shouldn't be back in Esmeralda for another day and a half anyway. Everything will be chill as long as Gram doesn't call, and why would she, all the way from Waikiki?

I have my fingers crossed. I have to get farther before Godiva knows anything. At least to Eden.

ELEVEN

It has mostly to do with Spider's smile. The way his thin face stretches almost painfully before the sudden flash of teeth and gum grabs me in the chest and squeezes my breath away. My thinking goes all haywire when he's around. He takes me in so many directions at once.

When he came back into Shoney's, he had flowers for me. No one has ever brought me flowers in my life. Where he came up with orange daisies and yellow carnations at 8:00 on a Sunday morning is a question I did not dare ask because what comes to mind is a church or a cemetery. He pinned the flowers in my hair like a crown. He says that his aunt who runs a beauty parlor in Tupelo taught him all kinds of hair tricks. I felt kind of silly, but nice silly. Getting back on the bus, I knew I was blushing and I knew I looked pretty and special to the crone patrol (as Spider calls them). Even the bus driver smiled.

It was such a beautiful morning. The dark tint on the windows could not keep out the sunlight, and the Virginia countryside was so much livelier than the Carolinas or Georgia, all blues and yellows and greens. More prosperous, the rolling farmland clotted with barns and houses, old-fashioned and neat, like the miniature Victorian village we helped Cleo set up under her tree on Christmas Eve, another holiday tradition. I unwrapped the colored tissue papers one by one to discover a house or a little store just like I do every year. I don't know why Godiva has always been so eager to spend so much time with Cleo and have all these little traditions with her when she can't stand to be around Gram, her own mother, for more than three minutes and never would think of spending a holiday with her. They're both old ladies so what's the big difference? Not that I care. She can spend as much time with Cleo as she wants now.

All through Virginia, Spider told stories about one or another of his great-great-great-uncles fighting a Civil War battle in whatever town we were passing through. Spider could tell me exactly how many people were killed on each side, what injury his great-great-great-uncle suffered and what act of heroism he performed. At some point I felt a tap on my shoulder. It was one of the more decrepit old ladies.

"I'm just on my way to the restroom," she whispered, her hand digging into my shoulder as she tried to keep her balance against the bus's sway while she offered me a mint LifeSaver, slightly damp. "You two look so sweet together."

It was a lark. Spider even had a soda can ring he pulled from a pocket of his briefcase. I don't know, I guess it sounds corny, but at the time I was all caught up in the mood. It was romantic, even when the flowers began to wilt and the petals started falling into my lap.

He was telling me about his great-great-uncle Morrison Peavy being taken prisoner of war at the Battle of Vicksburg when he stopped in midsentence, squeezed my hand tight and smiled. His eyes, yellow brown like a cat's, stared at me without a flicker, demanding that I not turn away. So I didn't. Hand and eye, he did not let go and did not let go. I could feel the strength in his hand, felt it traveling down his sinewy arm from somewhere inside his narrow back. I felt dull and tired in comparison. I didn't think about what he wanted; I just relaxed, letting the current pass between us back and forth. Then it was as if I were floating separate above myself, watching my mouth open and close. I began to tell him my story, about living out my childhood as if I'd been born by Immaculate Conception or something, knowing as little about who my father was as Godiva told me she knew, which I believed was next to nothing, then finding your picture. How that changed everything.

I never told anyone or even completely admitted this to myself, but I used to dream, daydream and night dream both, that you were Sam Malone, the guy on that TV show *Cheers* who owns the bar. Not the actor, but Sam Malone. He is funny and cute and lovable for an older guy, and he has no visible family. I used to imagine being part of the show one week, how it would be written up in *TV Guide:* "A beautiful young girl visits the bar and seems very interested in Sam. Diane is jealous until the girl confides she is Sam's daughter but is afraid to tell him." By the end of the episode, Carla, the waitress who's always pregnant, would make a joke about him being old enough to be my father. Then everyone, Cliffy and Norm and that psychiatrist, would roll their eyes, but I'd go into Sam's office and tell him the truth and there would be a big reunion scene and I'd end up with some kind of continuing role.

Well, I told Spider and he didn't laugh at me. So then I told about finding the wanted poster. He was still holding my hand. He opened his fingers and turned my hand over to study my palm.

"Ronald Reagan is a student of astrology," he told me. "The fact is not generally known, but it is one reason I admire him so much. He isn't all objective scientific method. Neither am I, darling." He actually called me that.

"I can finish your story studying this pretty little hand of yours."

I was blown away. Astrology and palm reading, weren't they on the same weirdness frequency as the *I Ching*? This had to be some kind of omen. I had not even mentioned that the poster was in Godiva's *I Ching* box.

"You are looking for him now and you don't expect a TV star anymore. But I see a family uniting here." He pointed to a spot right in the deepest part of my palm where three lines intersect. "And if your daddy is wanted by the FBI"—Spider's finger pressed a gentle crease from my wrist along the longest line of my palm— "I have connections that could be a big help locating him."

I don't know if I made a mistake, and I hope you're not angry, but I showed him the poster. I was really nervous. Part of me was saying don't do it, but I could not stop myself. Anyway, it is public knowledge, isn't it? I told him about the research I had done to trace you. As I was about to explain how I learned about Eden, the shadow of a face slid across the window glass behind Spider, just a slight darkening. Maybe it was a sudden jolt of the bus or a man's phlegmy cough a few seats forward, but I felt the warning was from you and stopped talking.

"So you'll look in his old haunts?" Spider kept stroking my hand, and I nodded, guilty that I was holding back, guilty that I had already said so much. He did not ask where I'm heading next; maybe he sees it on my palm, but I promise I haven't told him.

+   +   +

We didn't get to Washington until about eight tonight. The camaraderie evaporated as soon as the driver accordioned open the door. Filing down the narrow aisle, no one looked at each other. No one helped anyone else down the steep steps. Waiting for the bags to be handed out at the side of the bus, no one spoke. The air was dense with exhaust, unbreathable, no one could have spoken if we wanted to. Even Spider was a stranger to me again, and the possibility that I should not rely on a stranger leaned awkwardly against the trust we'd been building between us. I could see the stubble of a day's growth of beard on his chin. It seemed almost creepy that I'd been kissing someone old enough to shave every day. I've decided that he's older than I thought, maybe even twenty-five.

Spider left me alone by the island of plastic chairs while he disappeared to make one of his phone calls. The room was almost deserted. Two black men in their twenties stood in the corner playing a videogame machine and slapping each other on the shoulder, talking loud in a language I could not understand although it may have been a version of English. Every so often they looked toward me, not unfriendly exactly, but I pretended not to notice, any more than I noticed the stink of wine and urine on the five or six other men sprawled across or curled into the molded chairs around me.

I was the only female and the only white person. You might be disappointed in me, but I have to be honest. I guess I am a racist because, despite all those years of Godiva explaining racial oppression and the bond that I should have felt from being partly named after a black woman (who, I remembered as I sat there, was murdered during a criminal act, probably in a similar neighborhood), I was scared to death. When Spider came around the corner from the men's room I practically leaped into his arms. I couldn't see what interested him about a dumpy teenage girl with dirty fingernails and dead weeds dripping down through my stringy, unwashed hair, but at that moment I was just grateful he was sticking around.

I have no idea how he got us to this hotel room. He led me down various streets for what seemed hours. Then here we were. I was so tired I didn't catch the name but the lobby was bland and impersonal with lots of heavily bundled people wandering around, Christmas season tourists I guess. The lady at the desk who gave us the key didn't bat an eye at how cheesy I looked. Spider waved away the old guy who offered to carry our bags. Then up we went in the elevator to the twelfth floor.

"I'll be back in an hour," Spider said when we were inside with the light turned on and the bags on the little shelf. Of course, first we made out in the dark for a few minutes. His bony elbows with the little hollows were much sexier pressing me against the wall than scrunched into those bus seats.

I wish he'd get back. He told me to wash up and make myself lovely. That's how he put it. "Make yourself lovely, darling girl, then order us up two steaks, medium, and whatever dessert they have that's chocolate. Charge it to the room." Who talks like that?

I took a bath. To get out of my sweater and my jeans was heaven. The pants practically walked by themselves. I washed everything and used the little hair dryer the hotel provides until they were only damp. I put on a clean white T-shirt and my jogging shorts.

Do you condemn fancy places like this? Godiva would call it decadent. She refuses to stay in motels even. The few times we went anywhere, she always seemed to know a place we could "crash," friends or friends of friends or someone she met once and kept his address because he had a nice laugh.

In Esmeralda, of course, she's never really had friends, just old Cleo and now there's Mrs. Culpepper, too, I guess. But she's always had what she called her long-distance-call friends. There'd be calls every so often and letters from weird addresses in Oregon and Maine and North Dakota. I snuck a look through them to make sure there weren't any from you. Nothing doing. Not even a mention. Only a few references to me for that matter. Mostly the letters were about the letter writers. It was kind of pathetic, these grown people writing on and on about their love life, or lack of it. The letters all ran together: "Am I talented or just mediocre" . . . "If only I had enough time" . . . "I am lonely" . . . "If only I had enough money" . . . "I miss him but I wouldn't take him back" . . . "What I am attempting now is completely different" . . . "I am learning to grow up." Blah, blah, blah, blah. What did Godiva write back? They all wrote as if she felt the same way, but I cannot feature Godiva Blue ever admitting she didn't know exactly what she was all about.

Staying here is not really being disloyal to you, is it? I mean, the way I am doing it, on the sly and all. And it is amazing; I can literally see the Washington Monument from my window. How did Spider manage it? He says he has all these phony credit cards for his secret work, and they are all government supplied anyway, but who knows?

I wonder if this is the kind of place Cass stayed with her friend. By now they should be driving toward Esmeralda in her car, or did she park it somewhere when they met up? What does he drive? I'm picturing them tooling along in a cherry-red convertible, her mother's overnight bag stowed in the trunk? Holding what? A silk teddy the color of his car, a hundred dollars in single bills, Opium perfume, an ounce of cocaine? B.D., I never used to imagine other people's lives so much, but then I never imagined my own life much, either.

I'm frankly a little worried about Cass. I don't know much, but a couple of days before I left, she told me some crazy things she did this fall sometimes when she was not where she was supposed to be. Like the night of the lock-in. It's amazing what she got away with. Of course, who am I to talk.

Still, it was a little perverted. Some afternoons, when Mrs. Culpepper worked at school late and the boys had activities that kept them out of the house until her dad picked them up on his way home, Cass would cut last period study hall and drive all the way out Highway 7 to a spot where she could hear I-75. There's no exit there, but Cass told me that's why she liked it. She said she'd park the car and then cut through an abandoned field and some shallow woods to a grass embankment where she could sit and wave at the people driving by on the interstate.

"Sometimes I'd even take my shirt off and wave it around over my head."

"What?" I couldn't believe I heard her right. I made Cass repeat that part.

"Yeah, I'd wave around my shirt. It's like I could do anything sitting there. I was completely visible from the road but invisible, too. The cars go by so fast they can't be sure what they see."

We were standing by our lockers at school as she said this. She had on a black T-shirt and her narrow jeans. Watching her unwrap a piece of gum, I realized how otherworldly she could be with her pale skin and black chopped hair, a ghost in someone's rearview mirror. It gave me the chills, although considering Spider and me on the bus last night, groping each other, doing practically everything but IT, I can see how under certain conditions people do become, not invisible exactly, but beyond reach of everyone else's awareness.

Evidently Cass was doing her bare-chested thing one afternoon a few weeks earlier, enjoying the cool autumn sun, when a fancy sports car—she didn't notice anything else about it except its silvery peach color which she thought maybe she'd picked out slowing down another time—pulled off onto the shoulder. A short fat guy got out and walked up toward where she was sitting.

"I considered beating it back up the hills toward my car. But then I said to myself, what the hell."

There was a metal fence between her and the highway running along a narrow trough left from a dried-up canal. The man grinned at her and jumped the fence.

"I just laughed. I figured he wasn't about to hurt me or try anything with so many people driving by who could see."

"Cass, I can't believe you."

"Yeah, I was so stupid," she admitted. "It was only when he sat down and put his big sweaty hand around my arm that the light-bulb went on: There I was assuming I could do anything in front of the traffic. So why wouldn't he assume the same thing?"

He asked her name and she said Rebecca.

"It was the first name that popped into my head," Cass told me, laughing and pulling up one of her socks where it had run into the heel of her shoe. Then she leaned against her locker and started talking more quietly, as if she'd never heard the story before herself.

"He smelled nice, not sweet, but manly. Cigarettes and aftershave, and leather. He asked what I thought I was doing acting so silly, attracting attention to myself. His teeth were yellowish and uneven, but his voice was so easy, deep but not stern like my dad's. And educated. I bet he was a doctor or a lawyer or a business executive. He was wearing gray pants and shiny black shoes. I remembered reading somewhere that FBI men always wear black shoes so for a moment I thought maybe he was going to arrest me, but his shoes had tassels.

"I was scared. It took a lot not to start to cry, but I didn't. I asked him where he was heading. 'Nowhere interesting,' he said. Then he asked me if I wanted something to drink to cool off and he pulled a flask out of somewhere. He told me his name was Bill, that he was a pharmacist, divorced, and that he had a tattoo of the Statue of Liberty on the small of his back, would I like to see?

"I don't know what was in the flask, but I was more relaxed by then and thinking I would like to see a tattoo. I decided he was kind of cute close up, more teddy-bearish than fat, and not as old as I thought at first. I told him how I'd found this place and how it made me feel happy to sit above the rushing traffic. The same as I told you. Then I told him he was the first person who noticed I was there. 'Really,' he said, stretching out the word. You know, giving it all kinds of intimate meanings."

Cass kicked a wadded ball of paper down the hall.

"He had the sexiest voice. We were lying back on the grass by then. I was balancing the flask on my midriff so I could feel the cold damp tin on my skin. 'Well, you got my attention, honey,' he said and rolled over so one of his legs fell carelessly over mine. Then he began to rub my belly with his thumb. So I closed my eyes."

When Cass said that part, I said, "Gross!" but she didn't seem to notice, caught up as she was in the karma of her own story.

" 'Easy girl, you're some tiger,' I thought I heard him say, and then it was as if the cars were speeding inside my head. Next thing I remember, I'm opening my eyes and he's gone. My shorts and panties were all the way down by the fence in the canal ditch. Scrambling down there stark naked, I wasn't sure if I felt exposed or not.

"I stopped going out there after that. Not because I was afraid. But the episode was over if you know what I mean."

I didn't know what to say. I was shocked. She was so chill about it all. Maybe, though, Cass was more of an influence on me than I thought.

TWELVE

Okay.

Deep breath.

I am not sure what is going on. Or what I feel about Spider anymore. I am in the bathroom with the door locked, blow-drying my jeans dry enough to wear out of here. Spider is out there in the room, waiting for me, I guess. I've been in here for half an hour. I told him I was sick to my stomach, which is not far from the truth.

When he came back to the room he was different. He was cleaned up and shaven, wearing an electric green shirt and new boots to match, and the skinniest pair of tight jeans I have ever seen on a guy. He was different acting, too. He kept watching me out of one eye, not meeting my glance. He was less talky, and when he kissed me, he tasted funny. Of liquor or maybe something else, too, stale and sickly sweet.

I'm probably being paranoid. But it's all too bizarre, me and the whole situation. I'm trying to rethink the last hour or two, the "objective facts" as Miss Tilden in Civics would say. I'm ashamed but in the spirit of honesty I have to admit I just heard myself sounding like you know who. Godiva always uses that expression, "as so and so would say." Of course, I am not like her in any real way. Besides, Godiva is not around any more than you are. You will be soon enough, but in the meantime I am on my own. I have to figure out for myself whether I've got myself into a mess or not. And if I have, how to get out.

The first thing Spider did was take a bottle of wine out of a bag he brought back with him. He poured some into a paper cup, and I thought he was going to hand it to me. Instead he held the cup to my lips. Another of his romantic gestures, but he caught me off guard. I gagged a little and the wine dribbled out of my mouth, leaving a long stain down the front of my T-shirt.

So he gave me the cup. The taste wasn't too bad. I felt kind of floaty afterward. I have not had much sleep lately, so it went right to my head. I thought I saw a man, you actually, sitting in a straight-backed chair by the door.

I must have fallen asleep then, because when I woke up a while later I felt better. I was lying on the double bed though I don't know how I got there. Spider was talking on the phone. His briefcase lay open on the floor half in sight beyond the corner of the bed. As soon as he heard me stir he covered the receiver and whispered that he'd been in touch with certain people to get a copy of my father's FBI file.

"Not the one they edit, but the whole A to Z," he said. "All they've got on him."

"I don't get it. How can a regular person from Meridian, Mississippi—"

"Caledonia, Mississippi."

"Caledonia, Mississippi then. How can someone like you get that kind of information in the middle of a Sunday night?"

"It's only a matter of pushing the right buttons. Besides, I am not a regular person."

I was not totally sure I believed him, or even if I wanted to believe him, but after my nap I was feeling cheery and affectionate toward the world at large and him in particular. I wanted to give him the benefit of any doubt, and it only barely occurred to me to be worried by his claims. Mostly, I was impressed and flattered that he was taking me even half seriously. He made me feel protected and grown up at the same time. I was not used to so much attention from a man.

He leaned over to kiss my cheek, then turned away to hang up the phone. At the same time he kicked the briefcase closed with his boot, and I thought I caught a glint of something, a hard silver shape that gave me the briefest chill. But before I gathered the words to ask what I'd seen, Spider turned back to me with that crazy, irresistible grin.

"Well, darling girl, shall we eat?"

I nodded and said nothing.

The steaks must have arrived while I was asleep. He led me over to the little square table with its white tablecloth and the pink rose in a silver vase. Everything looked so expensive, the heavy utensils, like Gram's silver but duller, and the heavy water glasses tinted pale blue. There were two plates covered by silver domes.

Spider was lifting one to show me the baked potatoes and the string beans and the steaks themselves. White and green and brown, a nice coordination of colors, I thought idly, watching him cut the steak and spoon sour cream inside the potatoes.

He talked all through the meal. I was concentrating on the food. Rolls shaped like pinwheels came in a basket with chilled butter in a white bowl beside them. The green beans were the skinny slit kind you can't find fresh, or Godiva doesn't, and they had slivered almonds on top.

As for the meat, God, it was wonderful. Every piece I speared with my fork squirted bloody juice. I don't think I'd tasted steak since Godiva and I visited Gram last year. Red meat does not appear on Godiva's table, ever. And at the Brasletons', the meat runs more to pot roast and fried chicken.

Meanwhile Spider was explaining that he worked for a man named Que. I wasn't sure if that was the guy's real name and I was not hearing the pronunciation right or if it was just the alphabet letter as in a code name. Que worked for another man who was secretly working for one of those people who recently had to quit their big government jobs to protect the President. It took a moment for me to realize Spider was talking about Iran-Contra.

"Godiva would die," I said, looking at my now-empty plate, the hotel's initials greasy swirls in the center.

"A few people owe me a few tricks, *tu comprendes?*"

I didn't.

"They give me access." He was clearly proud, or awfully good at making himself sound important. As he was telling me this, he was unbuttoning his shirt.

On the bus last night, when it was so dark and everyone was asleep, we had gone pretty far, but this was different. I knew what was coming. I was afraid but not unwilling. I figured, this would be an initiation rite of sorts. If you were actually here with me I would never tell you this out loud, any more than I'd tell Godiva. But you are in my skin so it's different. It's as if you know everything anyway.

He came over to my chair, and I guess I stood up. I don't think he actually had to pull me up. Then we were on the bed, where, I guess if I'm honest, I'd been expecting us to end up. Dreading and hoping, if you know what I mean. He was reaching around me to turn out the light, only the bathroom light was on so we could still see more than I would have liked. He pushed my T-shirt up and pulled my shorts down below my thighs almost roughly. I felt awkward with the clothes half on and askew, constricted, more exposed than if I'd been fully naked. But it felt good when he ran his hands all over me. When he stretched and lowered the length of his own body toe to toe on top of me, I didn't know if I should be watching or closing my eyes. His eyes were closed, so I closed mine. I wasn't sure what I expected. What I felt was neither pain nor ecstasy. More like a hard fire pushing up into my stomach until I thought I was going to break into a million burning splinters.

Then it was over.

"You didn't tell me you were a virgin," he said, leaning across me again to switch the lamp back on. I opened my eyes to his stringy arm. I could smell our sweat. A red-brown stain oozed across the gray bed cover between us. Another stain we'd made together.

I hated the raw, lumpy body I'd exposed. I was ashamed for his nakedness, too, the straggly hairs on his chest, the raised veins running in lines along every bony angle, even his dick, shriveled and yellow-looking. How had I ever been attracted to him, or him to me?

"I have to pee," I said, pulling my shirt down and grabbing back my shorts which were gathered around my left ankle. He was lying on the bed with his ankles crossed primly on the sheets. As I stood, he glanced up and said something I didn't catch. My eyes were riveted on his arm, scarred with old scratches and bluish marks like cigarette burns.

With a wallop like I'd get from a belly flop off the high dive at Clearview Park, I saw clearly for the first time in days. At home I'd have stayed as far away as possible from anyone like Randall Spider Gervais. A man his age who would talk to a girl my age was weird, some kind of cowboy geek. And that talk about weapons. It was a gun I'd seen, wasn't it? He was scary. And if he was good-looking, that only made him scarier. Ted Bundy, the one who killed those college girls, he was good-looking, too. I stared at myself in the bathroom mirror, remembering Sex Ed class. Herpes, AIDS, not to mention pregnancy. I had given up my virginity with a stranger who was probably a creep. And what is more, I had entrusted the secrets of my life, of our life, to him. Why did I show him your poster? What a fool I am, what a stupid fool.

+   +   +

RANDaLL Spider Gervais is history. What happened is that I left. I came out of the bathroom in my damp clothes, wishing I didn't feel so clammy but ready to face the big confrontation with Spider I had steeled myself for, and he was sound asleep. I mean out cold. I'd never seen a naked male sleeping before. Curled up with the shell of his back to me, his head buried under an arm that only partly muffled his snores, he looked innocent and trusting. I decided it probably wasn't a gun I had seen after all. I began to wonder if I should have more faith in him and what we meant to each other, especially since if I left and if he was on the level, I'd be giving up the FBI file he promised. I hesitated, but then I picked up his shirt that had slid off a chair. The material was cheap and slimy. I had a second case of the creeps. Maybe it was superficial of me, but I like to think it was my survival instinct. I threw the rest of my stuff in my bag and was out of there.

Someday maybe I'll be able to laugh about the whole experience. "My First Time" and all that. I already have some mixed feelings. I'm not at all clear yet where he was coming from. I almost looked in his wallet. Maybe I should have. It was lying by the chair with his shirt and pants. But I didn't. Maybe I didn't want to know.

Actually, Spider did pass on some important information. I don't know when Godiva got it, but Spider pointed out that the poster is dated 1980. According to him, unless you've committed more felonies since the one listed back in 1970, the statute of limitations or something has already run out. 1970. I was born in January of 1971. 1970 was a bigger year for you than you even knew. Two events of historical significance. One changed your life, and one gave me mine, so to speak.

Meanwhile, I hope Cass isn't freaking out. It has been four days, so she should be back. She'll be looking for a postcard from me in the next couple of days; I'm supposed to send one every three. Unsigned of course. We rented the post-office box the week before Christmas. Actually, I stayed in the car with my sunglasses on. I could see Mr. Peden in there scratching his head when she handed him the month's rent. She told him she didn't want the Christmas presents she'd mail-ordered for her parents to come to the house. I can't believe he bought it, but he is just dense enough that he might have.

We have our whole plan worked out. Supposedly we went to Gram's, but Cass really spent the weekend with this new red convertible boyfriend. When she got back last night, she was supposed to call Godiva, though not until it was too late for Godiva to call Gram's. She was supposed to say I decided to stay a few extra days. Even if Godiva gets suspicious by today, she won't be able to track me down.

I wasn't sure if I should get Cass involved, but I needed help, and who else was there? After that incident at The Pink Heron, I had a feeling she'd be willing, but I was surprised how eagerly she jumped in. She came up with the idea of using a visit to Gram. Then when I talked to Gram and found out she was going to Hawaii with Uncle Jack, all the rest of the plans sort of fell into place.

Can you feel my approach? Some change in your blood, the electromagnetic field of your body actions or something, like I read about once in a science fiction book? Even though you don't know I exist, can you sense my presence homing in? Do we know ahead when something big is about to change our lives? That's something I wonder about a lot, every time I look at the poster. I try not to take my copy out too often, though. It is getting worn. What I really wonder is whether some part of me knew beforehand I was going to find your picture that day. Was everything pointing me toward that envelope on purpose?

THIRTEEN

I found my way to Eden almost without thinking about it. The gears in my brain finally clicked into place as soon as I slipped out of Spider's room. While the glass elevator parachuted down past rows and rows of sparkling gold lights, tiny as faraway stars, I stopped thinking and started knowing. Knowing I had to focus on one thing. Finding you. Period. Knowing I will find you, whatever it takes. Knowing, too, that I don't have much to go on except those books by Jane Alpert and your other underground friends, and that one radio interview with Gerry Flint.

On the bus into Delaware, I decided I should have worked out a way for Cass to accept long-distance charges at certain hours when her parents wouldn't be around so I could call some of the people on my list to ask if they knew where you are. I should have made those calls before I left. If I strike out in Eden, my next stop will have to be New York City, since that's where a lot of those people are. New York scares me, but the only way to avoid New York is to have success in Eden.

On the way here, I kept reading an article I copied at the Grassly. Four paragraphs and a grainy photograph that could have been a farmhouse. "The communist-inspired communal farm outside Eden, Delaware, has in the past attracted former self-proclaimed revolutionaries on the lam from radical hot spots."

Burrowed down in my seat, I read that sentence over and over, digging under each phrase for buried information or meaning. I didn't even notice who sat down next to me, a man or a woman or a kid, for that matter. I was concentrating on my hopes for this place. By the time the bus pulled up at the Texaco station, I'd keyed myself up like a cheerleader before the homecoming game. I was even giving myself little pep rally cheers. "I'll find you in Eden, I'll find you in Eden, I'll find you in Eden. Yes, I will."

As I guess you know, Eden is not much of a town when you first see it. Five buildings total, not including the abandoned ones with missing parts, here a window, there a roof. Believe me, I counted.

I stood shivering on a thin crust of dirty ice by the gas pump, watching the bus barrel away down the road. The gas station with its side garden of rusted car parts seemed vacant. I didn't know the pump man was sitting inside reading a detective novel, hunched down below the tire display so no one like me would bother him for change or directions. Next door was S&M Auto Parts. Set back from the road was a windowless cube of yellow cinder block, not unlike Godiva's studio, with the sign JIMBO'S TAVERN in red and black propped on the roof. Across the road and constructed of the same yellow cinder block stood Mount Zion Church, its front door chained shut. It turns out the real front door is around back, but I didn't know that then. And finally about twenty yards past the Church was Wyatt's, more cinder block but with an empty parking lot in front, a TruValue sign and a picture window through which I thought I saw two pairs of eyes watching me approach. You could say I was quaking in my sneakers.

As soon as I stepped inside Wyatt's, a blast of air overhead practically knocked me over with its roaring heat. I repeated my little cheer, "I'll find you, yes, I will," as I unzipped my jacket and forced myself to smile back and forth at the paunchy man and rather gaunt, gray-faced woman who were sitting behind counters at opposite ends of the room. On the hardware side, among a disarray of tools, fishing gear and paint cans, the old man puffed a smelly cigar and gave me a once-over. I wasn't about to let him think I didn't know what I was about. I hitched up my bag to strut over to the woman on the grocery side. A blue can of Maxwell House was the first thing I recognized on the shelf behind her, so in a loud voice I announced that I wanted a pound of coffee. She put down her *People* and nodded with the grimmest smile I'd seen since the Wicked Witch. "You must be looking for the Melon Place?"

I shrugged as if I knew what she was talking about. The article said nothing about melons or anyone named Melon.

"They expecting you to call?"

"Not exactly." I tried to sound forceful.

"Most of their visitors are unexpected, youngsters same as you wanting to see a real commune in action. You want I should ring them up?"

"Oh, that's not necessary," I told her, nonchalant as could be.

"Well, I'm Miss Jane. If you change your mind, just ask." She turned back to her magazine. When she bent her head I noticed she was wearing a wig.

"If you could just give me a local map."

She started laughing then. You probably remember her laugh. No one could forget it. Miss Jane has a laugh that takes over, fills a space and pushes everything else out. She screeches actually, like chalk scraped across the board only not unpleasant. That laugh is unnerving the first time you hear it. At least I was unnerved. After what seemed like forever but was maybe thirty seconds, she stopped to rub her mouth with a Kleenex. When she repeated her offer to call the Melon place, I lacked the will to resist. I nodded curtly, with as much dignity as I could scrape up, and she went into a back room to make her call.

I wanted to hear what was said, but I couldn't quite bring myself to follow her. The man was watching me. I pretended to browse through a rack of yellowed paperbacks, until she came back and said it was all set up, they'd send somebody as soon as they could. I don't know if I can express how elated the words made me. I had this crazy faith that a car would drive up and out you'd step. I'd walk up to the car, you'd take one look at me and know. You'd throw your arms around me and off we'd go, happily ever after.

I can picture you so exactly. The poster says 6'1" and 180 pounds which is pretty thin. But you've probably gained some weight as you've gotten older, become the burly, fatherly type who wears black-and-red plaid flannel shirts. And maybe, I don't know, just a hunch, you limp. Life on the run doing odd jobs and menial work has to have taken its toll.

To state the obvious, you didn't show up at Wyatt's. For a long time no one came into the store at all. Eventually, a couple of silent men hunkered over to the hardware side to buy nails and small goods from inside the case near the man, and a tired, raw-faced woman with a couple of heavily bundled, raw-faced children clutching her pants pockets bought a bag of groceries. Meanwhile, I took a *Newsweek* and stood leaning against the corner of the magazine rack, pretending to read. I was expecting to leave any minute. After a while, the store got pretty warm, what with that heater blowing all the time.

"I wondered how you was standing it," the man said when I finally gave in and slipped off my jacket. "Lewis is my name." He offered me a paper cup of Kool-Aid which I gulped down.

"Give her some of that fruitcake you're hoarding back there," he called over to Miss Jane. She went into the back room again and returned with a big white plate piled with sliced fruitcake. I hate fruitcake as a rule, who doesn't, but I had not eaten since Spider's steak dinner last night.

I finished off two slices fast and was debating my third when Miss Jane said it was time for lunch. Canned spaghetti warmed on an antique hot plate, cream cheese and apple butter sandwiches, hot chocolate. One of the all-time best meals ever in my life, better than the room-service steak or my first shrimp dinner in Florida. Lewis spread a striped towel over some low boxes where he lay out the food, then another towel for us to sit on, like an indoor picnic. That's how Lewis and Miss Jane eat lunch every day.

The next thing you know, the three of us are sitting together talking it up like old friends. Once those two start with their stories and jokes and questions there's no stopping them. I heard from Lewis all about Miss Jane's chemo treatments in Wilmington, the reason she wears a wig. I looked at every one of two albums' worth of photographs Lewis took of their six grandchildren when they visited last summer. Miss Jane and Lewis hate that they live so far away, one set in Idaho, the other in Nebraska. They can't even get together for Christmas.

"What's a holiday without family?" Miss Jane said, putting the albums in the drawer under the counter. She didn't expect an answer, luckily. Christmas last week with Godiva was a matter of going through the motions. I didn't know for sure if Godiva noticed, but I was counting the minutes.

Miss Jane and Lewis were obviously curious what I am all about, but unlike most adults they didn't push or dig. I could hear how lame my story sounded when I told them my name was Cass Wild and that I had a good friend at the Melon Place. They smiled a little oddly. It turns out they know everyone out there. Over the years they have lent Melon Place tenants tools and know-how, and probably, though they would never say so, money. They refrained from asking my friend's name and I didn't offer. I learned my lesson with Spider. Besides, I wouldn't have known what name to give them.

"Here, look at this." Lewis pulled out a small batch of photographs still in the developer's envelope. "Here's a picture I took out there years ago. And this one is from a few years later." Lewis is not the world's greatest photographer. The pictures were group shots, mostly out of focus and distant, but believe me I looked carefully. Your face was not there.

Which made me even more impatient for my mystery ride to appear and take me away to my future. I had to bite my tongue a dozen times to keep from badgering Miss Jane. The thirteenth time I couldn't hold back.

"Do you think maybe you should call again?" I asked her, casually sipping the last dregs from my mug of lukewarm chocolate as if the idea of another call had just that second popped into my mind.

"Sure she'll call," Lewis said. "But you know how it is around here, don't you, honey?"

I was beginning to. Every so often a car parked in the lot. I would tense all over until Miss Jane glanced up from her magazine and said it was the Smiths come for their daily milk and bread or the Grace boy from down the road or someone else equally inconsequential.

The afternoon was wearing out. What happened, I wondered, when the Wyatts wanted to close up and I was still hanging around. Lewis and Miss Jane were the kindest, nicest people I have ever been around. I was glad to know them, to know people like them could be part of my world. If it wasn't for you, I could imagine going back and staying with them indefinitely. If I asked, I had a hunch they'd let me. But I was not about to ask.

It was already dark enough outside for headlights to beam in at us through the glass as another car pulled up.

"Oops, here's Isaac come at last," Miss Jane said relaxed as toast.

Tickety tickety tickety, my heart began beating so loud Lewis could probably hear it straight across at hardware. I struggled into my coat and grabbed my bag.

"Tell Isaac to come in and warm up if he wants," Miss Jane was calling after me, but I could not wait. I had a destiny to meet. I was about to make my first connection. I mean, I could not believe I'd actually done it, really and truly connected with your world, just as I'd planned. And it was basically so easy. Mumbling thanks and goodbyes, I was out the door. A plank of cold walloped me in the face.

Standing by his car, stamping his feet against the cold was a small, elegant black man in a pinstriped suit and gray flannel topcoat. Isaac would never be taken for a hippie or a revolutionary, that's for sure. I'd say a businessman or a fancy lawyer. Maybe even an undercover cop, except the Wyatts weren't the kind to turn me in as a runaway unless they told me first. And besides, he was too polished and too beautiful to be police. With his close-cropped beard and narrow eyes, he suggested an oriental majesty.

"Haiku called me at the office." His voice was friendly, soft yet precise. He held out his hand, a thin blade of steel that gripped my hand and then relaxed. He smiled, but his eyes riveted in on me. In the news photos I studied this fall, many of the Black Panthers, Bobby Seale especially, had Isaac's same military elegance, but they never dressed in well-cut suits.

What could I say to this man? My tongue was not working. I could not form the words Henry and Fierstein.

Isaac did not seem to notice.

"We still get a handful of you kids every spring," he was saying, "but this time of year is a rarity. Marcus might even bake you one of his carob custard pies."

+   +   +

YoU never were in Eden after all, were you? I guess I'd begun to suspect as much before I got here. But that's okay, I'm the opposite of discouraged. I know it's only a matter of time until we're together. Besides, I have lived so much in this last week. Randall Spider Gervais was a whole lifetime and now Eden is another, a much better one.

I've never been on a farm before. What is ironic is that one night not that long ago, Godiva and I were eating dinner and she started in about farming, that farming was a lifestyle we should explore. She even asked me if I'd like to learn to ride a horse. When I said no thanks, she asked was I sure because Joe Rainey, Philip Rainey's father, whom I met at Thanksgiving, had offered to give me a lesson. I said I was sure; I fell out of love with horses when I turned thirteen. Godiva said okay, and that was it for our farm conversation.

Godiva obviously did not have the Melon Place in mind. The five days here have been a new experience. They've grounded me, as Godiva would say. I have felt more peaceful than I have in ages, despite being mixed up about where to go next. I would not have been ready for you before, but every day I am more and more prepared. I've had time to think; the farm has been teaching me to think. The pieces are all starting to fit into place.

You do exist. That's the main thing. I have to keep pinching myself, but it's no dream. Isaac, Haiku and the others all recognized the name right off although none of them has actually met you. The first night they told me what they knew about you, not a lot, but more than I ever learned from Godiva. For one thing, everyone calls you Henny, or did before you went underground. Hank Flint was probably a total coincidence; no one ever called you Hank that they knew. As for Gerry Flint himself, they said they were sick of talking about him. I guess reporters had tracked them down before I did. Of course, none of them ever heard of Godiva.

Isaac told me that you got into your trouble in Oregon, that you were part of a group that was indicted there, but he didn't know the details. At least he said he didn't. Which is fine. You can give me the details, if you want, when we are together. My new friend Haiku told me something else you probably wouldn't mention.

"He had a real way with women," was how Haiku put it, "but then they all did."

"All who?" I asked her, putting down my glue brush.

We were in Haiku's preserving shed, labeling preserves and packing them up to ship. Haiku sells them to health-food stores and cooperatives all over the Eastern seaboard under the brand name Life's Gift. My job was to adhere the labels after Haiku wrote "raspberry," "gooseberry" or "blueberry" in the matching color with her fancy calligraphy pen. Then Bethel and Dru packed them into the crates, eight of each kind to a crate.

"All the heavies. Radical rock-star types." Haiku took a jar. "At your high school, don't all the girls get crushes on the football players?"

"Gross, no," I told her, but I knew what she was getting at.

Crushes. That's what I was all about B.D. Dreams of popularity and love. I remember standing in the shadows of the Dairy Queen among the crushed cups, the dirty straws and sticky napkins, yearning after Jimmy Cryder. I always made sure to have an ice cream to lick while the others talked. They talked so easily, or so it seemed. Now I see it differently. Each of those girls, and the boys, too, had her own internal agenda I knew nothing about. Look at Cass. I'm beginning to think Cass may be miserable, yet everyone assumes she has it all. Just because people aren't unhappy in the exact way you are (you in the general sense, I mean, not that you are personally unhappy) doesn't mean they are happy. Anyway, I am not jealous anymore, or yearning.

There were no radical rock stars at the Melon Place that I could see. It got the name because Mr. Melon, who is about ninety, leased the farm out before he went into the nursing home. Eight women and six men live there now. I can't tell if some of them are couples or not. Are Bethel and Isaac a couple, the way they tease each other? But she has a single room this month. There are only so many single bedrooms and who gets a single changes on a rotating basis. There seems to be a code of unwritten rules that keeps order. Everyone except Haiku has an outside job plus farm chores. Haiku's job is managing the farm, or at least it was while I was there.

I was more or less assigned to her from the first night. No one else paid particular attention to me. At the big farmhouse dinner we ate together at seven o'clock sharp, conversation tended toward planning the next day's schedule. I don't think Magic House was like this. I have been trying to remember Magic House better since I got here. My memories are not very specific, but there seemed to be a lot of shouting and laughing, people always moving around me. Of course, I was little then. The Melon Place is more like some kind of monastery. No excess talk, a lot of enforced quiet time, rules and schedules. Yet from the occasional question or comment thrown my way, I can tell everyone knew all about me.

My guess is Bethel talked to the others about me. Not Haiku; it's hard to imagine Haiku blabbing. She is very quiet; it is impossible to read what she's thinking. The first night when I came into the kitchen with Isaac, she was leaning over the stove with her back to us stirring what turned out to be the most delicious carrot and lentil stew you can imagine. Isaac went over and tapped her lightly on the shoulder, then went off to change out of his suit to do his chores. Anyone else would have said hello and asked who I was and what I was doing there, but she didn't even look up. All her attention went into stirring the pot. Finally, she glanced over and gave me a short, but dazzling smile. "Welcome," she said, then pointed to a drawer full of silverware. "Please set the table for fifteen." I'm not sure why, but I felt a lot more comfortable then.

I admire Haiku in so many ways. Haiku's name fits her. She could be Godiva's flip side, the same and opposite if that is possible. Haiku is small and delicate but extremely strong. She can lift a fifty-pound feed sack and not even notice. She takes care of the goats and chickens and the three milk cows, not to mention the various dogs and cats. Her garden is huge. She's built a greenhouse. It's something to walk in there with snow on your boots and breathe in the warm wet earth, the green growing.

I think she is more comfortable talking to her plants, whispering them along, than she is talking to people. With plants she baby-talks and coos and flirts; with people she can be almost curt.

"Irrelevant." She cut me off when I began to complain how unfair it was of Godiva to keep secrets about you. "The past does not interest me at all, mine or anyone else's."

Maybe not, but this morning she woke me before dawn with big news.

"There is a woman, a friend of a friend, who says she knows Henny, or knew him."

"How did you find her?" I was in shock, electrified, as you can imagine.

"Never mind that. What matters is that she is willing to meet you. Get yourself packed and be ready to leave in half an hour. Isaac will drop you at the bus on his way to his office. She's in Ohio." Haiku handed me five twenty-dollar bills out of her apron pocket. Then she frowned.

"You should seek Henny only if he is part of your present and future, not if he's a relic from a past, yours or your mother's."

Yes, I know that's the kind of thing Godiva would say given half the chance, but I didn't resent Haiku saying it. Look what she's done for me. I started to tell her I'd write. She shook her head slightly, the way she does before she gathers herself up to speak, but she didn't say anything more. She took my face between her slim, powerful hands and kissed my forehead, then walked out of the room.

I'm sitting in the station cafeteria on my way to Cincinnati, Ohio. The wall I'm facing is all mirrors. When I stare straight ahead, I see a girl I know is me, but she's much prettier looking back from over there than I am sitting here. Past her I can see a man talking excitedly into a pay phone in the corridor out in front of the cafeteria. The mirror is divided into three panels. When he gestures with his hand, it separates from his body in front of me. At the only table between me and the mirror a woman is staring straight ahead, letting tears roll down her cheeks. I shouldn't know this since she has her back to me. All I should know is the back of her head, blondish hair fluffed above a starched baby-blue collar. But looking ahead, I can't avoid seeing the mascara running down the grooves of her cheeks. I'm embarrassed, not because I've caught her crying exactly, but because I can see all 360 degrees of her at once. That should be impossible. It's as if I have superpowers. The woman is almost close enough to touch. If I whispered, "I'm sorry," no one but her would hear. At the same time, her sorrow is all the way across the room. Close and far at the same time. The same sensation I felt at the farm sometimes.

Each day now, each place, each person I see is cram packed with so much mystery that cannot be deciphered. Here I am getting closer and closer to you. Yet a night ago, I almost broke down and called Godiva.

This was before Haiku told me about finding anyone who knew you. I didn't know she was even searching for anyone. Just the opposite. She said she didn't believe I'd thought my journey through enough and sent me out to Contemplation House for a few hours.

Contemplation House used to be the Melon Place outhouse before they added indoor plumbing to the main house. Then it was fumigated and painted white inside and out. Last night was my first time inside. There was one multicolored pillow cushion to sit on, a cross between Miss Muffet's and the giant caterpillar's from *Alice in Wonderland*, and a small wood-burning stove to keep the contemplator, in this case me, from freezing to death. Eden, Delaware, must be the coldest place in the world. I don't remember it ever being this cold at Gram's house in Connecticut. Even borrowing Haiku's down jacket and a pair of mittens, I shivered the whole time I was in there.

Which was good, according to Haiku, because my thoughts stayed crisp and I didn't fall asleep even though I dreamed. Haiku told me to let go, to follow my mind into whatever thought or memory it drifted. Which I did, and naturally my thoughts drifted to you, but then somewhere along the way they veered off.

I wasn't homesick or anything, but Godiva's description of Mrs. Brasleton popped into my head. "She's such a plastic purse of a woman," she told me after they met the first time. I was mad at her for being accurate. Back then, three months ago, I wanted to believe in the Brasletons, in moral blacks and whites. I liked it when Reverend Brasleton described evil as a tangible state we could battle by following the righteous path. But in Contemplation House, nothing felt that definitive, not even my hatred for Godiva.

At least she never tried to pretend that she was like other mothers. What I resented was not that she was different in the obvious ways, but that for all her talk to the contrary, she gave me no choice to decide who I was. She was too overpowering. She couldn't help herself; the force of her personality was a current too strong to swim against. When I was little I was perfectly happy being swept along, even if it meant never touching shore. As I got older, I could see what was being left behind, but by then I felt powerless to reach shore.

Don't get me wrong. Recognizing that there was no way Godiva could be different did not make it easier. I did not have to forgive her to feel sad for her. And sitting there shivering in Contemplation House, I faced how upset and worried she might be. I planned to call to say I was okay, not living on the streets or anything, but then the next morning I found out about Cincinnati. It's too important a lead to mess up, so instead of calling I've written to Cass, told her to go ahead and talk to Godiva, to tell her I'm fine and will be in touch soon.

+   +   +

WeLL, I've met Martha. Two days ago at a restaurant in Cincinnati called Mother's Earth. If Godiva ran a restaurant, Mother's Earth would be it. Vegetarian, with a lot of ugly paintings for sale on the walls, the plates all mismatched pottery, the tables and chairs all mismatched, too, for that matter. I wonder why

Godiva didn't end up in Cincinnati. A lot of people like her must live there.

Not Martha. Martha is dark and sly-faced, slick as an otter, as different from Godiva as two people could be. I wonder what you found attractive about her, if you really ever did. And if you did find her attractive, how could you find Godiva attractive, too? I also wonder if you remember her as well as she seemed to remember you, which was a lot better than Godiva ever did. I wonder not just about what Martha said but what she left out. Not that it's any of my business, Haiku's advice about letting the past be and all. But did you really live together for three years, the way she said?

When I came into the restaurant, she was already sitting at a table. I picked her out even before I noticed the green wool gloves she told she'd be wearing; there was a way she looked up and looked away. She said she knew me immediately, too. She said I have your eyes and your walk. How would I get your walk?

She had ordered her lunch before I got there because she had only half an hour break before she had to be back at work. She's a legal secretary of all things; she had on one of those secretary blouses that tie in a flat knot at the neck. Not that there was anything legalistic about the way she ate, shoveling in the brown rice and tofu sauté. She did not offer me any, which was fine. For once, food was not on my mind. She kept swiping at sauce at the corner of her mouth with her napkin while she answered my questions.

Only she wouldn't really answer my questions. Instead, she'd lift her napkin and say, "I don't know" or "I don't remember" or "That's quite beside the point."

When she finished eating, she handed me a ten-dollar bill, to cover the meal, I guess, and a folded piece of paper. Then she shook my hand, limply, and walked out of Mother's Earth. I left the ten dollars on the table and tried to follow her, but she was gone. I unfolded the paper. She'd written down the address of a restaurant in Velasquez, New Mexico. That was all, an address, but I stood in the street outside Mother's Earth laughing out loud. I wanted to tell everyone I saw, to hug every stranger. Instead, I sang, "It's a Beautiful Day in the Neighborhood, a Beautiful Day for a Neighbor, Will You Be Mine? Will You Be Mine?" all the way back to the bus station. When people looked at me funny, I was too happy to care.

I have an address. Your address. I still shake with the thrill of it every time I realize I have it tucked beside your picture in my pocket. You are becoming concrete reality. I have hard evidence where you may be, or at least where you for sure were some time that Martha knows about. This is incredible. Should I call the restaurant? I'm dying to, but it would be a bad idea, wouldn't it? I don't know what name to ask for, and I don't want you to get in trouble. Okay, I don't want to warn you too far ahead, either.

Thank God, I bought the thirty-day pass instead of the fourteen. New Mexico is far and I'm down to my last one hundred and fifty dollars. If Haiku had not given me that hundred I'd really be strapped. This should be enough, though. Even on the roundabout route I have to take I should be there in three or four days at the most. And I've all but stopped eating, anyway. I'm too knotted up with the possibilities that are only days away now. Mile after mile goes by without my really noticing. I've lost track where I am, Kansas or Arkansas.

Not that I'm just staring into space. I'm reading a book I found under the seat in Isaac's car on the way to the bus station. *The Tao of Physics*. Actually, I think Godiva has a copy. Isaac said it might be beyond my capacity to understand, which I thought was pretty presumptuous of him. He's a systems analyst, whatever that means. Something to do with computers. He is very smart and it was obvious everyone at the farm looked up to him, but both times

I was alone with him, on the ride from the Wyatts' to the farm and on the hour-long ride to Baltimore, we could not find a common ground for talking. He would ask me a question and I would try to answer, but my sentence would just lie there wilting until he asked another question. I mean, I am not the most sociable person, not like Cass, who can carry on a conversation with anyone from three to seventy-three, but I am not completely incompetent. I can usually make small talk. Not with Isaac, though. He was nice to me. He gave me the book and all, but I guess he scared me. He was too perfect, black and handsome, always immaculate, throwing around those windy, twisty sentences I could barely follow. I couldn't help wondering a little, more than a little, why he was at the farm, what he had done or been through to arrive there and to lead what had to be a pretty schizophrenic existence.

Is it possible you and I would have that kind of trouble talking? I mean, there are fifteen years for each of us to fill in, a lot of conversation. What if you are like Isaac? I'm used to adults who carry the conversational ball. Godiva could get anyone talking.

There was one afternoon the week before I left Esmeralda. Around 4:30, Godiva took a break from working in her studio, came in for a glass of water or something, and the two of us ended up on the back stoop, eating tangerines.

"Well, Noodle, are you feeling as moony blue today as I am?"

"No." I had no clue what she was talking about, but the calmness with which she spoke caught my attention. I could tell she wasn't fishing. Well, of course she was, but not only that. She was talking about herself, too.

"Lately something comes over me around five or six o'clock. Maybe it's the light fading or the drop in the temperature." She gave me a quick shoulder hug and dropped her arm before I could begin to resist. "You're so grown up now. I'm afraid sometimes of losing track. We don't have time like this alone together much anymore, do we?"

At that moment, despite everything, I wanted to tell her I was leaving to find you and why. Watching our legs stretched out in front of us, I was tempted to think she might actually understand. But I couldn't decide and hesitated. A few minutes later, she went inside to answer the phone, then drove somewhere and was still gone when I went to bed. It was a close call, wasn't it? She can really pull a person in.

+   +   +

ABoUT 5:30 this morning, I climbed off the bus from Wichita to wait here (I don't even know which town I'm in anymore) for a transfer to another town called Carousel, where I have to switch again. It was still pitch dark and I was half asleep, but I've got the rhythm of traveling by bus down now, so I felt pretty good. The stations are beginning to feel like home. The familiarity of the plastic chairs nailed down in facing rows, the Donkey Kong games going nonstop by the door, the fluorescent light that always makes me blink after a dark bus ride, the stopped-up toilets and the wet floor in the ladies' room, the juiceless air as if every bus depot in the United States were hooked up to a nozzle of the same giant vacuum cleaner.

Normally, I prefer to stake out a half dozen seats with my bag and coat so I can get some room to stretch, some space, after being cramped on the bus, but seating was more limited than usual. Most of the room was cordoned off with nylon rope while an old man dragged a wet mop across the linoleum. A whole row was taken up by old women with their Bibles open, even at six in the morning, swapping passages and ready to profess. Scattered among the remaining rows were a couple of younger women with children, and several ageless, raceless men with yellowed skin, drooping lids and missing teeth. A few leered up under their hunched shoulders and were kind of scary but not nearly as scary as the immaculately shaven, waxy-faced man in a bright-pink jogging suit who cracked his knuckles and smiled to show off all his gold inlays as I walked past.

Not to brag, but I'm pretty streetwise by now. I can spot who will be trouble and who won't. I always sit near the younger women. Even if they are prostitutes like Spider said (although I don't understand why prostitutes would bother to come around bus stations where none of the men have money anyway, or why anyone would want sex with these supposed prostitutes; they're half dead-looking most of them), they're usually less hassle than anyone else.

The woman I put my bag down next to was pretty typical. Depressing but harmless. Scraggly hair that lacked any specific color of its own. A used-up face, not old but used up, with bad skin and faded eyes you couldn't quite catch. Skinny as a broom handle, she still managed to be wearing clothes that were too tight. A couple of grocery bags stuffed with clothes and household items sagged around her legs; more were evidently piled under an old coat in the vacant chair between us. I knew sooner or later the woman would ask for a cigarette or the time or if I knew where to catch the bus for Carousel.

When she smiled, I smiled back and looked away. When she asked, with a nod toward the lump of child moving out from under the old coat, if I had any more gum, I gave her the rest of my pack.

"Say thank you, Crescent," she said to the little girl, who now sat rubbing her eyes with one hand and clutching the green sticks of gum in the other. "I'm Elise by the way. This here's Crescent. After the Crescent City, where she was born. I haven't been back there since. Day we got out of the hospital, Crescent and me hopped a bus north, didn't we, sweet thing?"

She flipped Crescent over on her back, grabbed a diaper out of one of the bags and changed her on top of the coat. "She's too young for gum, I guess, but it's something to do, don't you know."

I have never hung around really little kids, and I never had any interest in them, so I didn't have much to compare Crescent against. Her skin was light brown, the color of stale chocolate. Her hair was pinkish blond and curly, squashed damp against her forehead on the side where she'd been sleeping. Her eyes were dark brown, the thick lashes wadded together with bits of dried sleep. She didn't smile, even when her mother gave her the gum. She didn't cry, either. I thought kids that little cried a lot. Her face was flat and expressionless. She had yet to say a word. I would have guessed that she was retarded except that her eyes were so watchful.

Elise on the other hand was as chatty as her kid was silent. She told me she was twenty-one years old, only five, well six, years older than I am. She said she was running away from a man she called her husband.

"Not Crescent's daddy. We left him in New Orleans and no forwarding address, if you get my drift."

"Yes, I do." I got the drift all too well and offered Crescent a smile of more understanding. One fatherless daughter to another.

"Why are you leaving your husband?"

"To tell you the truth, honey, I don't have good sense for men. I always pick the wrong one. But my luck is about to change. You are my sign of good luck coming."

I didn't see why, but I took her remark as a compliment. When the Hardee's counter inside the station opened at six, I asked Elise if she and her daughter wanted to have some breakfast with me. "My treat," I added.

"Sure thing," Elise said, spitting out the last of my gum. "I don't have an extra dime to spend." She pulled Crescent onto her lap and changed her out of the stained red-and-white jumper suit she'd been sleeping in. Crescent submitted without expression to her arms being pulled out of sleeves and rearranged. Her chubby bare legs gave her a ruggedly healthy look, but they didn't kick like I thought little kids' legs always did. As Elise zipped her into a stained blue jumpsuit with a clown on front, I noticed Crescent had brand-new sneakers, the fancy kind with Velcro instead of laces.

I bought three egg biscuits, three juices and two coffees. I drink coffee now, black with a little sugar. I wanted a cinnamon raisin biscuit, too, but I couldn't spare the money for three of them so I lived without it. Standing in line, I glanced back and watched Elise combing Crescent's hair, kind of hugging her at the same time, but roughly. Crescent was just sitting there, not reacting to the tug of the comb or her mother's hugs. What a solemn little kid. Elise wolfed down her egg biscuit before she broke Crescent's apart into nice small pieces on the yellow Styrofoam plate. Gram used to cut up toast for me that way when she cooked soft-boiled eggs. Crescent picked up one piece at a time, removing the scrambled egg and chewing it first before she ate the bread.

Meanwhile Elise began to rummage through her bags, switching stuff like diapers and plastic bottles from one to the other. I assumed it was a habit from being on the road. I'd already decided Elise was a little strange, although she seemed to take good enough care of her kid.

I threw my biscuit plate in the garbage can and was standing up with my bag in one hand and my coffee in the other, about to go explore the ladies' room. When Elise grabbed my wrist, I just missed spilling hot coffee all over the two of us.

"You're a sweet girl," she said, "and I can tell you've got people who take real good care you don't come to harm."

I tried to pull my arm away without arousing notice, as if anyone was paying the slightest attention.

"So I want you to take care of things for me because I've got to meet a man about you never mind what." There was no way I was going to watch her things. I'd been too nice already, I realized. I should never have offered to buy her breakfast. What had I been thinking? Hadn't I learned by now?

"I've got a bus to catch in twenty minutes, Elise," I said, shaking my wrist loose and starting to move away.

"That's just fine. Crescent loves to ride the bus, don't you, sweet girl?"

I wasn't sure I'd heard right and turned back.

"What?"

Elise hooted a short, high-pitched laugh.

I stared like a dummy as Elise winked at Crescent, picked up a grocery bag and walked away. Fast. Without turning around.

Crescent didn't try to follow. She didn't cry. She sat still in the orange chair, her legs tucked under her, her face all smeary with margarine. I couldn't believe this was happening, not even when Crescent raised both her small grimy hands and waved them slowly at her mother's high heels clickety-clicking away.

I grabbed her up and ran after Elise as she began opening the door to the street. I was at the exit that fast but Elise was gone, whether around a corner, into a doorway or a waiting car there was no way to tell. No clue remained in the sooty morning drizzle. No sign of life period.

+   +   +

So here we are. I want to cry but not in front of Crescent because then she's bound to start. But what am I going to do? The bus will be pulling in any minute, and this kid is sitting next to me as if we belonged together. What did Elise tell her to make her stay? I mean, Elise obviously expected me to take her along wherever I was going, but she had the wrong idea about where I was going.

I cannot afford to be slowed down this way, not now. I almost blew it once. Just thinking of Spider gives me the creeps, what I did with him. Yikes. I guess I should be deeply depressed and traumatized by my first sexual experience. Actually, that part was okay. It had to happen sometime, right? And Spider was sweet in a way. What really creeps me out, though, is that I almost told him everything. How off the track I got. I don't believe any of what he told me was true. I don't believe he is likely to turn me in, either, but still, I was so naive. I risked so much. My only excuse is that when I met him, I didn't believe completely that this would all happen; you were still a fantasy.

Now you are very real. I have a real direction. Martha changed everything. Someone who knows you says I have your walk, your eyes. And Velasquez is not just a hunch like Eden was. It is an actual address where you've been known to be found.

But what do I do about this kid beside me—this baby? Whatever made Elise think she could hand over her own child to a stranger? And why me? Do I give off a scent? I think I'm too friendly. People keep attaching themselves. The problem is, I cannot turn in Crescent the way I did the old man.

The one in St. Louis. He was in front of me as I was getting off the bus. Skinny and frail, but natty, the way I remember Poppo when we stayed with him and Gram before he got so sick that he just stayed in bed. This man was wearing a green-and-orange plaid beret sideways on his head with a matching scarf knotted above his coat collar. All I did was carry his bag inside to the waiting area for him. It was a small square bag in the same orange-and-green plaid as his coat. Natty. He walked from one waiting room into the next and I followed, assuming he knew where he was going.

"Do you want me to put it anywhere special?" I asked, then asked again slightly louder when he didn't answer. I figured maybe he was hard of hearing the way he kept shaking his head.

"Is someone meeting you?" I practically screamed.

He gave me a toothless smile. I didn't know what to do. I kept repeating, "Is someone meeting you?" He kept smiling.

Then a man in a red sports jacket behind the renta-car desk called over to me, "Is there a problem, missy?"

I could tell he was the kind of man who chews breath mints, like my Algebra teacher, Mr. Curdy. He leaned over the counter and smiled, the same smile that twisted Mr. Curdy's mouth whenever he was about to pop a quiz on us.

I wanted to say, "None of your business," the way Godiva would have. Instead a tinny voice that didn't seem part of me answered, "Yes, please."

He smiled again and nodded as he picked up his phone. The next thing I knew, a guy in a police uniform was walking up to the old man. A policeman was the last person I needed to see or be seen by, but what could I do?

"You're not with him, miss?"

"No, I was just helping him with his bag, sir." If he asked for identification, I was sunk. There was bound to be some computer check to tell him I'd been reported missing, that is if Godiva knew yet, and by now she was bound to. There could be pictures of me in police stations and on cereal boxes all over the country.

"Sir, you need to come with me."

The old man didn't move or show any expression that hinted he had heard, but I had a hunch by then that he could hear fine.

"Where will you take him?"

The cop shrugged. "He's senile, sweetheart. Ten to one, he got to be too much work for someone, a daughter-in-law most likely, who shipped him off to the next in-laws on the list. Happens all the time. Maybe someone was supposed to meet him, maybe someone conveniently forgot."

I held out the old man's plaid bag and the cop swung it over his shoulder.

"Is someone picking you up, sweetheart?"

"Oh, no, I'm on my way to visit my dad." I didn't have to lie. That was good because cops are trained to pick up a lie.

"Well, you take good care of him when he gets old, you hear?"

"Sure thing," I said. "Don't worry, I will."

He took the old man's elbow to prod him forward a step. He looked so jaunty in his hat and scarf, I felt like the worst kind of traitor. What if someone had turned you in like that?

I can't turn anyone else over to the police. The police are the enemy, right? If I found out someone had turned you in, I'd want to kill him. But what am I going to do with this kid tagging along? I have to feed her and buy her a bus ticket, not to mention diapers. I have never changed a diaper. On the other hand, with her along I don't fit the description of a single teenage girl anymore. Sisters traveling together make a more convincing cover, don't they? I can't help thinking Spider would approve. The biggest problem is that I'm not sure I have enough money for the two of us. I think there's enough to make Velasquez, but what if you've already moved on from there? Please, please be there.

+   +   +

YeS, if you got a strange message yesterday, I admit I called the restaurant after all. I couldn't resist. I asked for Henry, but the lady who answered said no one with that name worked there. Maybe it's not where you work. Maybe it's where you hang out to drink coffee and talk politics. I've always wondered if those cafés really existed. I called five times altogether, asked for Hank the next time, Harry after that, then Henny, and Mr. Fierstein. No luck. I always got the same lady. When she said, "Los Combientes" with that husky voice, I could picture her in one of those fake Mexican peasant dresses with a flower in her hair.

Martha did not give me that address without a reason. She wouldn't send me on a wild-goose chase. That would be too cruel. Unless she's jealous. She did strike me as the type who could get jealous. But even then, why would she come up with this particular address? She could have had this address from a long time ago, I suppose, and didn't want to admit she'd lost touch since then.

If so, I'm screwed. No, I have to believe you are there. I'm going to bring Crescent along as an act of good faith. It's only two more days, anyway. We'll figure out together, you and I, what to do with her. I've got to write Cass about Crescent. She won't believe what I've got myself into. Here I am on a quest of mythic proportions for my long-lost father, and I am turning into some kind of long-term baby-sitter instead. Yikes.

+   +   +

CaN you believe the bus broke down? On top of everything else. And according to the schedule, we're only two and a half hours from Velasquez. I'm beginning to appreciate Isaac's book. The closer I get to Velasquez, the more the distance stretches out. Time lengthens and subdivides. The fractions keep getting smaller, but there are more of them. The bus goes slower. Now this. I keep having to remind myself, Velasquez is not infinity. I could drive myself crazy thinking this way. If Isaac was trying to tell me something, it doesn't matter. I left the book behind on a seat days ago.

With Crescent I don't have time to read. In a way, I'm glad to have her with me because she does keep me occupied. She has only about three changes of clothes, more than me but little kids seem to get dirtier. I wash her outfits off in rest rooms along the way, then dry them over the arm of an empty seat. The bus is so warm most of the time, they dry fast. Then she needs her diaper changed and she needs help eating. Not that she eats much, mostly just shares what I have. She doesn't cry or get cranky like other kids I see on the bus, but I try to keep her entertained. It's not hard. I tell her all those stories I remember Godiva telling me, teach her the little games we used to play.

It turns out she can talk very clearly when she wants to. She's quiet most of the time, but I can tell she's smart. She's very good at our favorite game, which is naming whatever we see as we pass it: house, tree, car.

Crescent is pretty good company, actually. She has a personality distinctly her own. She calls me "Dylly" and she won't let me out of her sight. She must miss her mother, although she never asks about her. She doesn't ask for much. When she's tired, she tells me. I hold her on my lap until she falls asleep, which is nice, how she melts into me, her head hard against my shoulder blade, the rest of her soft as a rag doll.

We happened to be looking out the window together, counting telephone poles, when all of a sudden, *chrunk,* the bus pulled up in short braking, jerk stops. Luggage went sliding. People gasped. One or two shrieked. I grabbed on to Crescent; she barely missed banging her forehead into the glass window. The driver stood up to calm people down, said he'd already radioed for help, but we would have to wait for another bus. Meanwhile, we were stuck in the middle of nowhere.

New Mexico is a lot colder than I expected. Actually, with all this traveling, I've lost track of weather the same way I have time. The landscape outside changes, but the inside of the bus stays the same. Once we hit New Mexico, the sky got emptier, but the air in the bus remained slightly overheated, too warm for me and Crescent to wear our heavy jackets.

Thank goodness she has one. The heater stopped working when the engine conked out. We had to bundle up. At first, everybody was pretty good-natured. It was almost like a party, the passengers walking up and down the aisle talking to each other, or at least smiling. There were a couple of boys near my age with a radio playing music I didn't recognize. The older people kept asking them to turn it down. One of the boys was kind of cute, with high cheekbones and dark serious eyes.

"Where you from?" he asked eventually.

"Back east."

"Where you heading?"

"Velasquez."

"Oh." His voice turned wary. "A ski tourist, huh?"

I nodded. I was a little disappointed when he turned back to his friends, but it was easier to agree than make up some other explanation. Several of the older women came over and offered Crescent cookies and fruit. I let them hold her. They asked how old she was and went on about how well behaved she was and how clearly she talked. I wonder if Crescent has ever had so much attention before. She actually began to smile and giggle a little, flirting for more sweets and compliments.

After a while, the new wore off. We ended up sitting out there for two freezing-cold hours. Toward the end, it frightened me how cold it got. Crescent started to whimper. I think she was hungry, too, but what could I do? I held her on my lap, wrapped inside my jacket, and rocked her so we could warm each other a little. My feet were like ice cubes when they finally came to take us off the bus.

They drove us to a mall at the base of a ski resort. Who knew such places existed? We all got a free lunch at a Mexican coffee shop called Bill's Cantina. I wonder if Los Combientes is like Bill's, in a mall and all. It would be easy to hide here for quite a while, I think. It's strange eating beef burritos and looking out at a mountain full of skiers. The snow is fake, the lady sitting next to us confided, because there's been a warm snap until today.

After lunch, they told us we had until three o'clock before they could put us back on the bus. So Crescent and I have been wandering around killing time. I took her into a shop called Slope Stuff and bought us matching hats and mittens—bright-red wool with black reindeer. It was crazy to spend the money, but they were marked way down, and it is cold here. Now we really look as if we belong together. We stood in front of a floor-length mirror, posing and making faces until the girl running the shop started to glare. Now we're sitting in the indoor courtyard, looking through the huge glass window at the ski slope.

The window is so large, the view so big, I keep thinking skiers are going to glide right through the plate glass. In fact, the lady who told me about fake snow also said that once someone completely lost control and did ski into the glass, but it was reinforced or something so it didn't crack. The guy broke his nose, though.

More than once this afternoon, it has occurred to me that near as we are, you could be outside right now skiing on that mountain. If you live here, you probably know how to ski. You could even be a ski instructor. That would be some cover, wouldn't it? What if I've been watching you for the last half hour and neither of us knew it?

Crescent has fallen asleep. Her cheeks get all puffy and damp when she naps. Her lashes are so long. She is really unusual-looking, but beautiful, I think. I can't believe Elise left her. Not even looking back. How could a real mother do that? And Crescent is such a good kid. When she falls asleep holding my fingers and doesn't let go, I feel important. I like being depended upon. I have not felt this close to someone since I was really little.

Back when I was Crescent's age, I took being cherished for granted. Godiva would never have left me behind anywhere. She needed me the same as I needed her, maybe more. The one thing I always knew was that she loved me. How long will it take for you to feel that way about me? I wonder. I don't expect hugs and kisses right off. I'll have to give you time to adjust to having a teenage daughter and all that. But eventually you'll know I'm really yours. Even if you've had other children since, I'll always be your first.

Physics or no physics, the fact is that if the bus comes by three o'clock, or even four, Crescent and I will be in Velasquez by nightfall. You and I could have a late dinner together.

I am so keyed-up. My brain can't sit still. It's jumping all over the place. The closer we get, the harder it is to think about, to think period. All I can do is run a hand over Crescent's hair, crinkly golden where it's escaped the rubber band. That and pray. I'm not sure anymore if I believe in God, but how else can I have come so far?

FOuR

Shit, this is hard, but damn it, I have to get started. Telling will help. Sorting it through, fitting the pieces into some kind of place, losing myself back where I was before. Where was I? I was right where I should not have been. On top of the world—my world, anyway. A little crazed, as usual, a little more scattered than usual, a lot more nervous. But flying high. Oh, yes. Flying high. Thanks to loose morals, as Elvira Brasleton would undoubtedly say, and that stupid stupid stupid infatuation with Joe Rainey.

I could make all kinds of excuses, but why bother? Why not face the damn truth, that for once in my life I fell off my high horse and broke all the rules. Godiva caught with her hair down but without a horse, screwing the horseman; ironic justice, wouldn't you agree? Not that I was so clever at the time. I had left rational thought way behind. I was flying by instinct. Instinct usually works for me, but even instinct can't be trusted all the time.

No, stop evading. The truth is that I was ignoring instinct. I was going by feelings. Feelings are totally different from instinct, much less reliable and much more dangerous. To hell with feelings. Stop the touchy-feely euphemism. It was lust pure and simple. I was acting according to lust and loneliness, a deadly combination in a woman of my age and temperament. As if there were ever a time it hasn't been a deadly combination for me.

And if I'm going for honesty here, the truth is I felt an itch all along, niggling in my inner ear. Why didn't Dylan call, why was I getting that damn machine all the time? I simply chose to ignore any off notes in the chorus that sang me through each day because they were inconvenient. My problem was not only that I'd thrown common sense out the window, but that I was keeping instinct at bay so I could have three days of la-la-land with Joe Rainey. God-damn, if he didn't seem worth it at the time.

That first time Joe and I made love in October, somehow I was able to write it off. God, how long ago that afternoon seems. Another lifetime.

I'd driven Dylan to her crazy lock-in. She was furious because I was late picking her up. It hurt, the way she squinched down in her seat as far away from me as she could get, stewing, withdrawn to a place I could not begin to touch. Not one word could I get out of that girl, not one. She was like a porcupine about to let fly her quills. I gave up talking and studied the storm in the rearview mir-ror. It was following us like a stranger in a trenchcoat, bigger and scarier the closer he came. Then the wind swallowed itself and turned the sky into an airless inner lining. Even with the windows rolled down, it was hard to breathe inside Miranda by the time we turned into the church lot.

Dylan slammed out of the car, not even a wave of goodbye. I can see her so clearly, running up the walk, the weight of the sleep-ing bag throwing off her balance. I hated to leave her. I wanted to run after her and clutch her to me. When she was little, she'd get mad and stamp "I hate you" until I squeezed and tickled her into submission. It got to be a joke. By the time she'd reach "I hate you," we both knew the tantrum was over. Such a loving child she was.

I cannot cry, damn it. I have to keep on with these rememberings, order them, find the pattern. I cannot fall apart.

I watched her open the heavy oak door to the church. A short wedge of noisy yellow light pulled her in and the door shut. Then I drove home, planning to close myself up in my studio. Close out every other thought I might be having by concentrating on my work. Body parts. That was the project I'd begun just after the accident. Freud be damned, Jung is my man. I began stringing black beads on wire bent into very large thumbs. Every now and then, I'd look up through the window to see a tail of lightning whip across the sky as thunder crackled somewhere off shore. After a while, my muscles clenched under the damp wool cloak of the early dark and I did some circle rolls with my head to loosen up. I took a drag off my cigarette and began to set a complicated pattern of ground glass into the underside of a hinged box. A chest cavity. When my thumbs got thick and spongy from handling the small sharp pieces too long, I took another cigarette break. A few minutes later, the rain came gusting in.

And then Joe.

"Go home, Joe Rainey," I said as he stepped inside the open doors, soaked to the skin in the short walk from his car.

I tried to stare him down, could not quite manage it, ended up gazing past his left ear at a collage portrait of Dylan that had always struck me as slightly off. Now I saw why. Her eyes were inaccurately painted, green like mine instead of her father's blue. Incredible eyes he had, like hers only deeper blue. I tried to concentrate on those eyes. How could I have made such an obvious mistake?

Joe took a step closer.

"Go home." I remembered his son's hand gripping mine so tightly in the ambulance. I stood up and my thigh knocked against the worktable's sharply mitered corner. The smarting pain brought tears to my eyes.

"Oh shit." It was all mixed up, what I felt for this man I barely knew while my daughter stared at me through the wrong eyes. The rain racketed down on the tin roof. The studio began to reel, the shelves of shiny objects circling in tighter and tighter toward some centripetal force.

"Blue, for God's sake." His breath on my cheek, my arms rising, his fingers in my hair, my mouth turning, his neck like velvet, his chest, his hips against mine.

"Damn us both."

Later, lying beside him on an old patchwork quilt among loose beads and broken shards, I realized that the rain had stopped. He described his life before Esmeralda, a paragraph of simple declarative facts. Born in south Georgia. One year of community college. A stint in the post-Vietnam service. His marriage in San Diego.

"Oh God, this is crazy," I interrupted him. "I do not live like this. I have screwed around in my time, but I have never ever been someone's other woman. I can't be that. You have to leave your wife. Oh Christ, what am I saying. I don't even know you. This is nuts. I don't even know you."

"Blue."

"Well, it's true, isn't it? What do we have in common? You are eight years younger than I am; our life experiences have been completely different. We didn't even grow up with the same music. Stop smiling, I'm serious. My life is my daughter and my art. Your life is, or should be, your wife and your son and your animals. I hate to tell you but I am afraid of animals, especially horses. Not to mention we are every cliché in the book. I refuse to be a cliché."

"Godiva Blue, you couldn't be a cliché if you worked at it for the next ten years."

"Yeah, like hell." I lay back down beside him and made him look at me. "About your marriage," I began.

"Mari wants to move back to California. She's had a definite job offer this time, in a big accounting firm in San Diego, and her family is there. She says she has never been happy here."

"I was about to say I don't want details."

"I know." But he went on as if he hadn't heard me. "Mari says that if she were the man and I were the woman I'd move with her. She says I might resent it, even hate her for it, but I'd go."

"She's right," I said, not wanting to.

"I know, but knowing doesn't solve a thing. I will not move."

"No more. I don't want to hear more." I peered down the lengths of our bodies, unearthly under the glimmer of watery stars through the high window, past our four feet sprouting comically like flowering stalks. His jeans and shirt lay jumbled with mine on the cement floor near cans of ochre and vermilion. There is no denying the longing that rushed over me. Shit, the no-holds-barred desire. Apologies will not make it right. Excuses will not make what happened go away. I put my arms around his skinny, naked male chest and held on tight.

We were not alone again, Joe and I, not that way, for over a month. We talked, of course. I told myself it was turning into friendship, that friendship was possible between men and women, right? Even highly charged friendship. I had been alone as a woman for so long; didn't I deserve friendship? He'd call and we'd yak like teenagers, on and on about God knows what. Amazing, isn't it, how much people who barely know each other find to talk about when the chemical mix is flowing. A couple of times we did meet somewhere for coffee or a beer, but if we were in a bar and his hand grazed mine reaching for his glass across the table, I quickly pulled my hand back so he wouldn't get ideas.

Bullshit. Let's get real, Godiva. I knew what I was getting into. Maybe I didn't admit it, but I knew. How we stood together between cars in the parking lot at the Waffle House in Perry three days before Halloween. Talking one moment, kissing the next, sucking together like magnetic dolls. Unavoidable as gasping for air to keep from drowning. Sure, I pulled back, eventually, but I was lost to desire. There is no other way to say it. Whatever conversation we had was beside the point.

In November there were two more encounters. Only two. One at a motel toward Gainesville, one at Cleo's while she was in Boca Raton, conveniently leaving me keys with, I swear, a wink. I never discussed Joe with her, never mentioned his name, but she made it clear she knew. If anything, she enjoyed the intrigue. Her artist and her cowboy getting together. Shit, getting it on.

I assume that's why she dropped Thanksgiving on my head, that tortuous afternoon with Joe and Mari and Philip, the slimy contortions of avoided glances and inevitable comparisons. I was chewing my turkey leg with fangs of jealousy I thought I'd left behind forever at the eighth-grade spring dance when Carl Epstein dropped me for Susie Ware. If the comparison sounds juvenile, that's the point. Closing in on forty years old, still under the sway of eighth-grade emotions. They did not make me any happier now than they had when I was thirteen. Stop and desist, I ordered myself. Go cold turkey on young Joe. But when he called later that night, off I went, God-knows-why.

I mean, I am not your typical middle-aged spinster aching with the lonely need to connect to others. I have never been a lonely person until this fall. I have always made a clear distinction between "alone" and "loneliness," just like they do in the women's mags. I have had good reasons to choose alone—well, alone with Dylan.

But I can't talk about Dylan yet, or I will break down and that will be the end of any sorting, any working through toward some kind of clarity.

Anyway, I always kept my life full enough with my art and Dylan. And this fall, I had actual other people in it besides. Louise and I were going for coffee after school a couple of times a week. She'd started a course toward her master's at the University extension center and credited me for her decision. She had no idea I'd faked the *I Ching*'s message, of course, and I didn't have the heart to tell her. She thought it was such a big step to take the course, and for her I guess it was. Her husband—a typical southern macho-man if I ever met one, though I didn't share that insight with Louise, either—was bent out of shape that she was spending evenings away from home. I mean, my God, it was only a Spanish course that met once a week.

Then there were the Franklins. We finished *Treasure Island* and were deep into *A Wrinkle in Time* when the doctors said David could go home the week before Thanksgiving. He was still bedridden with his injured spine, but much more lively. I brought him a magic set. To Myra's credit, she was a willing magician's assistant and even learned a few tricks herself. We'd begun to like each other, Myra and me, amazing as that sounds. She often invited me to go along when they drove back down for his physical therapy.

God knows, Myra is not someone I'd ever call my friend. I believe the hospital in Perry is as far from Esmeralda as she's ever traveled. And she chews gum constantly, wads of it. But our lives, seemingly so different in most of the particulars, have their similarities. For one thing, Myra has been a single mom all of David's life. When she was still pregnant, David's father went to prison on charges she does not talk about, and he hasn't been seen since. I caught inklings of the pressures she must be under, bits of conversation I overheard between her and her mother and her ex-mother-in-law and, once, that pompous Reverend Brasleton. Everyone in Esmeralda knows Myra's business and won't let her forget it.

So with all these new friends, not to mention Cleo and Dylan, I had no reason to be lonely. Shit, I didn't have time to be lonely. At school all day, in my studio until midnight most nights getting ready for Cleo's show deadline. But the idea of Joe would not stop interfering. I'd be working away and a net of missing him would drop over me, would tighten and cleave until I could not lift my arms to work.

Then last week, Cleo did her little number. Dylan tucked away at my mother's, right? Mari off with Philip to visit her family in California—leaving Joe behind, whether by his choice or hers I wasn't sure. So Cleo could not leave the erotic danger of coincidence to chance. Oh, no, she had to invite us for dinner.

I stewed for about half an hour, wasn't going to go, was going to tell Cleo to cool it. Then I said to hell with it, go for it, live it out. So I decked myself out in my gauzy embroidered dress, the only clothing I own that makes me feel female sexy, the way the light stretchy material clings and falls, and went off to chez Gallagher with bells on, literally, my Christmas bell earrings.

We ate shrimp and dirty rice, drank too much wine. Somewhere along the way, Cleo conveniently disappeared into the kitchen. Joe came around the table, leaned close and lifted a heavy twist of hair where it lay loosely braided on my bare shoulder.

"Oh Christ, don't do this," I said, not meaning one word. "I'm too . . ." His fingers grazed my cheek and neck and all I could think was how long had it been. To have a man stay all night in my bed, God, how long had it been?

The next morning, he was up before the sun. I heard him puttering around in the kitchen, making us buttered toast we ate on the back step wrapped together in an old cotton blanket against the early chill after the moon had set but before the sun had risen. Not dark exactly but as if all color had seeped out of the world. I have always been horrified by the idea of color blindness but for that half hour I appreciated the subtleties of a monochrome life. The lawn chair a darkish gray, the grass and bushes a lighter gray, his bare hand on my bare thigh gray upon gray yet distinct. By the time I could begin to make out the first pulse beat of palest beige which would gradually deepen into familiar rust reds, sandy browns, yellowy greens, Joe was gone to his animals and I was heading into my studio, our rhythm together as established as if it had been in place for years.

Three days, four nights, we lived our little dream life. As soon as Joe came back to the cottage after work, we ate grilled-cheese sandwiches or peanut butter, whatever was fast and easy. We made love in my old iron bed like two bear cubs. Furry, playful, animal sex. Afterward we lit a fire, and he stretched out on the carpet, his back against the clawfooted couch, while I sketched. Him mostly. Around ten or eleven, we drove to his place so he could check the livestock and horses. I did not go inside Mari's house. I sat on a bale of hay, stroking the barn cat or walked with Joe on his rounds. Neither of us slept much, but we didn't care. We were operating on pure adrenaline.

I reported to school for a few hours every morning, checked the systems, made the repairs I always make over Christmas vacation, cleaned up. It was easy work, almost restful. I spent the afternoons tearing it up in the studio, working like crazy on my razor-blade heart—a fitting choice as it has turned out—wowing myself on the oxymoronic beauty of the imagery. The razor-blade chips were a bitch to work with. I wore gloves and still ended up with a million cuts. I didn't care. A certain quality of pain was what I was after, along with a mirroring sheen.

I remember this afternoon, as if it were years ago, picking up a pair of ornate agate buttons, weighing them in my palm, trying to decide if I should use them. I ran my thumb over their swirly smoothness and realized I was disgustingly happy. I knew what we had was limited. I can't even say I pretended we were in love. But my creativity and sexuality were swirling together, giving me incredible energy. I was giddy, I was tipsy, I was dance-on-the-tabletop drunk with selfish carnal pleasure. Have the gods ever allowed selfish carnal pleasure to go unremarked?

When I heard the truck, I ran outside still holding the buttons, hoping Joe had somehow managed to get away early; it was New Year's Eve and I had champagne chilling. No Joe, only the mail truck.

I have always loved getting the mail, the delicious spark of anticipation walking to the mailbox. Back when we first nailed it up on the post, Dylan and I painted Day-Glo fish on the sides of the box. After ten years, the original metal was beginning to show through, giving the fish tails a phosphorescent quality that pleased me a lot. I was feeling kind of phosphorescent myself.

Bills, solicitations, a postcard. I laughed at the three-dimensional photograph of an erupting volcano before turning it over to read the greeting.

OAHU IS GLORIOUS. YOU'D LOVE THE LIGHT AND COLORS, JUDY, ALL BLUES AND GREENS. AND DYLAN, THE BOYS ARE ADORABLE. XXXOOO GRAM

P.S. DYLAN DEAR, I ENJOYED OUR LITTLE CHAT WHEN I CALLED. BACK AFTER THE NEW YEAR BEARING GIFTS.

People talk about their hearts stopping: Believe them. Everything stopped. Heart, lungs, nerve endings. The works. They started again, of course, in time for the heart to finish its beat, but I will be forevermore someone slightly else.

The brain, at least the conscious thinking part, must have stayed stuck longer. I found myself in the kitchen, the postcard in my right hand, those agate buttons still squeezed tight in my left. I was shaking uncontrollably.

"This is some kind of crazy mistake," I told myself over and over until the tremors eased. I rechecked the postmark—last Saturday and no return address, no hotel where she could be reached. There had to be some mistake. Where was Dylan if she wasn't with my mother? I called Hilton Head and got the machine.

But there had to be an explanation. Cass Culpepper would be able to explain; she'd gone with Dylan. I saw them drive off together with my own eyes. When Louise called me to say Cass had called her to say they'd arrived, I was in the middle of putting on my dress for dinner at Cleo's. I should have wondered right then why my mother or Dylan hadn't bothered to touch base, but I didn't. I was a fool.

Louise phoned again the other day to say Cass was back. And again I was not paying full attention. Joe was here. God forbid I give his presence away, and besides, I was impatient to get back to him. I did say to Louise, I remember saying it, that I hadn't been able to get my mother or Dylan on the phone. I did ask Louise what Cass said they had been doing.

"You know Cass, she is always so vague, but she did mention how nice your mother was," Louise said. That should have been the biggest tip-off of all.

I keep going over in my mind how I could let five goddamn days go by without communication. So many lost opportunities.

Why was I so nonchalant? I should have known in my bones that something was off. I did call. But when I left messages on my mother's machine and did not hear back, I let myself assume they were trying me when I was in the studio or taking a walk. After all, I didn't have a machine for them to leave messages in return. I even joked to Joe one evening that they must really be living it up, that, knowing my mother, Dylan was going to come home with a complete new wardrobe. Five days did not seem all that long at the time, but now.

I tried my mother one more time. The machine. I dialed the Culpeppers. The phone was becoming my lifeline. Cass would clear this all up. Five rings, six, seven. When I finally heard the girl's disinterested "hello," I was already in the act of hanging up. I could not speak.

Yet I was very calm driving to their house, walking up to the front door, knocking, saying hello to Louise's boy, the one with the freckles. Then I was inside. Louise and Cass loomed toward me, all out of proportion, as if I were staring at them through an empty soda bottle: Louise in a red sweater, her back against a table, a book clutched to her chest; Cass barefoot in a fluffy yellow bathrobe, the left side of her head covered in a towel, the right side a short thick mass of shiny black hair.

"Godiva honey, is something the matter?" Louise said and put her hand over her mouth like the speak-no-evil-monkey. I caught a whiff of myself in the mirror by the door, my shirt buttoned wrong, my face blotched and puffy although I had not shed a tear.

"You tell me, Cass." I stepped toward the girl, wondering at the strange sounds leaving my mouth.

Cass bent over and rewound the towel around her hair. Then she straightened and looked calmly into my eyes. She spoke without the least surprise, as if she were picking up a conversation begun some time before.

"She wants to find her father." Cass has perfected that non-committal half-dead voice girls her age aspire to. "The man in the picture. She says you kept him from her and the picture is proof."

Louise gasped.

Outside someone slammed a car door. I heard a male voice calling, "Barney, come on home." My fists clenched.

"She's doing fine, though," Cass went on. "I've heard from her." The girl's face was maddeningly blank. How much I hated her I could not begin to measure.

"Heard from her? She called here?" Louise asked, genuinely shocked.

"Wrote. I got the letter today. Not at the house of course." Cass glanced toward Louise, then me with what I took to be the beginning of a smirk. "She knows what she's doing, don't worry."

"Don't worry?" I began to laugh then, and I knew I was losing control big time. When I stopped laughing, I was choking. I had to work to catch my breath. "You will show it to me, now."

"I've already thrown it away, but she said to tell you she's fine if you asked. We hoped it would take until at least Tuesday before you figured out she wasn't at her grandmother's." She shrugged. "You're actually two days late." A cut to the bone and she knew it.

Speechless doesn't begin to cover it. Oh, the urge I felt to punch the words out of that tight little mouth was blinding.

I turned and walked out of the house. I don't remember driving home, but suddenly there I was in Dylan's bedroom, speaking aloud the names of her old stuffed animals—Squinchy, Target, Marshmallow, Pally, Momo—as if they knew her secrets and if I asked they'd tell me. The rain pounding the tin roof drowned out any answers they might offer. I left them, left the room as I found it, closed the door and went to stand on the back porch.

Another winter rain was building up across the Gulf. Behind me the screen door banged open and shut with the wind. Gusts of wet salty air pelted my chest and forehead and knees. My cigarette sputtered out in the ashtray already half filled with water. I had never felt such utter despair. The night Evie Pinkston's brother called and told me about Evie being shot in the neck, the night my father finally let go while I stood at the foot of his hospital bed, clutching the metal rails and sobbing, those moments of death were beyond my control. This, this was much worse. This was raw fear, with a slimy underside of guilt.

For almost five days I had been glad to have my child out of the way and here was my punishment in spades. She was gone God-knows-where—even if I threatened to break her legs, Cass was not about to tell me, that was clear. She probably did not know.

I tried to light another cigarette, but my matches were wet. Instead, I counted the red-tipped sticks like daisy petals. "She loves me. She loves me not." One at a time, I dropped them on the step until my hands were empty.

Empty. I knew I should be doing something, acting forcefully, making some kind of decision, but I could not think clearly. The sequence of events that formed my life had become a series of smudge marks run together. The poster. When was it that I found the poster? If only I had never noticed it that day with Louise. I remembered leaving The Oyster Shack, the glowering Indian summer heat that sucked the breath out of me as soon as I stepped outside the air-conditioning. I remembered the steering wheel hot against my palms and the swing of tires under me as I made a U-turn to park in front of the post office. Pure luck another car was not coming. Pure luck I went inside with Louise. Pure bad luck—if only I had waited in the car. Pure luck his face was the one on top of the stack. Luck and death, my father always said, come in threes. But it wasn't simply luck. I took the fucking poster.

I took it and hid it, and Dylan found it. Now she was gone and I had not noticed. I had chosen not to notice. Just as I had chosen to ignore the tension running in lightning streaks up and down her spine that last time I tried to hug her, the day she left, Cass honking from the yard. I had been so ready to let her leave that morning. Unforgivable.

"Dylan is gone," I said out loud. "Dylan is gone," I shouted over and over until I could hear the truth I had to face.

I started shivering, suddenly freezing cold. Joe would be back soon, in less than an hour. "Dylan has run away," I would tell him, and he would offer to hold me. But who was Joe? An outsider. An interloper. It was his fault, our fault. If I had been paying attention. Not that I had time to worry about men now. They were the past, both men, the one due any minute with innocent adulterous intent, the other who had inadvertently set the course of the rest of my life—burdened me with a child I couldn't live without anymore. Neither Hank nor Joe had the least interest in Dylan. That was the joke.

It was time to decide what to do. I packed up the few personal belongings Joe had left lying around, a shirt, a toothbrush, a few cassette tapes, and put them outside on the porch. I lined up the phone book, a pad, pencils. There would be agencies to call, organizations that put missing children's pictures on grocery bags and milk cartons. First, there was the police.

"Yes, ma'am. Now, you need to go a little slower." The cop who answered, a Sergeant Baines, was friendly, but that was about it. I gulped for air while he explained the procedure, which was not comforting. Kids ran away all the time, he said. They'd put out the standard APB they did for runaways. Yes, it would go nationwide. But kids usually showed up when they were ready, not before. I should come down and fill out the forms in the morning or, since it was the New Year's holiday, the morning after. No reason to rush over tonight, he could take down the basic description on the phone. He sounded tired as he went through the list.

"Name?"

"Evangeline Dylan Blue."

"Sex—female?"

"Yes, with medium-length brown hair. Five-foot-four, blue eyes, very trusting. Probably wearing black."

"They're all wearing black."

"Yes, well."

"How old did you say she is?"

"Sixteen, almost."

Dylan sixteen in three weeks. God, it is impossible to comprehend. I always thought I had been so different from Dylan when I was a teenager. Willful. Defiant. Much tougher than Dylan. More dramatic, melodramatic. At odds with my parents all the time. When I announced I was spending the summer as a volunteer at Freedom House in Roxbury, Massachusetts, my father bellowed over his plate of roast beef that if I left the house, I needn't bother to come back. Three mornings later, full of moral indignation, I packed the green American Tourister bag I'd been given for my last birthday and walked to the bus station, refusing to acknowledge my mother trailing half a block behind me in her Plymouth station wagon.

My father phoned the center a few times threatening to drag me home, but to my great relief, he never showed up. After a week or two, the calls stopped. Goddamn, what a time I was having.

Days I spent teaching crafts to small girls who mostly wanted to comb or touch my red hair. Nights I sat in shadowy apartments suffused with incense, listening to conversations I could only pretend to understand. It was wonderful. In August I called home to say I was thinking of dropping out of high school to stay on.

"It's your life," Daddy said and hung up.

I stayed another week. Two days before school started, I left a note to my roommates, college girls who'd treated me as a kind of mascot, and hitched a ride home. Underneath the bravado, I was not ready to stop playing the role of my parents' good girl after all. Of course, they took me back; they were always taking me back.

What gave them the strength to wait me out? I don't have it, that's for damn sure. At sixteen, unaware of the dangers slithering around me like so many cottonmouths, I had gone untouched. I had walked alone down unlit streets late at night. I had lied about my age to sit in smokey bars and drink tequila that made me higher than the pot and hashish available everywhere. I had hitchhiked for God's sake, picked up by two guys in their late twenties who gave me a joint before they dropped me off at the end of my block. But those were different times. Just the possibility of Dylan hitching rides now makes my stomach clench, Ted Bundy wannabes everywhere, especially here in north Florida.

"Now, don't worry too much, ma'am." The policeman was definitely trying, I'll give him that. "If, like you said, she promised to keep in touch with a friend, that's a good sign. And at least you'll know she's safe."

Is there such a thing as safe, some way to ensure that your child will grow up without encountering injury or evil? I'm no longer certain that there is. I keep thinking about David Franklin, less than two miles from his house. And Evie holding the package of chicken parts. I can still see Mrs. Pinkston's lumpish body prostrate across Evie's open casket, shiny white as new patent-leather shoes. I had listened to Mrs. Pinkston's keening wails, her unabashed outpouring of grief. I had listened with horror and, there is no other word for it, awe, that love could be so powerful.

Sixteen years ago.

"It's the letting go that's hard." Mrs. Pinkston, becalmed into weary dignity, handed me a glass of milk in her kitchen after the service. "The guilt is hard enough; I surely did not need those chicken parts so bad. But the letting go is worse. I just have to keep reminding myself it's the Lord's will. Alive or dead, you got to let them go sooner or later." She pointed to my belly protruding with my future daughter's knee or fist. "I expect you'll learn that soon enough."

No, I will do whatever it takes to bring her back, and then I'll never make the same mistakes again. Just bring her back to me, please.

Each minute passes so gradually into the next. My whole metabolism has altered, slowed to an amoebic crawl, only more slithery. I keep thinking of amoebas, what little I know of them, splitting apart to reproduce. And water drops, how they drip along wet glass into a kind of vertical puddle, hold briefly, and then separate. I am one of those droplets, only I cannot quite catch hold. Dylan's flight, disappearance, running away, whatever you want to call it, her going, has been pushing me to the furthest borders of my emotions.

Somewhere in the house I have a pen-and-ink sketch. Yesterday, I woke up, jolted awake the way I do these days, desperate to find it. I spent all day searching the cottage and my studio. As if the drawing would bring Dylan back. Dylan when she was, God, no more than five years old, sitting with her grandfather in that gray leather recliner of his.

He was teaching her to sing "Go Tell Aunt Rhody the Ole Gray Goose Is Dead," of all things. By then he was quite frail, close to death. He had to be in terrific pain. Bone cancer just wipes you out. But the two of them sat there, singing away, making up verse after verse about the reactions of all the different animals while I drew their faces and Mother did her ridiculous stitch work. I should have framed that picture years ago.

I found plenty of other pictures, but they wouldn't do. I had decided this one sketch was the only image that would ease the pain. I could barely bring myself to look at the others. I stood at my worktable, ignoring the pile under my hand while I stared through the open door into the tail end of an early winter sunset. As usual, my mind was wandering. Like a dog on a leash, it kept pulling toward Dylan. I tried to tug it elsewhere, toward chocolate ice cream or the tangerine sky, but then it would catch a scent and follow after Dylan again.

A flock of blackbirds scattered up against the lowering sun like blown ash as a car door slammed shut out on the road. I waited until the birds disappeared into the trees before I crossed the yard and made my way through the kitchen and living room to the porch. Cass Culpepper stood there peering through my uncurtained window.

What in God's name could she want? I wondered, and then wondered again, more excitedly, what information she might be bringing me. I had not spoken to her since our first ugly conversation. Louise and I had spoken briefly. It had been awkward. I had no energy to spare for Louise. Whatever friendship we'd begun was not strong enough for all this. She was not someone I could lean on. It was easier not to interact at all.

Cass I barely recognized. The heavy eyeliner and chalky makeup were gone. She'd washed the black dye out of her hair. It was now mahogany brown and long enough to cover her ears. She wore no earrings, no rings up to her knuckles. Holding a big white TIPTOP BAKERY box in front of her, she looked small, awkward and very young. A little pasty, exactly how Dylan used to look beside her, I realized with a pang.

"Are you going to send me away?" she asked quickly, breathlessly, as if she was afraid I'd slam the door in her face. A realistic fear, actually. "I got another letter from Dyl, and she asked me to tell you she's okay."

"And you decided to tell me in person." I summoned all the self-control I had left. "Well, come on in." As much as I resented her presence in my home, I wanted whatever information this girl had and bullying her would not get it.

"It came a couple of days ago." She shifted the weight of the box from one arm to the other but did not step forward. "I guess I should have come right away."

"Yes, that would have been nice. But hey, I'm not going to eat you, I promise." I opened the door wider so she could fit through with the box.

"If I didn't know better, I'd say you brought me a birthday cake."

Cass stared at me. I thought of Dylan's sixteenth birthday coming up so soon and possibly away from me. I wouldn't put it past Cass to bring a cake as some kind of perverse adolescent joke. I repressed a new flare-up of hostility toward this girl. "So what is in there, anyway?"

Cass shook her head, expressionless. "Nothing like that."

I led her into the kitchen. She put the box in the middle of the kitchen table, then turned to face me, one hand resting on the cover behind her as if otherwise something might pop out. All the cockiness of the other day was gone. I could not read this kid at all. Hell, what was new? I obviously couldn't read Dylan either, as it turned out.

"Some tea?" I asked, walking pointedly wide of the table on my way to the cupboard.

"Instant coffee would be better."

"Don't keep the stuff."

"Really?" Her eyebrows raised. "Then tea's okay I guess."

"Lapsang, Irish Breakfast, Constant Comment, Lemon Zest."

"I don't care. I don't know the difference."

"We'll have Lemon Zest, then." I forced myself to smile and put the pot on to boil. "So?"

Cass met my eye. She was not hostile toward me after all, I decided. Stubborn. A little shy. Maybe even apologetic. I began to calculate what it would take to get her to tell me what I needed to know to find Dylan. I leaned my tush against the sink. "So, it's a pretty crazy time here, huh, for all of us?"

"What has my mother told you?" Her sharpness caught me off guard.

"Nothing," I said honestly.

Her chest heaved once. "I can't let you see Dyl's letter."

"I'd like to read it, to be honest, but I figured you wouldn't let me." I worked to keep my voice level. "You certainly are a girl who keeps her word, I'll say that for you."

"Right." She nodded solemnly. "The police called me to find out what I know. Are they going to bug me until I tell them something? Because there's nothing I'm going to tell them."

"Hey, they are just doing their job." Can you believe me saying that? "So what do you know, anyway?"

"I came by here the first night I was back. I looked in the window. You were here with a man."

"Yes." I breathed carefully. "I was, but he's gone." I wanted a cigarette, but my last pack was in the garbage can. I had quit cold turkey. Call it superstitious, but oral deprivation to expiate my sins seemed in order.

"My mom doesn't know, does she?" Her voice was not threatening. Not at all. She was trying, in her awkward way, to let me know she could keep my secrets as well as she kept Dylan's.

"No." I shook my head and shrugged. It occurred to me for the first time, I'm almost ashamed to admit, that if Dylan and Cass didn't go to my mother's, Cass must have gone somewhere else. I wish I could say I was curious, but, frankly, at that moment I did not much care.

The pot began to sputter. I took down two mugs and we sat at the table, the bakery box between us.

"I don't have any cookies to offer you, so if you have any in there, we should break them out now."

"Afraid not." A meager smile flickered across her lips. She sipped her tea while I pretended not to study her. "Those are pretty paperweights," she offered eventually.

"They are actually prettier earlier in the day, when the sun catches them through the window and brings out the colors."

"Where did you get them? I bet they were expensive."

"I made them years ago, when Dylan was a baby."

"That is way cool." She finished her tea and refused more.

"You don't make them anymore?" she asked.

"Don't have the time or equipment it takes."

Cass seemed genuinely interested. She was no surrogate Dylan, far from it, but it was nice to smell once again that young-girl scent of soap and cheap perfume that could fill a room like laughter. Also, there was about Cass an eager nervous energy, a hunger. She had sought me out, and I could not help respecting the courage it must have taken to face me here. She did have spirit.

I explained a little about working with glass, the heat it takes, the delicacy and precision. It had been a while since I thought about those days: the constant warm roar of the furnace, the pure power surging through the blowing iron, squeezing, stretching, bending molten formlessness into glass.

Cass chewed on a straggle of hair. "I wish my mom were more like you." The compliment startled me. She seemed sincere but I smelled a trap.

"Your mother is great. Caring. Natural. A regular earth mother in panty hose and polyester."

Cass studied her hands.

"She's okay, I guess." I could see she was holding back tears. If I asked the right questions, God only knew what I would hear.

"Shall we open this?" I asked instead, pointing to the box.

Cass immediately leaned forward and slit the taped flaps open with her fingernail. She pulled away the cardboard top and sides.

"I patched it back together the best I could, but it's not perfect."

I stared, speechless with astonishment, then ran my palm across the oval top of the ceramic egg, along hairline cracks stitched with dried glue.

"Where did you get this?"

"I bought the pieces."

"It was broken?"

Cass nodded. Standing side by side, I realized she was not much taller than Dylan, coming up just above my shoulder.

"And you put it back together?"

"All the silver people are inside." She was proud of her work, separate from its meaning, whatever the meaning was. "It's taken me a while."

I was horrified and spellbound at the same time. What was this girl doing with my Egg of Life? I thought of Joe. The day we ran into each other at the gallery, the Egg was what had caught his attention. And Cleo. Cleo told me specifically that she'd sold this one. She paid me for it.

"It's a goddamn wonder." I lifted the top to count my silver babies, to check how many were actually missing.

Cass cleared her throat and waited until I glanced up.

"I had an abortion."

"What?" This I did not want to hear. I put the ceramic top down and waited with a sinking heart for whatever else was to come.

"Instead of going to your mother's, I went to a clinic in Gainesville. All the girls from the university use it, so I knew it was okay."

"How did you pay for it?" I was in no position to judge her. Cass was what, five, six years younger than I had been when Dylan was conceived. Nevertheless, I was horrified. Poor Louise.

"I had some money saved."

I took a breath and plunged on.

"Did Dylan know?"

"No." Then in an avalanche of jagged words, Cass explained that she'd been sleeping with boys—and not just boys, men—for quite a while.

"I can't tell you why. I just kind of liked it. At least at first." She didn't say where she met them or how often, and I did not ask.

"Don't worry. Dylan was never involved." Was I supposed to thank God for small favors? Thank you, Jesus, because even if Dylan was living on the streets tonight, prey of every rapist and heroin addict in America, at least she was virginal when she ran away? Thanks, but no thanks. "Does your mother know?"

"Not exactly." She looked at me, pleading. "Not yet."

Poor Louise. Still, I would have traded problems with her in a heartbeat. At least she had her daughter safe at home now. Shit. Who was I kidding? No one was safe.

"I'll have to tell her. You know that?"

Cass nodded. That was why she'd come, wasn't it? For some reason this girl had decided to trust me. As if I had the strength to deal with another family's nightmare. Was this some mutant angel's idea of therapy, a perverse method for getting me to give my Dylan fears an hour's rest? Was Cass's dropping her secret in my lap supposed to be a gift? Or was it a test? Maybe the gods had decided that only if I made up for some earlier wrong by doing the right thing for this girl would they open the way for me to get Dylan back.

As if life were simple rights and wrongs. All that bullshit I fed Dylan about truth and honesty, purity and beauty. I don't know if it was bullshit exactly, but virtue was easy for me all those years because I had no hard choices to face. And I had no hard choices because there were no people in my life. Now people have been coming at me as fast as they've been leaving me, and when people are involved, damn if every choice doesn't have its cost. Well, I am paying, God, I am paying.

Fear. Anger. Guilt. My new mantra.

I have been drifting through the hours in a makeshift routine of desperation for I don't know how long anymore. I have been to every bus station within a hundred-mile radius and put up posters. Even if she were long gone from the area, somebody might remember her buying a ticket and to where. No one has. I have called Sergeant Baines down at the police daily. I have called the FBI. Me calling the FBI. It was odd, but they were very nice and referred me to a runaway hot line. My schedule has become: get up early, since I haven't slept anyway; make more posters and get them copied; send out posters; call hot lines; take calls from people who mean well but I don't want to talk to; sit sipping lukewarm tea while staring out the window until it's time to lie down and stare at the ceiling some more.

Joe? There is no way I could reconcile what went on with Joe, the pleasure and visceral expectation he raised in my molecular structure, with the slough of Dylan's absence. I told him we were finished, that I could only handle one loss at a time, that there was too much electricity on the line, and I was shorting out all over the place. Actually, I don't remember what I told him. I was in such a state. He called a few times, but hearing his voice was like twisting the knife. I don't deny I miss him, but whatever was between us seems so sordid now. I gave him up for the same reason I gave up all my other bad habits, even smoking—to get those stars aligned.

I used to say I was alone but never lonely, didn't I? Well, now I am both. I have not completely abandoned the Franklins, but David is getting better and doesn't need my visits, and Myra has gone back to work at the mill. Cleo tries to be supportive, but we are both aware that I am going to screw up her big spring show. There is no way I can concentrate enough to complete the pieces I promised her. As for Louise, when I told her about Cass, I can't deny experiencing a certain glint of, shall I call it, satisfaction along with my genuine sympathy and empathy.

She seemed almost relieved. "At least I know something concrete and can go from there," she said and thanked me.

That was that. I have heard nothing more from her or from Cass. I don't expect to. I don't imagine Louise is comfortable with my knowing her family secrets or with knowing mine. But I do miss her. She always managed to ask the question that could get under my skin. Even that last morning, as we stood saying our perfunctory goodbyes on her front porch.

"Do you think she'll find him?" she asked.

"Him? You mean her father?" I rummaged pointedly in my bag for my car keys. "I have not considered the possibility."

"Perhaps you should." She spoke kindly, but I stiffened as she turned to go back inside. After all, she knew who Dylan's father was.

I was not about to admit it to Louise, but of course I have thought about the possibility. I have thought about little else for days. At first a big steering wheel in my brain kept turning all thoughts away from Hank. Why bother about him? I told myself. Hank was not an issue. Hank did not count anymore. Never had. He was not part of our life. Only now he is because Dylan wants him to be. Because every clue that might lead to Dylan counts, and Hank is a central clue. The jilted mother, and lover, may hate to give him that much credit, but the practical, do-anything-to-get-my-daughter-back mother knows I have to.

The local cops obviously do not know where Hank is, much less who he is. Why bring up his name? I asked myself, after my first short interview with Sergeant Baines. Considering who manned Esmeralda's police station, there was a good chance whatever I disclosed would be all over town in a heartbeat. I wanted Dylan back with as little humiliation as possible. As little as possible for her, that is, not me—humiliation was the least of it for me—because why should everyone have to know the hurtful truth about her father? How many of her friends in Esmeralda would be able to understand that he was not a bad man, not evil in the sense that their Bible teaches about evil. And anyway, what were the chances that Dylan would actually find him, assuming Cass told me the truth?

But somewhere along the line, I decided there was no holding back where Dylan was concerned. Even if I knew for certain that she didn't know where Hank was, the police might think she did, and that might matter enough to them to ignite their efforts to find him. And her.

"What if you guys had reason to believe," I asked my new best friend Sergeant Baines in our first face-to-face meeting, "—isn't that how you put it?—that a missing runaway girl might be in the company of someone who was a fugitive from the law on serious felony charges?"

"I'm not sure I'm following you, Mrs. Blue."

"A criminal. Someone wanted by the police. By the FBI."

"How serious? Are you saying the minor would be in danger?"

"Well, I don't know about that."

"You should." I decided I liked Sergeant Baines a lot. "If we had knowledge of a felon who might be dangerous to a minor, the priority on finding that minor goes up."

"Pictures?"

"Yeah, I suppose so."

I didn't hesitate. I spelled out Hank's name for him in capital letters. Under the circumstances, what I was doing was the only thing to do. I wanted my daughter back, damn the cost. I know there are people I used to respect who would say I was betraying him. I might say so. I had betrayed Dylan by not showing her the damned poster in the first place, and now I was betraying Hank, using him as bait. It was crazy for me ever to think of protecting him. I don't owe him anything; he owes me.

God, I had been so young once upon a time. And Hank had been so, so what? It seems crazy but the word that comes to mind is "dashing." I knew him for maybe three days. We were together nonstop for all of seventy-two hours minus a little sleep here and there. Yet I was probably as in love as I have ever been with a man; in comparison, these last few months of Joe Rainey have been a mere blip on the old radar screen. What a thing to have to admit to myself while Dylan is God-knows-where, going through whatever she is going through; but because of her, I have to admit it. Not that I hold any illusions that I still love Hank. That dashing young man no longer exists, except intertwined with my genes within Dylan. Children are the reincarnation of the living. Dylan has inherited pieces of my psyche and his.

Meanwhile, the days keep passing. A lot of the everyday things in my life have begun to take on more ominous souls. The plastic food containers in the refrigerator, Miranda's steering wheel, the tub and sink faucets. Every one a different animal, ready to bite. One morning, Dylan's chenille bedspread became rows of chattering human teeth. I never hallucinated exactly, but the world that used to comprise my life has become less than solid, and I am not always sure anymore what's what.

By this afternoon, I had to force myself to pick up my mail because the fish on the mailbox reminded me too much of sharks. I reached in and grabbed the envelopes lying there, then hurried back up the sand path to safety, pushed open the front door with my shoulder and bolted inside. A tan card slid loose from the pastel bundle of bills and flyers I was holding. It fluttered toward the floor and lodged at the bottom of the doorjamb like a wounded wren. I bent down automatically to pick it up, then froze. I didn't have to read one word to recognize the crabbed left slant. "Unladylike," a narrow-minded fourth-grade teacher used to condemn across the top margin of every assignment Dylan handed in.

"Who wants to be ladylike, anyway?" That was my easy answer to cheer Dylan, but Dylan would shake her head, sobbing against the injustice. This was before she stopped being interested in my opinion or in needing my advice, before I became an embarrassment, before adolescence drove the first wedge between us. We were still a pair then, to hell with the rest of the world.

"This is the writing of strength and independence, Honeybunch," I told her, "of an intense depth of mind and soul."

Now I crouched down, afraid to take the postcard in my hand. I could swear I saw a copperhead about to strike. The other unopened envelopes fell into a ragged skirt around me. Strength and independence. What was it my mother stitched on one of her pillows during her Early Americana period? "If you plant peas, don't expect to reap beans." I traced my name with my index finger, each spindly, pressed-down letter. G O D I V A B L U E. The letters sunk in, flashed out.

I AM FINE. AM NOT RUNNING AWAY FROM YOU. AM GOING TO MY FATHER. I DON'T HATE YOU OR ANYTHING. I AM NOT IN TROUBLE. CASHED THE SAVINGS BOND SO HAVE ALL THE MONEY I NEED. DON'T WORRY TOO MUCH. DYLAN.
  P.S. FORGET TRACING ME THROUGH THE POSTMARK. I'M LONG GONE.

Long gone. The eggshell in which I have been hiding cracked. What spattered out was not relief but pain. No, not pain. Anger. Building toward fury that Dylan could do this to me. Gone off on a wild-goose chase to search for what? A father who for all practical purposes did not exist. As far as Dylan was concerned, whatever he and I shared once was merely an accident of time and place. I was the mother who willed her into being against all odds, who worked like a dervish to create a life for the two of us. Okay, not the perfected, artistic vision I've been telling myself, but a damn good life all the same.

"The ungrateful brat." I grabbed the postcard and was about to rip it apart when, thank the gods, I caught my face in the mirror. Red and distorted as the wicked stepmother witch in every fairy tale I ever acted out while reading to Dylan. I stuck out my tongue, screwed up my nose and lips into a misshapen leer, crooked my finger.

"Come here, my pretty, all my young pretties." The mirror leered back. As I blinked, a hard chip dissolved. I became merely an almost forty-year-old woman with crow's feet and a sagging jaw. I looked at myself a second or two longer. Then, and maybe this is pathetic, I picked up the phone and called my mother.

We spoke one other time since she returned from Hawaii. She called to ask what all the messages on her machine were about and I had to break the news to her that Dylan had run away. She offered to come stay with me, but I told her absolutely not. She called several more times, but each time I let the machine pick up. Oh yes, I have a machine now. I can't afford to ride my anti-technology high horse anymore. What if Dylan phones while I'm out buying milk?

"Hello," my mother said, her brittle New England precision intact. I'd seen through that voice years ago, recognizing without much sympathy the shyness it masked, but hearing it now—what can I tell you?—I burst into tears at the comfort of its old familiarity.

"What do I do?" I heard myself asking, I who never sought my mother's advice, assuming ahead, and always dead right, what it would be. Every decision I ever made, including and especially giving birth to Dylan, had been made against that woman's better judgment.

"I don't know what I would do, knowing the reason she's gone, not knowing where she's gone." In other words, I told you so. I began to regret the call. "Even that summer you ran off to Boston, we knew where you were. We talked to the settlement-house director frequently."

"Nathan Pearl? He never told me." God, everywhere I turn I meet betrayal. Mine and everyone else's. Or was it just my family? A genetic glitch.

"That's not the point, dear." Shit, I have always hated it when she calls me "dear." First she'd zigged me one way, now she was zagging me the other. "What can you do more than you already have? I'd hate to see her become one of those photographs on the back of my cereal box."

"That's exactly what she *has* become." The need to justify was disintegrating in the face of my own culpability.

"Judy, I know you are worried sick. You should be, but give the police a few more days, and then we'll hire a private detective."

It was too much. My own mother talking this way, probably fingering her pearls genteelly as she contemplated Humphrey Bogart finding her granddaughter on the Orient Express.

"Mother, I hate to tell you." I took a deep breath. "I've already hired one."

There was a moment of what I took to be stunned silence. Then she started to laugh. So did I. The insane logic of it all was too beautiful not to. The miles of phone wire between us cackling and swaying under our unhappy mirth, we laughed into each other's ears for ten minutes. Laughed until we cried. What else is there left to do?

FiVE

Stepping into the kitchen, Dylan forgets for a moment why she is here, forgets Crescent clutching her hand, forgets everything in the rich grease-flecked steam that envelops her. She breathes in the freshly brewed coffee, the meat dripping fat on the grill, the seared peppers cooling on the chopping block, the sugared pastry dough still in the glass oven, the onions sautéing with garlic and cilantro in an iron skillet. Some smells she recognizes. Others she cannot place, but the delicious wisps of sweet and spicy and tart and even bitter swirl together knotting her stomach with hunger.

At a long table, a group of men and women she assumes is the staff of Los Combientes sits finishing a meal. Another man and woman work at the counter and the stove. It is like a dumb show, everything happening in slow, exaggerated yet hazy motion. Even Crescent letting go of Dylan's hand registers only at a remove, the slight lessening of warmth beside her. As Crescent shyly approaches the table, Dylan stands rooted to her spot, disembodied more than paralyzed. A woman who introduces herself as Margie puts a phone book on an empty chair and lifts Crescent up. A plate is placed in front of her and a glass of milk. Crescent takes a piece of chicken in one hand and reaches for the milk.

The glass tips over. Blue-white milk flows down the length of oilskin into a plate of butter. Margie laughs while she and two of the others spread napkins where the milk has collected.

"Oopsie," Crescent sings out, waving her chicken gaily at the mess she is creating.

My god, I am here, Dylan thinks. Everything, the voices, the faces, the smells, jar back into sharp clear focus, the same way she used to find herself startled awake on the bus by a sudden swerve, unaware she'd dozed off to the rhythmic forward sway in the first place.

Iris, the pretty dark-haired woman she approached a little while ago in the parking lot, comes in and rests her hand, light as a bird's wing, on Dylan's shoulder.

"She's looking for a guy named Henry Firestone," Iris tells the others, and Dylan feels a welling up of gratitude that someone else is doing the asking for her.

"Ain't me," says one of the men with a heavy Spanish accent. Everyone laughs as Iris gently leads Dylan to the table and sits down next to her.

"We know it's not you, Manny," Iris says, "but I haven't worked here that long, and I thought maybe one of you would remember him and be able to tell this young woman where he is now."

Dylan smiles at how lucky she was to meet Iris first. Standing in the parking lot, screwing up her courage to walk through the front door, Dylan watched Iris come out of the restaurant with two other women, women in heavy fur coats. Iris wore only a black turtleneck and kept her arms folded on her chest against the cold as she walked the others to a station wagon. She was turning to go back inside when Dylan, spurred by an adrenaline rush of bravery, picked up Crescent and jogged up to her.

"I'm looking for someone who works here," Dylan called out.

Iris stopped and glanced over her shoulder briefly. "Your boyfriend?"

"No." Small icy clouds carried Dylan's words ahead of her. "My father."

"Well, come on in, then." Iris gave her a sharp once-over, maybe searching for a resemblance, before she opened the heavy wood-framed door. "You look as if you could use some warming up. Both of you."

And yes, at that moment, Dylan felt chilled straight through, but not now. Now she is warm, melting like a block of ice inside her clothes.

"What's he look like?" asks an older woman with hair in a tight topknot, as she carries the wet napkins to the sink.

"Dark hair," Dylan answers hesitantly, not sure how forthcoming to be with these strangers.

"Well, that narrows it down," someone snorts. Every man in the room fits that description.

"He might have a beard."

"Like Orey said, that narrows it down."

Dylan flushes. They are teasing good-humoredly, she knows, but what if this place turns out to be a dead end?

"Crescent." Dylan speaks softly but urgently. Crescent leaves the game she has been playing, wrapping and unwrapping a napkin around some spoons, to climb down from her chair. Dylan lifts her onto her lap, clutches her tightly and takes a deep breath.

"So does he know you're looking for him?" the woman named Margie asks. Her freckled redhead's complexion and loose sloppy ponytail remind Dylan just slightly of Godiva.

"My father does not know I was born," she answers with more force than she intends. Everyone stops eating and stares at her. In the suddenly tense quiet, the only sound is the *tck tck tck* of the man at the counter chopping vegetables on a wooden board with machinelike speed. Instinctively, Crescent shifts her sturdy little body into a protective curve against Dylan's chest.

"Why don't you eat something first?" Iris passes Dylan a plate of glistening vegetables slashed with grill marks.

"No, thank you. I don't think I can."

"Eat." The man at the chopping block speaks for the first time. It is the kind of low, quiet command you do not argue with. Dylan picks up a miniature carrot.

Iris stiffens slightly and turns toward the counter.

"David, you don't remember anyone who could be this man, do you?" There is a tentative undercurrent of something Dylan cannot put her finger on, a stickiness she has not heard in Iris before. "You're the one who'd know if anyone would."

"Iris Morales O'Neill, you can't help getting yourself involved, can you?" He is almost chuckling, and Iris blushes. Then Dylan understands: Obviously they are boyfriend and girlfriend. Dylan can see that whatever they are talking about doesn't have to do with her.

The man turns to smile at Iris, pushing his bottle-thick glasses up on his high creased forehead. He has an old-fashioned handlebar mustache, salt-and-pepper gray like his hair, what little there is of it. The white T-shirt under a stained white buttonless jacket is too tight and shows a soft ridge of fat above the belt of his pants. Dylan finds it a little pathetic how he is trying to look hip, with black high-top sneakers and a turquoise earring dangling from one ear. Why would someone as young and pretty as Iris mess with such a weird old guy? Iris gets up from the table to stand near him. She reminds Dylan of the actress Cher, willowy and exotic. She has to be at least twenty years younger than he is.

"Dylly wants her poppa," Crescent murmurs in a sleepy singsong.

"David, you're a jerk, but I forgive you," Iris says under her breath, almost whispers really, obviously hoping no one else hears. Her gums show pink above her teeth and her lips curl into creases as she tries not to smile too broadly. Dylan knows that feeling.

David shrugs and grins back, cutting his gaze away from Iris just long enough to take Dylan in.

"I'm sorry, kid, I don't remember anyone named Fierstein." He cocks his head slightly, whether apologetically or ironically Dylan never decides.

She bites on her lip so hard she tastes blood. His face. There is no cut-and-dry similarity. But she sees something, something an inch past comprehension, half an inch, not quite familiar, a shift of eye and muscle.

"Dylly wants her poppy." Crescent sings again louder. A sketch, half-remembered, swims up to the shore of conscious thought like a snatch of melody she cannot quite hum. A rough crayon sketch like so many Godiva did over the years, scrapbook after scrapbook Dylan flipped through randomly to entertain herself on rainy days. Faces her mother found interesting in one way or another, some she'd known long and well, others she'd seen once but memorized. Something in the narrow bumped nose, the calm, controlled gaze, the set of the jaw. Sad and knowing.

A steely rod of light shoots up through Dylan's chest and flames across her horizons.

It is him.

Approaching awareness, Dylan hears nearby murmuring, water over smooth pebbles. She opens her eyes to face an endless blue, the pale, pale blue of mid-morning's horizon across the Gulf from the flat rocks on the Point. Then her head clears and it is a blue wall she sees, and she is lying on a bed, the crisp starchiness of a fresh pillowcase under her cheek, the murmur not running water but conversation somewhere behind her, too far away or low to catch its particulars.

Slowly, deliciously, it comes to her, the fact of where she is. She almost laughs out loud with the pure wondrousness of it all, savoring her anticipation, how when she rolls over she will meet her father's welcoming arms.

"Dylan, are you all right?"

A woman's voice. The girlfriend. She has forgotten about Iris. They like each other, she and Iris, so that is something. She starts to sit up, to reach for her father, but her head is heavy on her neck and her arms tingle.

"You really scared us." Iris touches Dylan's forehead. "You fainted, you know."

Dylan does not care about that. Seeing him standing beside Iris, she shakes her head carefully and wills Iris to leave now. Doesn't she see she is extraneous? But Iris shows no sign of leaving. She keeps chatting and fiddling around with the blankets.

Meanwhile, why doesn't he say something instead of pulling at his crazy mustache? Dylan tries to read concern into his expression, but he is looking at the bedpost as much as at her. She has to concentrate. He takes a glass off the small table and fills it. For me, she thinks. First food, now drink. He is giving her a sign, that must be it. But why is he so distracted, so distant?

She remembers them all together in the kitchen, what she said, and is mortified. What was she thinking? How could she have been so stupid? No wonder he is upset. To toss out his real name in front of all those people had been dumb, possibly dangerous even. He is on the lam, after all. He cannot risk giving himself away.

What does he call himself now? Dylan reaches back into the welter of names batting around the kitchen—David, David Balboa is how she will think of him from now on. Even this girlfriend Iris probably has no idea about his true identity. Dylan will have to wait until they are alone, that is it.

The water has a mineral taste, but Dylan drinks it down greedily. He has taken off his jacket. His bare arm touches Iris's at the elbow as if they've been folded and cut from paper. Both of them dark and long limbed, they could be brother and sister except he is so much older; father and daughter, then. Iris her sister, that is a spooky thought.

What is he like? Dylan shivers at a quick cold gust of worry that all her fantasies have been just that, fantasies.

"We wondered," Iris begins slowly, carefully picking up and laying down each word like a precious stone, "about your parents, your mother. If you want us to contact her or something."

"My mother, Godiva Blue, or Judy Blitch, depending when you knew her, can be a crazy woman," Dylan begins, watching for a sign of recognition that does not come. Immediately, she wishes she had described Godiva with a more positive adjective. He might remember Godiva differently. "I mean, she's probably no crazier than most mothers. It's okay between us. I sent her a postcard and all a few days ago."

"So she knows where you are?" It is the first time he's spoken to her directly since she woke up. His tone is colder than she expected. Tears gather in her throat but she wills them away.

"Not exactly."

"Well, then, you need to let her know."

"We'll deal with it later," Iris breaks in, protecting Dylan again, as if Dylan needed her protection. "Meanwhile, David and I have talked and decided to let you stay here for a few days."

"Here?"

"Above the restaurant," he says. "My apartment."

"They let you live at the restaurant?"

"I own the restaurant." Dylan could swear he almost smiles.

"You do? Really?" Her father is no longer Henry Fierstein, the fugitive Weatherman, a communist, an anarchist, or whatever he was. He is David Balboa, restaurant owner. A new future begins to spin itself out in her head.

Iris puts an arm around David's waist and crooks a witchy finger in his belt loop as if she owns him, then clears her throat.

"About Crescent," she begins.

"Crescent!" Tears of panic rise in her throat. "Where is she? What have you done with her?"

"Hey, your sister's fine." David speaks more kindly this time. "She's eating nacho chips in the bar with Orey." He has a way of pulling his mustache and winking that reminds Dylan involuntarily of an old Groucho Marx movie she saw once with Godiva. "She's so busy flirting, she's forgotten you completely already."

Dylan begins to sob and cannot stop. The most important day of her life and, though she knows he is kidding, she feels suddenly bereft.

TWENTY

Iris and David stand in the doorway of David's study where the girls lie sleeping on a fold-out sofa bed.

"Dylan's obviously a runaway, poor kid," Iris whispers, as David turns away. "But the little one, for her mother to palm her off on a stranger, a kid. What kind of monster is she? We'll need to notify the police."

"Give them one night," he says grimly over his shoulder. "Recovery time. They'll need at least one."

"Oh sure, one night won't matter." Iris follows him down the hall to the bedroom. "I feel bad for Dylan, too, all this way for nothing." From that first moment in the parking lot, when the half-frozen girl spoke out so proudly, Iris has felt a kinship. "I like her. She has some grit."

"Like you did at sixteen, maybe." David pulls her against him in a light half-hug. Iris sighs and leans into him. Apparently David is as willing as she to forget last night, their first serious argument in three months of being together. It came out of nowhere. They'd been sitting in the pantry office at midnight, snacking on the day's leftovers and flat champagne, a ritual they've evolved for when they are feeling particularly tired and close.

"I don't want a damn restaurant to be the rest of my life," she'd blurted out half-kidding and then realized she meant it.

"No one's asking you to." He laughed, scooping up a spoonful of zabaglione to wave temptingly in front of her. When he touched her bottom lip with the tip of his spoon, a metallic taste, longing and anger in equal overlapping measures, filled her mouth.

"Why not?"

"Iris Morales O'Neill." He likes to call her by her full name when they make love. "I have traveled alone for a long time, and I doubt I could change now even if I wanted to."

"Even if." The strength of her fury brought tears to her eyes. "Which means you do not want to. Well, I never said I wanted you to."

He did not move to soothe her or seduce her back although she'd have been willing enough for either. He merely sat there, his head tilted back, his mouth gone crooked, as if the sweet cream of the zabaglione were souring on his tongue. She ran out of the room and out of the restaurant, ran the three blocks to her cousin Connie's, where she spent the rest of the night keeping Connie awake with her pacing. It served Connie right, since she was the one who suggested the job at Los Combientes in the first place when Iris moved back to Velasquez in September. If it weren't for Connie, Iris would never have met David.

This morning she went through her routine chores at the restaurant without seeing David, wondering nervously just where she stood with him, aware that her outburst had given away how dependent on him she'd become. When he finally made his appearance in the kitchen, they avoided actually speaking, and throughout the busy prep and lunch they circled wary as cats.

Then these girls showed up, and in the general excitement, David and Iris forgot they'd been holding their breath around each other and started to breathe together again. It might only be a respite, not a resolution, but Iris is not ready to push beyond the unspoken understanding of David's arm around her shoulder, leading her to his bed.

+   +   +

WITH*i*N the next twenty-four hours, it is clear to everyone at Los Combientes, whether David chooses to acknowledge it or not, that Dylan has decided David is going to be her father. She does not say the word "father" again, but she watches David constantly. She is filled with questions about his life, where he grew up, where he went to college, where he was in December of 1968 or August of 1969 or May of 1970. He always has an answer, but Dylan keeps asking. She'd make a good lawyer, Iris jokes to David, but privately she finds it painful to witness.

David is clever in deflecting Dylan's questions, switching the spotlight back on the girl to get her talking. He is trying to weasel out enough information to contact her family and send her home. The first morning, he gets her going on about her mother. For a girl who's run away, Dylan seems to love and admire her mother greatly. But she catches herself when he pushes too hard. She will not say the name of the town, or even the state where she's from, although from bits and pieces it is evidently somewhere warm and near water.

"We need to call the police," Iris keeps insisting, but David wants to wait.

"Just another day or two. Maybe she'll drop this delusion and decide to go home on her own. Wouldn't that be better than dragging in the authorities? All that trauma?"

Iris knows the ramifications if they don't contact legal authorities soon. She has already explained them to David several times. But she understands his hesitation. He's formed an attachment to the little girl, Crescent, and hates to think what lies in store for her once she leaves Los Combientes. Crescent has no mother waiting. She'll become a ward of the state, possibly for good. Iris finds his protective concern endearing.

"Maybe you could adopt her," she suggests, attempting to lighten the issue. "Adopt them both?"

"Do I look like a father?"

"No, but Dylan's so desperate, she seems willing to take you as a last resort."

"I'm taken."

He gives Iris a kiss that surprises her with its intensity, and Iris, stroking his cheek, finds herself bemused that the two girls' predicament has drawn David closer to her. Whether it is having a problem to solve together, or an awakening of parental instincts, or their helplessness before the kids' needs, whatever it is, the relationship seems to be turning a corner.

Rather, David seems to be. It's a corner Iris turned months ago. Barely two weeks after David Balboa hired her last October. The night she stayed after closing time to celebrate the restaurant's third anniversary. Until then, she'd avoided socializing with the staff, not out of a sense of superiority, although she imagined that's what the others thought, but because she intuited that she was at risk, because nothing about David Balboa would let her relax.

Everyone was drinking tequila that night. Acutely aware of the symmetry of blue glass and yellow and pale-green rinds on the white linen cloth, Iris was alive to the sexual tension everywhere around her. How Orey the bartender flicked cigarette ash in Manuel's direction with a short dangerous snap of the wrist. How Rolf and Estelle accidentally touched their glasses at the same instant every time they drank, while Estelle's husband sitting between them winced. How David's eyes followed Iris whenever she laughed—she laughed a great deal that night—and how the women, especially Margie, narrowed their smiles in her direction. Sucking a wedge of lemon, Iris speculated briefly and distantly which, if not all these women, had slept with David, but she put the lemon down and let the question float away as she imagined, knew, really, as if it were already memory, the weight of his hand cupping a heel, a shoulder, a breast.

"Free-spirited" Iris, according to her grandfather. "Clever" Iris, according to her high school principal. The first woman in her family, or man for that matter, to attend college, let alone graduate third in her law-school class, only to disappear from Albuquerque on the eve of the bar exam to escape certain emotional entanglements she had decided were suffocating her. That same independent-minded young woman has not been able to avoid the obvious since the first night she made tequila-drenched love in his bed: that she has become totally absorbed in David Balboa and his world.

All along she has recognized an imbalance between them. Even in their most intimate moments, he remains, not remote exactly, more like a room she cannot quite see into all the way. She has to remind herself that no one is completely open or honest, but the shadowy corners she senses in him both worry and titillate her. It's been a turning of the tables. In the past, she was always the one not quite knowable. At the end of previous relationships, the men she was invariably rejecting would accuse her of having pretended the whole time that she was someone she was not.

Someone who loved them or might someday, someone pliable and ready for commitment. She'd declare that she never lied. And she hadn't, not technically. But now, given how she is with David, she admits that what she did with those others was not lie but omit. She had always been herself, but less, holding back in a way she cannot with David. With David she exposes every inch of herself and all her raw hungers.

So she understands that this girl Dylan cannot help herself. It doesn't matter whether Dylan wants David to be her father for reasons that, as far as Iris can see, make very little sense. Dylan's desperation is palpable. It makes her claim. Like Iris, she is not about to relinquish David Balboa without a fight.

Twenty-ONE

The truth: Things are not working out the way Dylan hoped. Once the first opportunity passed, pride has kept her from saying more until her father does. She keeps waiting for a sign from him, but it does not come. She feels sure it will, if she could catch him alone, but he never is alone. When he's not in the kitchen sorting out the day's supply of produce with Iris and Manuel, he's cooking, or he's working the front rooms, gossiping with stern-faced old ladies and getting his back slapped by heavyset men in cowboy boots and string ties.

The boots remind Dylan of Spider. It is hard to believe that less than two weeks ago she was sitting next to him on a bus in South Carolina, his feet in those smelly socks crossed at the ankles, and the boots stuck halfway under the seat in front. Maybe he was from New Mexico. Wouldn't that be ironic?

As for her father, or David Balboa as he calls himself now, when he isn't tied up with the restaurant duties, which is most of the time, he allows that stupid Iris to attach herself to him like a safety pin.

Really. Dylan was mistaken to think, when they first met, that Iris would be an ally. She is pretty much the opposite. She cannot keep her hands off David Balboa. It would disgust Dylan even if it didn't infuriate her, how Iris will not get out of the way. Dylan is positive David Balboa must want to talk to her as much as she wants to talk to him. Why doesn't he just tell Iris to get lost? The situation would be unbearable, but one thing Dylan has learned since she found the poster three months ago is patience; the other is to keep her own counsel, except perhaps with Crescent. Crescent is so little that she doesn't count.

Dylan knows she has to wait. Meanwhile, she studies him constantly. She has to be sure. Absolutely one-hundred-percent sure. She looks at herself in the mirror and then at him and then at herself again. Feature by feature. He definitely has the eyes. No question. And the walk. In Cincinnati, Martha saw the walk immediately.

And Dylan is convinced he is sending her signals. Especially when they're together in the kitchen. She loves helping out in the kitchen. She loves the good smells, the easy joking that occurs between Margie and Manuel, and David himself when Iris isn't butting in, but most of all she loves that she can feel him watching her. He might work to cover it up, but she can tell he is genuinely interested in finding out more about her, as much as she is about him.

He asks her questions, what her high school was like, what subjects she liked, what she did for fun. The kind of questions adults always ask. When she tells him, in vague terms, about the Youth Fellowship, he starts teasing her about leaving behind some boy with a broken heart as he pinches off bits of dough to form balls to fill with a cheese and apple mixture.

"So you're Baptists, you and your mother. Hey, Margie, aren't you a Baptist?" He wipes his high round forehead with a towel; the kitchen gets very hot with all the burners going. Dylan wonders when he first started going bald. That photograph must be pretty old. He still has hair but it's definitely getting thin.

"No way," Margie cackles. "They won't let me past the front door anymore."

Dylan laughs along with the others, but actually she could care less if Margie were a Baptist or a Zen Buddhist like Coyote Sikes. If Dylan gets a chance to show him the poster, he'll realize she knows about him being an atheistic communist.

"My mother hates that religion stuff." Dylan tries to mention Godiva every chance she gets, looking for a reaction. "I only joined for my friends. I'm sure you've heard about peer group pressure in adolescence."

He nods, but the way he twists his mustache after he puts the apple-and-feta cheese pastries in the oven makes Dylan nervous. She thinks he is wonderful, of course; he is her father even if he does seem a little stuck on himself. She keeps looking for the right thing to say to please him and charm him into growing so attached he could not bear to part with her.

As long as he lets her stay, that's a hopeful sign. But she still cannot figure out what he is thinking from moment to moment, cannot second-guess him the way she could Godiva. Dylan could always make her laugh.

"Godiva is very spiritual, actually, you know, in her own way. And I've been more or less rethinking my religious beliefs." It's crazy, but Dylan finds herself missing Godiva a little. Or not her exactly, but lying in bed at night and hearing the waves hit the rocks, then looking out to see the light on in the studio. Or sitting on the back stoop with her, the easy silence. Most of all, though she cannot put it into words, she misses being the center of some-one's life.

"What religion are you?" She watches him slyly.

"Foodist. The preparation of wonderful food is my religion." He reaches for a clean bowl to mix up cactus and cilantro chutney, then wanders into the other room to wash his hands, or look for Iris.

Meanwhile, Dylan stays put on her stool, peeling carrots and adjusting her plans. If he really cares about this restaurant, he is never going to want to leave, that's obvious, but it also occurs to her that his reverent attitude toward food and Godiva's toward her boxes might be compatible. She is beginning to see how they might have been attracted once, and how they might connect again under the right circumstances. Once he accepts how much he wants to keep Dylan with him for good, her and Crescent both, maybe she'll suggest bringing Godiva out here, at least to visit. Dylan is not particularly in love with Velasquez as a place to live. Almost everyone is Mexican or Indian or something and the town is even smaller, not counting the tourists, than Esmeralda. The sky is too big. But if the restaurant means that much to him, she's willing to adjust. Godiva might be willing, too, once she and David Balboa/Henry Fierstein rediscover their old passion.

"Dylan!" Margie's shriek breaks the reverie. Dylan looks up and then down at her hand. The scraper has slipped and dark red blood is dripping onto the clean shredded carrots from the ball of her thumb.

+   +   +

MORNiNG number three, or is it four? The days have been running together for Dylan in her concentration on this battle to win her father. She wakes up to television noises and walks into the apartment's living room to find the three of them, David, Iris and Crescent, squeezed together in the big leather chair, rawhide he calls it, watching *Sesame Street*. In Spanish at that hour. Dylan has been left the sling chair, but the others don't seem to notice. They're too busy singing along with Big Bird and Maria. Crescent has on a diaper although yesterday Iris was the one making a big deal about toilet training.

"She's got to be close to three, and she needs to be trained so she's not ostracized," Iris told Dylan when she took them shopping for what she called a few necessities.

"Ostracized?" Dylan asked.

"By other kids."

"Like in an orphanage, you mean?" Dylan sneered.

"No, not an orphanage. A school. Three-year-olds go to school, preschool anyhow."

Dylan bristled. "I know all about educating little kids, a lot more than you probably. My mom works in a school."

They were coming out of a clothing store down the block from Los Combientes. Iris had just purchased Dylan a pair of stretchy black pants. They had already been to a shoe store and were on their way to a children's shop for Crescent, who was holding hands with both of them so they could swing her up between them every other step. The black pants would definitely have looked better on Iris but she refused to buy herself a pair.

"This is your shopping spree," she kept saying.

If Iris wanted to spend money on Dylan and Crescent, let her. But that does not give Iris the right to take over Crescent. Crescent is Dylan's responsibility. Maybe David Balboa's, too, if he wants, but not Iris's.

"There you are, Dyl. Are you hungry?" Iris gets up from the rawhide chair as soon as she notices Dylan in the doorway.

Dylan shakes her head, holding on to yesterday's anger. She was mistaken ever to think she could like Iris. She is not about to let herself be taken in again, no matter how sucky sweet Iris acts. Iris is the moat keeping Dylan from David Balboa. Would any man leave an Iris, with her quiet, delicate elegance, for a big lumpy Godiva Blue? Not likely.

Dylan sits down in the sling chair. A bigger problem is David Balboa himself. She's still trying to figure him out. He is not like any father she met in Esmeralda, that's for sure. The pierced ear and his mustache could go. Gross. On the other hand, everyone around here likes him which is a good sign. Yesterday, in the shoe store, Dylan flushed with pride when another customer spent about twenty minutes raving to Iris about the restaurant and David.

"David has a certain magnetism," Iris boasted afterward. "He always seems to have the answer to a question no one else thought to ask."

Magnetism is good, but Dylan finds herself picking at a new worry: With a mother like Godiva and a father like David, how will she turn out? She used to worry, long months ago, about being considered ordinary. Back then all she wanted was to be ordinary. Now there is no hope of ordinary. In Esmeralda she will forevermore be the one who ran away.

"I've got to get to the bank," David says standing up, "and then I was going to stop by Hernandez Brothers to check out that new oven of theirs."

"Why don't you take some company?"

Dylan catches the meaningful bend of Iris's head in her direction and blushes in resentment at Iris's patronizing meddling. At the same time, she hopes against hope he will invite her along. Instead, he gathers up Crescent, who has been perfectly content playing with a set of tin measuring cups and spoons, and zips her into her parka without a word to Dylan. Not even see you later.

"What you need, girl, is a manicure." Iris turns to Dylan as soon as David Balboa leaves, Crescent riding on his shoulders. "You know I worked in a beauty parlor for a while in high school. I'm known for my manicures."

Dylan shrugs. Less than enthusiastic, she sits cross-legged on the floor as Iris sets up a little folding tray between them.

"I was always good at manicures, but God, how I hated working at Hollywood Hair. The chemical odors that invaded my pores were bad enough, and all that constant gossipy chatter. But what got to me most of all was how ugly the women looked in their stripped, naked faces."

"I'll bet." Dylan has never been to a beauty parlor. Not exactly Godiva's kind of place. Godiva always cut Dylan's hair for her, at least until last summer when Cass gave her the punk cut. Modified punk, really, because Dylan was not sure how far she was ready to take the punk thing. The cut is practically grown out now. Her hair hangs loose and slightly ragged, but pleasantly heavy against her neck.

"The truth is we have a lot in common." Iris lifts Dylan's limp hand and turns it over to check the Band-Aid on her thumb.

"Yeah, sure," Dylan mutters, but Iris rattles on as if she hasn't caught the sarcasm.

"When I was nearly your age, a little younger, I took a bus to see my father, too." Dylan's hand stiffens slightly.

"You didn't live with him?"

Iris shakes her head.

"But you knew him. It's not the same thing at all. You knew where he was whenever you wanted him."

"I knew all right. In the VA hospital in Albuquerque." Iris begins pushing back Dylan's cuticles.

"My dad went to Vietnam in 1965. I was barely three years old. I don't even know if he was drafted or enlisted. Did they draft married men with children?" She opens a small bottle of moisture cream. "When he came back he was what they called 'dysfunctional.'

" 'A walking basket case except he can't walk so well, either,' my mom would tell her girlfriends. The same tired, sick joke over and over. I cringed every time because the joke meant Mom was getting mean drunk again. When she got bad enough, she'd storm out and not come back for days, even weeks." Iris switches to Dylan's other hand and begins massaging it, rubbing in lotion one finger at a time. "She finally went away for good a month before I turned nine.

"She left a ten-dollar bill under a spoon along with a strip of snapshots she'd taken of herself at the five-and-dime in her favorite white off-the-shoulder blouse." Iris lifts Dylan's hand and turns it over, then pauses almost as if she's forgotten for a split second why she's holding it.

"I lost the photographs years ago, but I can see them as clearly as if I had them in my hand right now. Five shots. In the first one, my mother is smiling. In the second, she stares deadpan straight ahead. In the third, she is chewing a finger and flirting up through her eyelashes. The fourth is in profile as if she were praying, and in the fifth, she has her eyes closed."

Dylan considers asking if Iris is telling this story to make her feel bad, but she holds her tongue. She wants to hear more. She wonders if David Balboa knows Iris was abandoned by at least one of her parents, and if that knowledge might affect his attitude toward Dylan.

"My trip to visit my father was not as long as yours, I guess. I figured I could get there and back to my grandfather's house on

Front Street in a day, so I ditched school to see him for his birthday. At the hospital my father was sitting in a garden in his wheelchair. It was late afternoon by the time I got there. Almost sunset. The last bus back here was at nine. I had worked out the timing all wrong, not taking into account an extra hour for the walk from the bus station to the hospital." Iris rubs more lotion into the skin on Dylan's fingers. "Have you ever walked on a dusty road in socks that are too thin and keep slipping down into the heel of your shoe? Boy, did I get blisters."

Iris laughs but Dylan has an unpleasant flash of sensory empathy, for the skinny girl with a long braid down her back trudging along the side of the highway, choking exhaust from the trucks that threaten to brush her from the road as they roared past, while trying to ignore catcalls from the drivers.

"The colors that evening were incredibly beautiful, the sky streaked yellowy and gray, like marble. So when I finally got there I said to him, 'We'll watch the sunset together. It will be nice, special.'" Iris begins carefully painting the nails on Dylan's left hand a deepish, pinky beige.

"We were sitting there, not talking or anything, but it was pleasant enough, what I thought a father and daughter together should be like. Then a plane flew over us. No big deal, right, except that Daddy went nuts. Started shouting obscenities, real ugly ones, and there I was with everyone watching and listening."

"You were embarrassed, huh?"

"I could live with it. I knew he was sick and so forth. But then he started grabbing me, pulling and twisting my arm."

Iris wipes excess polish off the brush and takes Dylan's other hand.

"He dislocated my shoulder. I wasn't sure what was wrong, but the pain was excruciating. I was afraid to let on, thinking he'd get in trouble for hurting me, which he might have. I hitched a ride back to the station with one of the nurses and then rode the bus back to Velasquez, hours and hours it seemed, holding my arm so no one would notice. I had planned to slip home as if I'd never been gone, but I hurt too much. I called my grandfather as soon as I got off the bus. When he picked me up at the station, he said my face was like a death mask. He took me to the doctor, but he did not ask and I did not offer to tell what had happened."

Dylan holds up her newly painted pink nails and breathes in their varnishy shine. Does Iris's shoulder still hurt sometimes? She wonders what that kind of pain must feel like. How did Iris manage, riding the bus home?

Physical pain is not something Dylan has thought a lot about. It has not been part of her personal realm of experience. The closest she's ever come to witnessing pain was David Franklin, the kid in the bicycle accident, and he was so connected in her mind to Godiva, that she never let herself wonder about him much. She paid very little attention to Godiva's description of the actual accident, and when Godiva began to visit him all the time, Dylan was less jealous than annoyed that her mother was off on one of her tangents. The day of the lock-in, when Godiva was late coming back from the hospital, Dylan burned with indignation at first, until she found the picture. Then she was actually grateful that he'd kept Godiva away long enough. After that night, Dylan was caught up in her research and dreams for her future; she barely thought of David Franklin again.

Now she remembers an afternoon before the lock-in, when Godiva dragged her along to the hospital on one of her visits. Dylan wanted to leave as soon as she arrived. She found the hospital creepy, the way nobody looked straight at anyone else passing in the hall, afraid of what they'd catch, some whiff of death.

David Franklin was in a room with another kid. "Temporarily," his mother whispered. There was a screen between the beds. Dylan never saw the other boy, but his low constant whimper made her skin crawl.

David himself did not look particularly glad to see visitors. He lay wrapped in his white cast like a Martian mummy, staring ahead while Godiva read him a book she'd brought along, one of Dylan's illustrated classics. At the time, Dylan assumed he was uncomfortable with Godiva, a stranger acting as if she were someone important in his life. It would be like Godiva to exaggerate the relationship.

But studying the nails Iris has shaped and painted so precisely, Dylan realizes David Franklin had ignored her because he'd been unhappy that Dylan was there. He'd wanted Godiva all to himself. He resented Dylan, maybe envied her. And he was in real pain. What a baby she'd been.

She glances at Iris, with genuine curiosity.

"Did you ever see your father again?"

"Many times. Not that it made any difference."

"But you loved him?" Dylan is embarrassed by her own question.

"I still do." Iris screws the brush back into the shiny pink bottle, like a genie back into a magic lamp.

Twenty-TWO

Dylan hears David Balboa's car pull into his reserved space. When he doesn't come to the kitchen, she decides he must have taken the private stairs to the apartment. She finishes folding the pile of napkins in front of her and slips away upstairs.

David Balboa is lying on the rug, stomach-down singing softly to Crescent. Dylan recognizes the song from one of Godiva's old records. . . . *I get the urge for going, when the meadow grass is turning.* . . . Crescent is riding his back, giggling, but as soon as she sees Dylan, she stands up and waves around her new book of nursery rhymes.

"We read the big-girl book." She plops back down on David Balboa, who groans and laughs at the same time.

Dylan ambles over to the rawhide chair but does not sit down. David Balboa begins to read in a gentle, playful voice Dylan has not heard from him before, even kidding around in the kitchen. What would it have been like if he'd been there to read to her when she was Crescent's age? Dylan's stomach turns to ice. They are as close to alone, she and David Balboa, as they have ever been so far. It is now or never. She watches as he carefully, gently sets Crescent in the chair with her book. She has known him for less than a week, but time is already running out. She is scared to death.

While she is gathering her thoughts, he clears his throat.

"We need to talk," he says and faces her directly. She knows how important it is to stay calm, now that they're about to talk adult to adult, but how can she? This is the moment she has been waiting so long for.

"You are my father, aren't you?"

David Balboa walks over to the window, which faces north to the mountains. She follows him. It is the kind of winter bright morning, late morning now, when a metallic sheen brushes every surface. Looking through the window is like looking at the world reflected from inside a spoon, and her heart is so full that her chest hurts.

A bird is pecking around the empty feeder Iris usually keeps filled.

"She must have forgotten to fill it this morning," he says.

"Aren't you?" Dylan is not sure she can wait for another second.

"Your father?" he says, staring at the feeder. "What has given you that idea? I told you I don't know any Henry Firestone."

"Stein. Fier*stein*." Her voice cracks. "You said Fierstein the other day. I heard you. You *are* him. I know you are. Sure, you have to hide it in front of the others. I can understand if you have to. But we are alone here." She begins to tremble despite her best efforts. "Look at my eyes. Look at how I walk."

She crosses the room to Crescent. "Your friend in Cincinnati said we walked the same and we do."

"I have no friends in Cincinnati."

"Yes, you do. Martha." She touches the top of Crescent's head, bent over the book, and walks back to him, hoping to catch a reaction that doesn't occur. Does his forehead wrinkle, just a little? Does his frown deepen? She wishes she knew Martha's last name. It is too easy for him to deny knowing someone without a specific last name.

"I know all about you." She hates the pleading tone with which her words emerge. "More than anyone. More than Iris. You are my father, you have to be."

He folds his arms across his chest and frowns.

"If I were, which I am not, would it honestly make much difference?"

"Yes, yes, it makes all the difference in the world, yes." Look what she's gone through to find him. "How can you think it doesn't make a difference?" She is panting.

He steps toward her, rests his hands on her shoulders to quiet her. She's been waiting what seems her whole life for him to touch her with this kind of parental concern, but she breaks away. "If you don't want me, just say so."

"Poor Dylly, are you sad?" Crescent is watching attentively from the chair. They are not alone after all, even now. Dylan shakes her head and attempts a smile so Crescent won't begin to cry herself.

"It is not a matter of my wanting you or not wanting you." He speaks slowly and calmly. "I cannot be your father."

"Because you're afraid."

"Dylan, stop. I am not your father. I am not part of your life. Be honest with yourself. Do you really want me to be?"

"Yes," she says without a pause, "I do." But her heart shudders.

He shakes his head and sits down on the rug beside Crescent's chair. Dylan sits down, too, so they are facing each other, their legs crossed Indian style, the way she sat for her manicure with Iris.

"Listen, Dylan. Your trip here, the way you describe it, it's as if you were traveling back in time. And it was a strange time, I'll grant you that. Living on the edge. No, over the edge a lot of the time." He pushes his glasses up on his forehead, begins to twist his mustache, then stops, a habit Iris has told her he is trying to break. "Everything was so important then, every decision, every act. All the clichés we lived by."

"What clichés?" Dylan asks, but she knows what he means. Here he is talking to her for real at last. She should be ecstatic but the conversation is going all wrong. She has no control over the sentences coming out of her mouth.

"If you are not my father, where were you on May 5, 1970?" Tears of fear and accusation start again and this time she does hold them back.

"Sweetheart, I haven't the slightest idea."

At the window, the hungry bird begins to peck the glass. Crescent climbs down from her chair to see.

"Poor birdy." She taps the glass in a helpless attempt to comfort. "Please, Davey, let him in."

David Balboa does not move.

"Please, Davey." Dylan startles, but no, Crescent did not say "Daddy." "I share my Cheerios."

He nods to Dylan to fetch the birdseed from the cupboard, and like a robot she obeys. As soon as she opens the window to fill the feeder, the bird flutters its wings to hover inches out of reach. Dylan pours the seed onto the flat tray and closes the window quickly, her hands already reddening from the cold. While Dylan puts the box of seed away, Crescent stays at the window to watch as the bird circles the feeder before it lands and begins to peck.

David Balboa watches Crescent watching the bird, then stands up and walks over to Dylan. He takes her face between his open hands, the way she's dreamed he would for so long. He shakes his head once, emphatically.

"I'm just a man in the restaurant business." He is old and tired. He smells of coffee and aftershave. Lacy red lines trail across the whites of his eyes.

"I hate you. I wish I never found you." Dylan's cheeks burn, held stiff in the vise of his dry, hard palms.

"You need to call your mother and tell her you are coming home," David Balboa says calmly, coldly. "You have reached a dead end here. It's over. The quest, or whatever it has been for you, is over. *Se acabó.*"

+   +   +

No, it is not over. Not for Dylan. Not by a long shot. She runs into the study and slams the door. Crescent calls her name in a perplexed little-girl whimper, but Dylan is beyond responding, even to Crescent. She leans against the door, choking down sobs. She hears them out there, the two of them, Crescent's soft, high-pitched questions and the male grate of his answers, hears them moving around, then the foot treads on the stairs down to the restaurant. She is alone, more alone suddenly than she's ever been in her entire life.

She sits down on the edge of the unmade fold-out bed. T-shirts and jeans jumble together on the floor nearby. Crescent's sweater and a new pair of corduroy pants lie draped over the desk chair. It is his desk but with nothing of his on its surface except a phone and an adding machine. She has inspected the contents of the desk drawers several times already, has found not one clue she could use as proof that the man who calls himself David Balboa is someone else. Not that she will ever think of him again as David

Balboa. No, she will never think of him as anyone but The Man Who Refused to Be Her Father.

She opens the top drawer again, with the methodical care of someone who has memorized the contents, which she has. She touches the now familiar ledger books, the folder of printed menus from other restaurants, the scheduling charts. She is still hoping to discover what she's missed—a stray newspaper clipping, a letter, some scrap of physical memory he saved the way Godiva saved Henry Fierstein's wanted poster.

Godiva. It would be late afternoon in Florida now. Godiva would be sitting on the porch smoking. Dylan can see the smoke wavering up, smell the bitterness of burning cigarette in the salt air, see her mother's wide back, the loose flyaway braid that hangs down so long Godiva could almost sit on it. Dylan looks at the phone, her fingers itching to dial home to that unfailing source of too-easy love, but instead she moves to the narrow bank of bookcases across from the bed.

She begins pulling cookbooks down off the shelves, one at a time, then as fast as they'll come. She read a novel once in which the villain hid a missing will inside a book, but Dylan cannot remember how the other characters discovered the hiding place. She holds the books upside down and jiggles them. From one a small paper card flutters down and she grabs it. A recipe for mango soufflé. She tears it up. Similar cards fall from other books. She looks at each. All recipes she tears into pieces and more pieces, then drops into a metal wastebasket. She takes a match from one of the little sliding boxes with LOS COMBIENTES printed on the front in flowing turquoise script. She strikes the match and drops it, lit, into the basket, a little offering to the gods of orphaned and half-orphaned children. The paper is old and dry and burns quickly down to ash the color of dirty snow.

Not fair, damn it.

She picks up a book lying open on its face. *How to Cook a Wolf.* The problem is that he caught her off guard today. She should have shown him the poster. She should have shown him the first day.

But how? The first afternoon was such a disaster. She admits she messed up then, saying his name to everyone. But was anyone really paying serious attention? No. And she never said anything about his being wanted by the police, being a criminal, being on the lam. Besides, she has been careful to protect his identity ever since. He knows she's said nothing to the others. Not even Iris; there is no telling what stories he's fed Iris. Dylan has eavesdropped on enough of their conversations by now to make a good guess.

Dylan puts the book aside. From the inner pocket of her backpack, propped against a desk leg, she removes Henry Fierstein's picture. Flattening the edges of the paper, she smooths her father's face against her hand. With all this travel, her copy is no longer very clear, but she still likes the way he looks. How many kisses has she placed on his smudged forehead? All those conversations they'd shared in her head while she was on the bus. Weird, what a fun time that seems now, the future so full of possibility just a week ago.

She imagines the conversation The Man Who Refused to Be Her Father must be having with Iris about now:

"Where's Dylan?"

"She needs a little space, some time alone. She's going to call her mother and get out of our hair. Or else."

Or else what? He couldn't very well call the police on her, could he? That's probably why she's been able to stay as long as she has—because he doesn't know how to get rid of her without drawing attention to himself. He's afraid. She looks at the paper in her hand. Maybe she has more power than she realized.

The Man Who Refused to Be Her Father won't call the police, but she could. If he could betray her like this, and denying his own child has to be betrayal in the deepest sense, what does she owe him? Besides, he has broken laws and criminals should pay for their crimes. Godiva used to talk about how she knew the risk of getting busted was part of the package when she went to antiwar demonstrations. She was critical of some former friend who wound up in jail and then bellyached about the bad food. "God, Honeybunch," she proclaimed, slapping her hand into the dough she was kneading. "The whole point was to get arrested, wasn't it?"

And if Dylan is mistaken, there'd be no harm done then. If he really is not her father, if David Balboa really is David Balboa, then no one has anything to lose except Dylan herself. She'll have to go back to Esmeralda while he and the cops share a laugh. But at least she'll know.

"Dylan, are you okay?" Iris opens the door. "Is something burning?" She surveys the mess, sniffing, but does not come in.

"Did he send you up here to check on me?" Dylan quickly folds Henry Fierstein's picture and tucks it back in her pack. "Well, you can go right down and tell him I burnt his recipe for mocha cheesecake, among others."

"God, Dylan." Iris begins to ask the obvious why but stops herself. Dylan can see her mentally backing up as she stares at the scattered books.

"David didn't send me up. In fact, I haven't seen him since this morning." She frowns not so much at Dylan as to herself. "Evidently he brought Crescent into the kitchen a few minutes ago and left her with Orey, then took off. I thought you might know where."

"Oh sure. He tells me everything." Why doesn't Iris just leave her alone. "Isn't the lunch crowd due about now? Who's going to seat people if you're up here baby-sitting me?"

"Dylan, don't be so angry at us." As if Iris were part of the equation. "You need to go home. To get on with your life. You can't hide here indefinitely."

"Why not, Miss Almost Lawyer? Isn't that what you're doing, hiding here with your David?" Dylan locks eyes with Iris. A direct hit. "How much do you know about your beloved boyfriend, anyway?"

Without answering, Iris turns, slowly closing the door behind her.

Dylan is immediately sorry. Not at what she's said, but because now she is alone again. She stares at the phone. Late afternoon in Esmeralda. Godiva might still be at the elementary school working. Christmas vacation ended over a week ago. The secretary would have to page Godiva from the office.

No. Calling Godiva like a homesick baby would be way too easy on him, Dylan decides. No. He is denying her rights, and she is not going to let him. Carefully, she steps around the scatter of open cookbooks toward the desk. Carefully, almost reluctantly, she picks up the receiver and dials 911.

SiX

I practically tripped over myself to pick up by the second ring. I already knew. Maternal instinct, it doesn't weaken with age or distance after all, not as long as you're paying due attention, which believe me I am these days. And when I heard Dylan's voice—well, you can imagine. It was not simply a weight lifting off my heart and lungs and big toe. No, I swear to the gods, when I heard the soft slur of her S, the quick, so-familiar emphasis of her long vowels, my whole being lifted.

"So, Mom, it's me," she said, and I began to hover, literally hover, inches above the pull of this earth's gravity.

She was safe. She was coming home.

"I'm in New Mexico."

"New Mexico," I echoed back, not mentioning the call I'd received a few days earlier. A Detective Marks from Albuquerque, letting me know a girl fitting Dylan's description had been sighted in a mall, not in Albuquerque itself, but near Velasquez, some ski resort town I'd never heard of—skiing has never exactly been my sport. A security guard noticed her acting suspiciously, whatever acting suspiciously might mean. The details Detective Marks had available were fuzzy; the report mentioned two girls, one much younger, which made no sense. But who knows?

Anyway, I'd been living on cigarettes and the edge of my seat ever since. Up to three packs a day again. I know I'd quit as part of my bargain with the gods to get Dylan back, but after I heard from the detective, I had to smoke to calm down, and I had to calm down so I could breathe. It was almost worse waiting to hear more than when I'd heard nothing at all. No, nothing was worse than that. I just had to have faith. And I did. I knew this call was coming. I knew it in my bones.

"The police guy wants to talk to you," Dylan was saying. She had not made the call of her own volition. A tug of disappointment on the old heart strings but I can't say I was really surprised. Nothing could surprise me anymore.

"How did they find you?" I wanted to keep her talking to me, mouthpiece to mouthpiece, just a little longer, to regain some kind of rhythm between us.

"They didn't." Her voice, so flat, the way Cass Culpepper's used to be. "I contacted them."

"Oh, Honeybunch." Yellow warning light flashing. "Why not just call me?"

What had she been through during these last three weeks? Which of those fears that I had blocked out of hitting range was about to come true? I thought of Cass and Louise. Was it better to know everything, "the concrete details" as Louise would say? I took a quick steadying breath.

"Dylan, did something bad happen? Was someone trying to hurt you?"

"I found him."

It didn't quite register. "What?"

"My father, I found him for them."

"Hank?" I think I spoke out loud then, but maybe not. How in God's name could she track down Hank Fierstein when the FBI had not been able to find him for twenty years.

"Why didn't you tell me he was a wanted man?" Her voice pitched upward toward anger. "Why didn't you show me you had his picture all along?" I could hear the pain almost break through a thousand miles away, but then she paused, collected herself. Even as a toddler Dylan could do that, stop mid-tantrum and pull herself back into control before she really let loose.

"How, Honeybunch? Where?" I couldn't believe it.

"How I found him isn't the point. I just did. But Mom, he said he wasn't." And she began to sob, my disconsolate little girl. I wanted to put my arms around her and rock away all that pain the way I could when she was five and she woke sobbing from a nightmare. "He said he didn't remember you, as if anyone ever forgets you. He was hateful and mean and I didn't like him from the first minute, just told myself I did because he was my father. And he was a fake, a big fake. All the people here thought he just hung the moon. Well, he didn't and I proved it to them."

She sniffled, but I did not know what to say, what to think. Hank could not have forgotten me, could he?

"Here's the cop," Dylan said, her voice gone flat again.

"Mrs. Blue?" The policeman was surprisingly polite. Well, they'd all been actually, the FBI men, too. But this one's Western twang softened his official formality even more.

"Yes." My hands were shaking so badly I could barely hold the phone. "Where's my daughter? I want to talk to my daughter."

"Your daughter's right here beside me doing just fine. We'll be getting her back to you quick as we can."

He said he wanted to outline the situation first though, and that's all there was, an outline with next to no details. He did not know how Dylan had ended up in Velasquez, New Mexico, and of course she refused to say. When she phoned the local police with a supposed tip about the whereabouts of a wanted felon, no one paid her much attention at first, he said. They figured she was just another kid making a crank call, but then the computer kicked out her name as a runaway in possibly dangerous proximity to a possibly dangerous felon.

"We'd gotten an APB on her almost two weeks ago, but there are so many kids. Now her calling, this was different. And she was naming a pretty respected citizen around town. The guy runs one of those trendy new restaurants, way too high priced for the likes of me," the cop added.

Dylan had somehow finagled to stay with this man David Balboa for several days. His name and the cop's physical description added up to nothing, a tallish man between forty and forty-five with a mustache, a receding hairline and a ponytail.

"By the by, do you know a David Balboa, or anyone fitting the description I just gave?"

"No, I honestly don't." I tried to imagine the Hank Fierstein I knew running a restaurant. It seemed completely improbable. How did Dylan come up with this particular man?

"Well, if he is Henry Fierstein, he's a wanted man. No statute of limitations on federal crimes."

He couldn't be Hank, could he? Not my Hank, safely tucked away in the deepest pocket of my soul for so long, long before the afternoon at the post office, way back since the first time I felt the baby kicking inside me and knew that through that baby, Hank would be with me, to be cherished and loved whether he wanted me or not.

Had I bartered Hank's freedom for Dylan's return? Yes, and I'd do it again. Except, as usual, I was probably giving myself far too much credit. Whatever went on out there in New Mexico had very little to do with me or my mess-making anymore. Dylan found this man on her own. She called the police against him for her own reasons. But what had happened between them—after she went through God-knows-what to find him—that made her feel the need to call the police? Had he been arrested?

"Did he hurt her?" I asked, afraid to hear the answer.

"No, nothing like that it appears."

"So where do we go from here?"

While the cop explained about minors in custody and possible travel arrangements to get Dylan home, I hoped and prayed to God and the devil both, for Hank's sake and Dylan's—not to mention my own—that the man in New Mexico was not her father.

"We've got his place under surveillance," the cop was saying. "We've questioned the girlfriend extensively, but she doesn't seem to know a thing. He seems to have flown the coop completely, but we'll keep searching. Don't worry. Your daughter's safe and sound."

"Thank the gods."

"Yes ma'am." So polite, missing my point entirely.

Twenty-FOUR

A *few* rows forward a child squeals. Dylan presses her head against the small rectangle of cold glass and tries to pretend she's on a bus. Which bus though? To Delaware? To New Mexico? To Atlanta, before it all began? No, it all began before she got on the bus, even before she found the poster. Anyway, she's on a plane now, not a bus, and there is no pretending otherwise. She is too tightly strapped in, and the view, even if she ignores the tip of wing, is too forever blue to be anywhere else. Like the wall when she woke up her first afternoon in the bedroom of The Man Who Refused to Be Her Father. Only now it is eleven in the morning and she is probably over the border into Texas.

Texas. She missed Texas coming. The route back will be a lot shorter: a little over an hour and a half to Dallas, then two hours more to Tallahassee. It is laughable. It is unfair.

Since the terrible conversation two mornings ago, everyone in New Mexico has slabbed up an impenetrable wall of vague kindness. Someone is always asking if she's okay, promising things are going to work out for the best.

"What things?" Dylan spits back, but they pretend not to hear or answer with more mumbo jumbo that avoids saying anything at all.

To hell with them. They are all strangers she'll never see again, and The Man Who Refused to Be Her Father has turned out to be the most menacing stranger of all. So now she is heading back to Godiva. To Mama. Los Combientes is closed up. Margie, Manuel, Orey, they are all out of a job.

The Man Who Refused to Be Her Father walked through the kitchen that morning, got into his car and drove off. Not particularly unusual, Orey and the others thought, although it was strange that he showed so little interest in the lunch prep. Not particularly unusual except that he never came back.

She doesn't see how he could have known that Dylan was going to turn him in since she didn't know herself beforehand. But then the police came. Everybody was there in the kitchen, staring at her. Not angry exactly (well, that, too), but more in a state of disbelief.

No sign of him by dinner, which the staff went ahead and served. Iris jumped every time the reservations line rang, but, of course, he never called. By the next day, it was obvious, even to Iris, that he wouldn't. Dylan overheard one of the cops tell Iris that he had cashed in two big CDs when he took Crescent on his little errand run. Over $50,000 at two different banks. They found the car yesterday by a railroad crossing. The four doors wide open, nothing inside but the owner's manual. Did bums still ride the railroads?

What did Godiva say to her years ago, when Dylan begged to watch *The Wizard of Oz* on TV at Gram's. "Oh, Honeybunch, you're old enough to face reality. There is no magic at the end of the rainbow. The magic is in the color itself."

The baby has stopped squealing, but another somewhere toward the back of the plane begins to howl. An elderly woman in the seat across the aisle puts down her knitting and takes out a stick of peppermint gum.

"For the air pressure. They say it really helps."

Crying babies and old people. Plane travel turns out not to be much different from bus travel after all.

"You know, this is my first time flying, too, and I'm seventy-three."

Dylan is disappointed that she looks so obvious.

"I have to admit I'm a little bit afraid at my age, but we'll be fine, both of us, won't we?" Both of whom? Dylan wants to somehow make it clear that she has no connection to this woman. None at all. Damn, she does not want to cry again, but her throat constricts.

Crescent did not cry at all when Elise walked away. She did not cry in Velasquez this morning, either. Less than two weeks they were together. For less than two weeks, Crescent has been motherless, or rather Dylan has been her mother. It may as well have been two years. Fifteen years. As if Crescent could tell the difference. Will she even remember, let alone distinguish that Elise chose to leave her behind while Dylan was forced to leave? By next week, what place will Dylan take up on her little memory shelf? Crescent almost never mentioned Elise once they reached Velasquez.

What good will remembering do anyway if Crescent is going to grow up in an orphanage or group home or whatever they want to call it these days, the faceless, dreary dark building of Dylan's nightmares when she was little, with a concrete play yard where other children, mean and oversized, would torment her?

Dylan takes out the Polaroid snapshot Iris made the day she took Dylan and Crescent shopping. The two of them in their matching scarves stand under a sign to the Gold Mine, a video arcade. Crescent had refused to smile, absolutely refused, shaking her head with great emphasis. Iris tried making faces, sang goofy songs in a squeaky voice, promised her bubble gum, but Crescent would not smile. Finally Iris gave up and stood the two of them in front of the sign so that in the picture the big gold-painted coins appear to be falling around them from the sky. Dylan has not noticed before that Crescent has her hand in Dylan's jacket pocket, as if she were dropping in a coin while they gaze straight ahead at the camera. Dylan can just make out the underside of a grin despite her tightly clenched lips. How alike they look, the jut of their chins down and to the left. They could be sisters.

On the ride to the airport, a long ride which seemed to Dylan never-ending, Iris promised there would be no concrete playground for Crescent. She had called a friend with connections days ago, a lawyer in Albuquerque who has already begun working on alternatives.

"Please, don't worry, Dylan." If Iris was trying to sound convincing, she was failing. "No matter what, I'm not going to send her away."

Iris tried to reach across the seat, but Dylan shrank back against the locked door.

"Do you really want to stay? Be honest with yourself." Iris was red-eyed and haggard. Her unwashed hair was stringy. She did not look pretty anymore.

"Stay? With you? Of course not, but Crescent was mine. She liked being mine."

"People don't belong to other people."

"Oh, please." Iris is such a phony. Dylan hates her. "Everyone seems to think I belong to my mother."

"You're fifteen."

"Sixteen in a week."

"You've got a life to work out for yourself. So do I, as it turns out." Iris smiled grimly. Since The Man Who Refused to Be Dylan's Father vanished, Iris has been making plans to leave Velasquez, too. Heading back to the big city.

"Frankly, Dylan, I don't know whether to hate you or be grateful."

So maybe Iris is beginning to get it after all, to realize that Dylan has saved her. How could she practice law while involved with a wanted criminal at the same time, even by mistake? Besides, for Iris to think she had a chance with that man she had to be nuts. If Dylan had not come along when she did, Iris was destined to become just one more in his harem of ex-girlfriends who never got over his slimy charms.

"As for Crescent, I'll let you know where she is. You can be a kind of aunt. Gifts and visits even."

"Sure," Dylan answered to shut Iris up as the car sped past trashy rundown shopping strips one after another. New Mexico turned out to be as ugly as everywhere else, with subdivisions full of artificial haciendas. It particularly bothered Dylan how the garages dwarfed the attached living quarters. But then she decided, after considering all the plaster animals on the lawns, that the garages weren't so out of keeping, were the one hint of authenticity, because they took the place of what would have been mule sheds a hundred years ago. Maybe, but the houses were depressing any way you looked at them, the pastel stucco peeling from the sides and the grass in the yards uniformly brown.

Dylan is glad to be out of it, up in this airplane where geography loses its harsh edges and becomes only an outline. Up here she can look at the hard facts from the distance of altitude.

Fact one: Dylan will never see or hear from Crescent again. It is stupid to pretend otherwise. Crescent, who has already forgotten Elise, her real mother, will forget Dylan at least as quickly. Probably by next week. And despite Iris and her good intentions, Crescent will end up, if not in an institution, then in foster care. Dylan has seen the kids from foster homes passing like phantoms through the halls at school over the years, the ones who are not out-and-out juvenile delinquents. Crescent's childhood is going to be as miserable as any of theirs.

Dylan remembers now what it was like for her to be little like Crescent. She remembers Magic House much better than she did six months ago. The wide porch overlooking a river, crowded rooms spilling with music and people she knew less by their faces than by their hands. Not male or female, but rough or gentle, quick or slow. They picked her up and dressed her, fed her and tickled her. Some tickled. Others were more businesslike. No matter what, Dylan felt safe with Godiva watching over her. Yes, Dylan admits to herself, there is something to be said for having a mother who loves you. It's like owning property that no one, not even The Man Who Refused to Be Her Father, can take away.

At fifteen, what memories will Crescent own? Won't she wake up one morning and want to solve the mystery of her existence? But her only physical clues, her physical self, are not clues at all. She won't have as much as a walk to go on. Will some early vision of Elise return to haunt her, will she cling to some secondhand description from Iris, if Iris is still around? If Elise was Crescent's mother. There's no knowing for sure.

As for a father, Crescent won't have even secondhand stories of a father. Stories of a father are all Dylan still has herself, and few enough of them. She looks out the thick oval window at the sky, milkier now with clouds. She considers, what if they track down The Man Who Refused to Be Her Father and he turns out to be somebody else altogether?

He is obviously not David Balboa, that much is clear. She hates him for rejecting her, despises him for denying who he really is—whoever that might be. If he told the truth, if he is not her father, he is still a creep and a jerk with something to hide or why would he disappear? Dylan would be glad to know she doesn't have to claim him as a relative. Maybe she'll try to find Henry Fierstein again later, when she is truly independent, maybe in a year or two. She could pick up the trail where she left off in Eden. Even if the clues are colder, she will be more experienced and more savvy. A lot more careful about whom she trusts, whom she cares for.

No, because of fact two: The search is finished. This trip has used up every bit of her energy.

Beyond the wing, a cluster of small clouds float by. In buses Dylan could always see past the electric wires and phone poles to the horizon, the magic line where sky joined land. In an airplane she has to depend on the wing dipping down toward earth to make sure it is still there below, waiting for her. From buses she could count houses, trees, all-night gas stations, ugly but essential mileposts of the dreary everyday life to be passed on the way to what she considered at the time her superior destiny. Now, craning her neck for a glimpse of what looks like a sheet of lumpy brown paper bisected by thin lines but which she must assume are highways or rivers, she is nostalgic for the old bus landscape.

That landscape had not been much different than the landscape she left behind. Travelers passing through Esmeralda on

Route 7 and Highway 12 look out on littered vacant lots, a sprawling narrow-windowed school, Esmeralda Estates subdivision, gas stations, the Ocean View Motel with no view of an ocean in sight, the Dairy Queen.

Fact three: Leaving home was a more public act than Dylan intended. More likely to draw embarrassing attention than anything Godiva ever did. And now she is going to return empty-handed, with nothing to show for the time away. What will people think? Over the phone Godiva did not mention how she has been explaining Dylan's absence to people. Knowing Godiva, she probably hasn't bothered, or else she's casually broadcast every detail.

What about Cass? Dylan put a lot of trust in her. How much has she let on? Assuming she received Dylan's letters, has she kept them to herself? Has she kept them period? What crazy stuff Dylan wrote. She isn't sure anymore what actually happened; already it seems, most of it, so long ago. But those letters. If they still exist, Dylan wants them back. They are her only record.

The trip has not been all bad. Eden was a good place. She wishes she had stayed there longer. She wishes she had the book Isaac gave her, the one she misplaced half-read on a bus somewhere in the Midwest. She wonders if he or Haiku ever think about her. If she shows up again in a year or two, will they welcome her back? The Wyatts will. They'd welcome anybody.

She even feels a certain fondness for Spider now that she'll never see him again. To think she was even briefly won over by his peculiar charms. For that matter, to think she once considered Jimmy Cryder crucial to her happiness. He was nice, though. Oh well, by this time he is sure to be dating someone else.

Dylan gazes out across the clouds. More than anywhere else in the world right now, she wishes she were sitting in First Period English, Mrs. Cadwallader knocking her erasers together, Danny

Morris and Travis Crain in the row ahead, the soft indentation of pale skin above the rim of their T-shirt collars as they hunch over their books. Cally Jasper's sharp concentrated profile to her left and Judy Bellamy's sleepy one to her right. The fake-wood desk with a thin rind of dirt under its metal edging that Dylan likes to scrape with her pencil point. The torn pieces of notebook paper, folded twice so the writing inside cannot be read, her name written in Jimmy's broad scrawl. The smell of chalk dust and sweat that all schools share.

Two weeks, two years. The clouds and sky dissolve into a mist, silvery and transparent, but endless so that the plane seems to be roaring in place. Dylan's eyes begin to close. Relaxing into the drone, she allows herself to doze off.

"Coke, fruit juice? Would you ladies like something to drink?" The flight attendant takes Dylan's silence at face value, but as soon as the cart rumbles on to the next row, Dylan is wide awake and starving.

She pulls up her backpack from under the seat in front of her and takes out a white insulated bag with LOS COMBIENTES printed in iridescent shades of yellow and turquoise. She took it from Iris grudgingly at the departure gate when her flight was called. Now she is glad to have it. Inside are two pieces of coriander lime chicken, a green apple wrapped in tissue, and a wedge of what Dylan has to admit is the best cinnamon chocolate pound cake in the world. She eats greedily, but when she comes to the cake, it is inedible, dried out and stale. The Los Combientes she knew would never serve stale cake.

Fact four: There is no more Los Combientes. She thinks about a conversation, one of the few when The Man Who Refused to Be Her Father talked at all about himself.

"I didn't just design the menu." He was describing how he'd created Los Combientes out of an empty warehouse. "I hung the Sheetrock, refinished old tables and chairs, put in the kitchen stove, worked twenty-four hours a day cooking and serving and cleaning up." He was talking but it could have been Godiva Dylan was hearing.

"And, damn, if I don't love what I created." Godiva got excited the same way about Point Paradise, about her boxes.

"I love to watch customers eat my food and fill my rooms with their best moods. It's all in the details, kid." For once he smiled at her or at least in her direction. "The pepper in the pepper mills, the paintings on the walls, the temperature of the wine."

How could she have ended up with two parents so alike? Aren't opposites the ones who are supposed to attract?

Dylan sits up and grips her armrests, almost ill at the enormity of what she may have done. What if Martha in Cincinnati made a mistake? Got her aliases wrong? What if he is another man hiding from another past? What will his life be now? What if Dylan has destroyed it for nothing? The truth remains too unclear, too unresolved. She refuses to feel guilt or remorse, yet. She forces herself to swallow the saliva gathering under her tongue and to breathe in and out. Still, she can hardly bear the claustrophobia taking hold. That and a breathtaking impatience to hear the certain rhythm of the Gulf tides breaking against the shore at Point Paradise. She has been inland too long.

Twenty-FIVE

This morning's plane was already over an hour late. I was a wreck, a zombie, hair on end like the bride of Frankenstein, sweat on my palms, all nerve endings on red alert. I paced the corridor between the escalator and Gate 22 for God knows how long, going back through my dreams one at a time. For weeks now, I've been making notes as soon as I wake up, sometimes several times a night, in my old dream diary which I've begun to carry with me at all times, the way I carry my pack of cigarettes.

I was too nervous to sit down, also dying for a cigarette, but my God, with Dylan in the air I did not dare tempt fate. I tried to think about other things, about which clasp to use on the necklace I'd been commissioned to design for one of Cleo's better customers, about the light in the third-grade classroom that kept shorting out, about what Dylan might like for dinner tonight. Dylan. I couldn't not think about her. So unlike me, but I kept trying out what I'd say to her. I knew I needed to strike the right balance, let her know, yet not laden her with how worried I'd been. No free lunch but no guilt trip, either.

A man in a three-piece suit asked me the time. Ten years ago, hell six months ago, I would have written him off as an uptight idle-class white guy, but I guess I've lost that judgmental edge. Besides, he was carrying one of those giant stuffed pandas they sell at airport gift shops for inflated prices and I liked his looks, kindhearted in a pale, slightly pudgy and self-deprecating way. A man with a sense of humor. But after I took the mint LifeSaver he offered, I turned back to the window, grateful he didn't push a conversation, half-wishing he would. Beyond the glass wall, the planes rolled past like lumbering giants.

Then the woman at the check-in counter picked up her telephone as if it had just rung, but it hadn't. I was sure it hadn't. The woman frowned. I walked nearer, trying to hear, apprehensive, afraid of the obvious, that something had happened to Dylan's plane. Living out the scenario in my head—the announcement, being herded into some room to be consoled—I found myself strangely becalmed, the horror mitigated by the removal of any need to face the future: If my future were robbed from me, I could live in the past, live and relive those golden years of Dylan's childhood without the distraction of the present. But then I shook myself. God, what was I doing? What possibility was I creating by even considering such dangerous thoughts?

For once my mind games didn't matter—thank God—because suddenly, Dylan's plane was there. One minute it was an idea, a concept, DYLAN'S RETURN, happening completely inside my head, like an inspiration I might take back to my studio and shape into a papier-mâché box. I don't mean fantasy. More like expectation, real in my head, but not yet decided. Without substance until there was proof.

And then the loudspeaker's voice was announcing Flight 76 and I heard the roar of the engines as the plane appeared outside the glass, its huge face coming forward as if about to swallow us. When it stopped, there was a flurry of activity beyond the ropes and people, real people, began to shuffle through the arrival door with dazed relief at having made it back to earth.

My friend with the panda waved to a pleasant-looking older woman carrying a plastic bag with knitting needles poking out between the drawstrings. At the sight of the panda, the woman, who had to be his mother, cackled with laughter until she had to grab the man's arm to keep from toppling over with hilarity.

"Oh Ned," she wheezed. "You are still the silliest boy in the world."

Now there was a fresh surge of passengers. Some melted into the crowd heading for the terminal. Others clotted the hallway in chatty groups blocking my view. I gripped the aluminum knob of a guardrail and watched for Dylan. More and more passengers passed, some smiling and waving, some in a grim rush, some in a sluggish lonely fog. I squinted toward the last stragglers as the gate door closed.

A young businessman switched his briefcase from one hand to the other. A woman not that much younger than I am carried a small baby against her chest while dragging a folded stroller behind her. What would that be like, to have a small baby again? She looked anxiously for whoever was not there to meet them. Another young woman, raggedly chic in cowboy boots with a red scarf flapping rakishly against her open jacket, slung a backpack over her shoulder.

Dylan? I had to blink twice to be sure, but it was Dylan, my Dylan, and wouldn't you know, almost the last one off.

"Dylan!" I shouted.

Her head jerked up, searched over the heads around her. I called out again and waved. I'm not sure, but I think—I want to think—she brightened when she saw me. She definitely nodded and waved back. I rushed forward, although my arms and legs were trembling. When had my mousy pudge of a teenager transformed into this slim girl, her pale locket-shaped face framed by a glossy sweep of bangs? Her eyes were sterner, her expression, her whole demeanor unreadable.

I took a deep breath. Forget the anger I'd felt on and off for days, forget how crazy with worry she'd driven me. Dylan was back with me now, that was what mattered. The next few days were bound to be awkward; we might be a little shy around each other at first. But, I told myself, we'd talk it through until we found some degree of reconciliation. Wouldn't we? We'd laugh together before long. Maybe. If I am very very lucky.

God, I wanted to grab hold of her and never let her go. It seemed to take forever, but we finally reached each other. When I did press my arms around her, Dylan did not hug me back. Had I really expected her to? No, but I was still hurt, stung, even though I'd been warning myself to take it easy, take it slow. Not that she was hostile, merely stiff and slightly formal. For once, I didn't push. I dropped my arms.

"No marching band to welcome me home?" she asked with a wry smile.

"Afraid not." I forced myself to smile back. The Dylan I knew never made sardonic jokes, but this Dylan was different, almost another being. Experiences I would never know about had shaded and molded her into the young woman facing me, compellingly intense yet self-composed. Across my visual memory flashed the image of Evangeline Pinkston in a blue dress, practicing her music, not much older than Dylan. The truth began finally sinking in, the brutal truth.

It was not a matter of tensions easing, of angers and guilts receding with time. It was not even the unsettled question of her father. Whoever that man in New Mexico was, he was gone. Vanished into the mountains or desert or wherever the railroad tracks lead beyond the New Mexico horizon. He could be dead for all anyone knew. But I didn't want to think of him or what had become of him; there would be plenty of late nights ahead to lie awake wondering at my culpability in sacrificing him. And after all, I had been willing enough to sacrifice him. Dylan and I had that in common at least. Our motives may have differed, but motives are individually exclusive, aren't they? Like fingerprints except that fingerprints can be recorded. Motives are indecipherable to anyone but the person who acts by them. A mother's desperation doesn't cover the why any more than a daughter's sense of revenge or justice. Who's to say which is more valid? Law-abiding citizens would say we were both right, wouldn't they? Even if neither of us was. As for the man in New Mexico, he'd decided to disappear for his own reasons he didn't choose to share.

Anyway, the matter was no longer Hank Fierstein. Never had been really. The matter was that I had lost the power to shield my little girl from the world. I wasn't kidding myself anymore about my less-than-perfect record as Dylan's mother: I had not paid attention. Not only this fall, but all along. How else could it have escaped me that Dylan's needs might be as different from mine as mine had been from my mother's? I wasn't about to absolve myself from that responsibility. Far from it. If anything, I wanted to take more responsibility for my maternal screwing up. Because, in a way, this was worse; the fact that whatever choices I had made over the last sixteen years, however I acted, whatever I did or didn't do, I still would have lost control over Dylan's life. Maybe not now, and maybe not so dramatically, but sooner or later, one way or another she would have abandoned me. Monday they're yours and Tuesday they're not. I was no different from every other mother, from Louise Culpepper or Myra Franklin or Mari Rainey. Or Mrs. Pinkston, Evie's mother, whose first name I never learned. I wondered if she still lived in the old apartment. Still played organ for her church choir. What pictures of Evie hung on her walls? I should have written to her when Dylan was born, should have kept in touch all these years.

Because, my God, I was different from Mrs. Pinkston, and much luckier. Dylan was alive. Dylan was standing there in the airport next to me, alive, stronger in fact than I ever imagined, or to tell the whole truth, probably ever wanted her to be. Not my little girl, but nevertheless my daughter, even if she hated me for the next twenty years. And she might. She just might.

A man in a Hawaiian shirt hurried up to the woman and baby I'd noticed earlier. After a short exchange of words, he took the baby from her arms and they walked off, whether together or separately I wasn't sure. I stopped watching. Dylan hoisted up her pack, and we made our own way through the thinning crowd as the loudspeaker announced that the next departure from Gate 22 was delayed indefinitely.